THE CHRONO SLASHER

AN ALICE BERGMAN NOVEL
BOOK THREE

DREZHN

PUBLISHING

THE CHRONO SLASHER

Published by Drezhn Publishing LLC
PO BOX 67458
Albuquerque, NM 87193-7458

Print Edition - July 2022
Version 1.2

Cover design by Dan Van Oss, CoverMint

HARDBACK ISBN: 978-1-947328-58-7
PAPERBACK ISBN: 978-1-947328-59-4
EBOOK ISBN: 978-1-947328-44-0

BOOKS BY DANIEL KUHNLEY

SUPERNATURAL SERIAL KILLER

<u>Alice Bergman Novels</u>
*Birth Of A Killer (novella)
*The Braille Killer
*The Night Mauler
*The Chrono Slasher

EPIC DRAGON FANTASY

<u>The Dark Heart Chronicles</u>
*† The Dragon's Stone
*Reborn
*Rended Souls
True Heir

Scourge (novella)

CHRISTIAN YA SCI-FI/FANTASY
(As Daniel Luke Kuhnley)

<u>VR Academy</u>
Kiara Kole And The Key Of Truth

* - Also available as an audiobook
† - Previously released as Dark Lament

Visit Daniel's website to find these books and more!
danielkuhnley.com

READ *BIRTH OF A KILLER* FOR FREE

Curious how Alice gained her sight as a teen?
Want to read about the attack that started it all?

danielkuhnley.com/become-a-conqueror

Sign up and read *Birth Of A Killer*, An Alice Bergman Novella. Be the **FIRST** to get sneak peaks at my upcoming novels and the chance to win **FREE** stuff, like signed books.

A paranormal serial killer thriller that'll keep you turning the pages.

Be careful what you dream when murder is on your mind.

My name is Alice, and I'm a sixteen-year-old ghost. No, I'm not actually dead, but I was born blind. The sad thing is the world's more blind to me than I am to it.

That is, until the day he noticed me. A bully. He ruined my life and turned my dreams into nightmares, so what could I do? The same thing any girl my age would do—I wished he'd die.

Then… he turns up dead. Naturally, I freaked out. Am I to blame? Did my nightmare kill him? Would anyone believe me if I confessed?

It's absurd. I know it. Nightmares don't come true… do they?

Birth of a Killer is the suspenseful prequel novella to *The Braille Killer*. If you like unique sleuths, origin stories, and a hint of the supernatural, you'll love Daniel Kuhnley's nail-biting tale.

Buy *Birth of a Killer* today to see how Alice's story began!

AN ALICE BERGMAN NOVEL BOOK THREE

THE CHRONO SLASHER

DANIEL KUHNLEY

CHAPTER ONE

SEVEN ROWS FROM THE front of the nave within Notre-Dame Cathedral, the man I've hunted for the past nine weeks kneels on the black and white diamond-patterned marble floor in front of his chair. He's no priest. No saint.

A parasite.

God or not, no matter how much time he spends on his knees, forgiveness will evade him. He's damned himself to hell for what he's done. Honestly, though, it's irrelevant. All that matters is what happens next.

Beads of sweat glisten on the back of his bald, misshapen head, the left side of his cranium cratered and scarred. Had I an ounce of empathy for the man, I'd inquire as to how the grotesque injury came about. But he deserves nothing.

Soon, the whole of Paris will know the name of the man I've come to call the Chrono Slasher: Jacques Milan. A horrible man. Ruthless serial killer. Friend of none.

A quick glance around the nave reconfirms that he and I are alone. The privacy both comforts and alarms me at once, given the man's unique gift. And, speaking of said gift, it's the only thing that keeps me from putting a bullet through the back of his skull. A relentless curiosity.

What can I say? Perhaps I'm part feline. Or maybe just a curious zealot.

Either way, my mind refuses to contemplate anything else.

Sweaty palms and a racing heart root my feet to the marble floor. Both ailments cloud my judgment and ratchet up the tension in my shoulders. But the tension grows beyond me. A virus spreading throughout the entire nave. It leaves a dense, acrid taste upon my lips.

Two deep breaths slow my pulse as I clutch a golden FNX-45 Tactical FDE between my hands. The piece isn't mine, and no matter how tight my grip, it still feels loose. Not a good combination, especially given that the fear of it jamming or misfiring ceaselessly runs through my mind. It scares me almost as much as he does.

Another slow, deep breath frees my feet. Clears my mind.

Now or never, Alice.

Eyes forward and barrel raised, I take several steps toward him. "Jacques Milan—" My voice echoes through the cavernous cathedral, shattering the silence. "—place your hands above your head where I can see them and rise to your feet," I say in French.

Black, bell-shaped sleeves slide down brown, lanky arms disfigured with pinkish-red scars as the man raises his arms and rises from his knees. Two fingers are missing from his right hand. The middle one and his pinky.

Jacques steps into the aisle and turns toward me. As his head slowly rises, the shadows surrounding him withdraw, revealing facial features I'll never be able to unsee. Pieces of skin hang from grayish, cracked lips, the lower one split and crusted with blood. A small nub and two gaping holes lie between his eyes and lips.

My God… he's a monster.

Then, his gaze meets mine. No number of deep breaths could stave off the fear radiating from my bones as I stare into his unmatched eyes. Green with flecks of gold on the right; its yellow sclera fissured with angry red veins. An inkwell as black as death itself consumes his left eye. At least the part of it that remains intact.

A dry, raspy breath escapes from my parted lips as we stare each other down. Fear will not force me to break eye contact with the man. I won't give in. Doing so would give him the upper hand.

Nostrils flaring, I inhale a mixture of stale sweat and incense. The former smells of my own brand. It triggers my mind to trace back to my last shower.

Days…

I shake off the query as the man's head tilts slightly to the right. For a moment, I imagine he does so because of an unevenly weighted head, but then his lips pull apart, forming a crooked, gapped smile of nicotine-stained teeth. Tendrils of saliva and fresh blood connect his upper and lower lips.

Hairs rise on my nape. Thunderous drums pound in my ears. Sweat runs down the sides of my ribcage.

He smells my fear.

Just twenty paces separate us. Two hundred wouldn't be enough. My left foot slides back several inches. Its traitorous act infuriates me, and I'll be damned before I let the other one retreat as well.

Reflected light glints off the twisted silver cross that hangs from his neck on a cord of twine. It demands my attention. Pulls me forward a step.

Disfigured, like him.

Jacques slowly reaches down and grasps the wretched cross between finger and thumb. The impulse to do the same with my necklace is so strong that my left hand jerks back awkwardly, leaving the gun flailing in my right hand for half a beat.

Jacques doesn't seem to notice, his attention glued to his own pendant. Beads of sweat roll down the small of my back as I shrug off the misstep and regrip the gun.

I motion with the barrel. "Arms up." The words stick in the back of my dry throat like sand.

Jacques's fingers linger on the cross a few more moments before his arm rises again. "Simple, right? Yet such power." His rough, French accent turns my head ever so slightly as my mind works to decipher his words.

A speech impediment?

At first, I think I'm right, but then I see it. A dime-sized hole through the tip of his tongue. Could be larger. Another glance of the man's features and the way he stands and holds himself reveals just how disfigured and maimed he really is.

An abomination. God's punishment.

His words finally sink in, but their reference point lost. "I don't follow."

Jacques motions toward the raised, golden altar behind him with his head. "I speak of the Christ. A single deed to rid humanity of its sin. Once, for all. Simple. Powerful."

Christ.

The word reminds me of Mother. Of home. I can't wait to unshackle myself from Paris and the filth that accompanies it.

I shift my weight, fully aware of the consequence it might bring about, especially while handling a weapon that isn't mine. "Is that why you kill? You believe you're already forgiven?"

His head tilts farther to the side. Awkwardly so. "You wear a cross, but you're no believer, are you?"

There's no hint of accusation in his tone, yet his words pierce my heart. Draw blood. Send anger coursing through my veins. Jaws clenched, I can't help but lash out at him, a vile murderer condemning me. "You know nothing about me or what I believe."

"Our bodies speak for us. Tell the truth when our lips lie." Jacques, arms still raised, takes an awkward step toward me. Then another. The unsteady, yet bold moves leave me breathless. "I can see the pain in your eyes, Detective. The way you reached for your cross when I grasped mine nearly drove me to tears. You're lost, but there's no need for you to be. I can help you find solace."

"You help me?" I'd be pissed if the suggestion weren't so ludicrous. "How can you stand there and act like you're the better person between us?"

"Better?" He chuckles. "We are all sinners, Detective, yet salvation is close at hand." His fingers grasp at the air above his head as he inhales through the two holes above his mouth. "Ahh. Can you feel it?"

"Salvation? What would you know of it? The ground you stand upon bulges with the bodies of your victims."

Jacques's gaze pierces me. Sends my heart into a frenzy. "Come now, Detective. The ground you tread does not differ from mine. In fact, I'm inclined to believe that it's our similarities that drive fear through your veins."

"I'm no killer!" My banshee voice shrieks through the nave, but the ancient, stained-glass windows hold strong.

His right eye glistens in the pale light as his smile fades. "Nor am I," he whispers.

Anger flares. Tightens my grip on the gun. "Eleven bodies say otherwise."

"Do they?" Jacques takes another step. Three more. Only a dozen paces separate us now.

My finger slides down and caresses the side of the trigger. "One more step, and I'll send you straight to hell."

Jacques's brow wrinkles as his gaze falls to the floor. Mine follows his, and it's then that I notice his bare, disproportioned feet. One foot lacks all toes, and the other foot part of its heel. "One more step will end my suffering, and I so long for it, but doing so will not save…"

Drops of water splatter on Jacques's feet and pummel the white tile he stands upon. When our eyes meet again, I notice the light glistening off his tear-streaked cheeks. Several drops cling to the underside of his narrow jaw. Sparkling little jewels.

This time, it's my feet that draw us closer. Dangerously close. I steady my hand and level the weapon toward his gut, easing my finger away from the trigger.

Silence gathers around us as we continue to stare at one another. Two strangers. Different worlds. United by death.

He's the killer.

I remind myself of this fact repeatedly, yet I'm one, too.

But we're not the same.

Empathy he doesn't deserve creeps into my voice. "Finish what you were going to say, Jacques. Killing you will not save what?"

Jacques's gaze returns to the floor, and the pool of tears puddled at his feet continues to grow. A waft of booze masked with peppermint hits my nostrils when he exhales. After a handful of seconds in utter silence, he finally responds with a hollow whisper, "Him."

CHAPTER TWO

Nine weeks earlier…

AIRPLANE TOILETS ARE BY far the worst. Not only are they cramped, but they smell just as bad as an outhouse. Plus, I'm always afraid of flushing while still seated. The hole that opens in the bottom of the toilet might only be a few inches in diameter, but it sounds like it could suck me right out of the plane. Never a good thought.

I stand up and smack my head on the wall in front of me. It's almost impossible to turn around. "Ugh! Why do they have to make these bathrooms so tiny? There's no way any couple could ever join the thirty-thousand-foot club in here."

And why would anyone want to?

After pumping the sink several times with one hand and cupping as much water as I can with my other, I splash it onto my face. Despite it being lukewarm, it's still refreshing. Crouching down, I stare into the mirror and begin wiping off the remaining water from my face with a hand towel. Ghastly, bluish-black sacks hang beneath my eyes, evidence of months of insomnia.

Pushing on the sacks somehow makes my reflection worse. "Lord, I'm a disgusting mess."

Just as I'm about to turn away, I notice something odd happening with my eyes. The vibrant green hue of my irises dulls and grows darker. Becomes more of a hunter green as they shrink in size. My normally large pupils shrink to beady pinpoints, and the sclerae become pink with angry red veins. Then, I notice the pea-sized mole nestled between my cheek and the right side of my nose.

"What the hell—"

"Hello, Alice. You miss me?"

Voices are my thing. I never forget one no matter how long it's been. "Reagan?"

Two hands reach through the mirror and grab hold of its sides. I stutter backward. Slam into the bathroom door as the impossible happens right before my eyes. The mirror expands in width and height, and Reagan begins pulling himself through it and into the cramped space with me.

Reaching back, I fumble with the door lock but can't seem to get it to unlatch. I risk a quick glance over my shoulder and see the problem, but it's too late. Reagan's fat, sausage-fingered hands wrap around my throat and slam me against the door repeatedly.

The latch gives out, and the door flies open and slams against the back of the plane. We tumble out of the bathroom and onto the floor. The combination of landing on a hard surface and Reagan's excessive weight coming down on top of me knocks the wind from my lungs. I can't catch my breath as his fingers tighten around my neck.

Clawing at his hands does nothing, nor does punching him in the gut, and his girth has my legs pinned to the floor. He grins deviously, then smashes my mouth against his dried, cracked lips.

His tongue probes for an opening and leaves a trail of slobber across my lips and down my chin when he finally pulls back. "I relish the moments we've shared."

I'd spit in his face if I could, but a grunt is all I can manage.

Reagan releases his hold on me and rolls to the side, then stands. I gasp for air and massage my neck, but the reprieve is short-lived. He grabs me by my hair, yanks me to my feet, and shoves me against the airlock door. I scream, but no one comes to my rescue.

Pressing himself against me, he yells in my ear, "Time to fly, Detective. Hope you packed your parachute."

The airlock door swings open, revealing the night sky. Reagan grunts as he shoves me out of the airplane.

Wind rushes through my hair and billows my shirt and pants as I plummet toward a dark plane. At first, what my eyes see makes no sense, but then I realize it's the ocean rushing up to meet me.

"God, no!"

* * * * *

The jolt and screech of wheels touching down on the runway pulls me out of my nightmare and thrusts me back into the uncomfortable leather seat of our Boeing 777 just moments before impact with the dark ocean. My heart thunders in my chest, but not from the jolt. Seth's hand caresses the top of mine as our eyes meet. That simple gesture chases away the nightmare. My pulse slows, and I force a lazy yawn, but Seth's no fool.

His brow furrows. "Another nightmare?"

Reagan's beady green eyes fill my mind. "It's noth—"

Words catch in the back of my throat as a second and third jolt come in quick succession before the plane finally settles on the runway. The taste of grilled chicken and vegetables mixed with stomach acid bubbles up the back of my throat, an unwelcome encore from our earlier dinner. Or lunch. At this point, I'm uncertain as to which meal it was supposed to be. I swallow hard, forcing it all back down.

A few deep breaths settle my roiling stomach, but then my entire body careens forward as the wing flaps rise to slow the airplane. My hands punch the back of the seat in front of me with jarring force. Guilt draws me back into my seat as angry brown eyes stare at me through the narrow crack between the seats. Fringed by deep troughs of cracking foundation, the eyes belong to a middle-aged white woman. Given the accent she spoke with when addressing the flight attendant on several occasions during our forever-long flight from Dallas, TX, I'm certain she's British.

"Sorry," I mouth to her. She responds with an eye roll that sends her eyeballs all the way up into the back of her head before she finally turns around.

Not sorry.

The captain's voice fills the large cabin, welcoming us all to Paris-Charles De Gaulle airport in Paris, France in both English and French. He drones on about the current weather, time, and various connecting gate assignments, but his voice fades as my gaze meets Seth's grayish-blue eyes once more.

Concern fills them and wrinkles his brow further. "Your nightmares are becoming more frequent."

"You think I don't know that?" I say through gritted teeth. Regret sweeps in, forcing me to bite my lower lip and look away. "I'm sorry."

Seth slides his arm around my back. Squeezes me gently. "I know, and it's okay."

"No, it's not." The cabin blurs. I blink back angry tears, then quickly wipe my eyes with the back of my hand before facing him again. "You deserve better than me."

"You're probably right, but you're better than the best of them, so I guess that means I'm stuck with you unless I want to be alone in life." The corners of his mouth rise, parting his lips and exposing a set of pearly whites. A dimple in the center of his left cheek deepens.

God, I'm the luckiest person in the world.

Even after fifteen months of marriage, I still don't understand what he sees in me. Lifting his arm back over my head, I slip my hand into his and intertwine our fingers. His soft skin sets me adrift on a blissful sea.

He graces my forehead with a soft kiss. "You sure you don't want to talk about it?"

I look around the plane. No one seems to be paying attention to us, but it still makes me uncomfortable. "Not right now. I'll tell you everything later. Promise."

"Fair enough." His gaze moves beyond me and settles on a point somewhere outside the small cabin window. Tiny wrinkles form around his eyes. "Can you believe we've just landed in Paris?" Excitement strains his voice as he crushes my hand and thrusts it against the rigid plastic armrest between us.

I pat the top of his hand with increasing force. "Seth, stop."

His brow furrows as he looks down at our hands, then his grip loosens. "Oh, right. Sorry about that, babe."

Pulling my hand away, I verify no bones are broken before flexing and then shaking off the pain. Out the window, the taxiway glides by as we head toward the airport apron. Excitement builds in my chest as the reality of where we are begins to set in.

I can't believe we're in Paris!

"First time on foreign soil," I whisper, afraid I'll sound like a schoolgirl if I try and speak with greater volume.

Seth shakes his head and grins. "Not for me, but this is at the top of the list of places I've been."

Occasionally, I find myself trapped in a moment where I question how well I really know this man I call my husband. This is one of those moments. In all honesty, it's a bit frightening. I turn in my seat and stare at him. "What other countries have you been to before?"

He waves me off and stares out the tiny window. "Nowhere important. Just forget about it."

The plane pulls up to the skybridge and comes to a halt, and then a loud ding signals we can remove our safety belts and disembark. As per the usual, most of the passengers have already done so. Everyone's always in a rush to disembark.

Where's the emergency?

An hour and a half later, Seth and I emerge from customs and into the main part of the massive airport. In the distance, I spot a man dressed in dark slacks, a white, button-up shirt, black dress shoes, and a brown overcoat. He's holding a sign that reads "Bergman-Ryan." Short-cropped, salt-and-pepper hair parts the right side of the man's scalp. A pleasant contrast to his aged, olive skin. Wire-rimmed glasses hug his clean-shaven, narrow face, but it's his sagging cheeks that bring a smile to my lips.

He looks like Droopy Dog.

Pierre or not, I'm already fond of this man.

Recognition sparks in the man's eyes as we approach. A grin spreads across his face. He folds up the sign and shoves it into one of his overcoat pockets as he heads toward us.

The three of us meet in front of Le Grand Comptoir, a French coffee shop. The man proffers his hand toward me, and I accept it. Warm fingers wrap mine and lift my hand toward thin, parted lips as Pierre leans over. His moist lips greet the tops of my knuckles.

Grey eyes meet my stare as Pierre releases my hand and straightens. "Detective Bergman, it is a pleasure. I am Special Agent Pierre Lamont. We spoke previously over the phone."

I nod. "Yes, of course. I recognize your voice."

Pierre dips his head toward Seth, his gaze breaking from mine for only a moment. "Detective Ryan. Welcome to Paris."

"A pleasure." Seth folds his arms over his chest, a stance I'm all too familiar with.

Pierre's smile broadens as he looks me up and down. "Your police photo does you no justice."

A flash of heat toasts my cheeks. "And you're not what I pictured."

The man cocks his head. "Good or bad?"

I shrug, heat still in my cheeks. "I haven't decided yet."

He frowns, then nods. "Let me know when you do." Turning away, he beckons us to follow. "Come, we have no time to dispose."

Time is money, I guess.

Seth glances over at the counter of Le Grand Comptoir, and I know exactly what he's thinking, so I grab his arm. "Not a chance, babe. You'll have plenty of time to consume French coffee later."

"Unlike you, I didn't sleep most of the flight. Just one sip will fend off my jet lag."

Sleep? As if.

"No." I tug on his arm. "Come on. We need to get moving before Pierre loses us."

Seth scowls. "Might not be the worst thing."

"Lighten up. I kinda like him."

His scowl deepens. "That's what worries me. Him and his fancy French accent."

"It's barely noticeable," I say. It's true, but I still like it. "Besides, he's probably old enough to be my grandfather."

A crack surfaces in Seth's armor, the corners of his lips inching upward. "Maybe so."

"I know so, and you're one to talk. I saw how you soaked up the attention of that brunette in customs. Her eyes barely glanced at your passport, but she gave you several scans."

Seth chuckles and shrugs. "Ah, yes. Natalia. No harm in appreciating the fact that someone took notice of *me* for once. You're always the star of the show, so give me my moments when they come."

"It's the red hair that makes me the star." I twirl a finger through it.

Seth sweeps my hair back with his hand. "It's not just the hair. You've got the entire package, my sexy wife." He reels me in and kisses me but pulls away far too fast, his attention lured away by our surroundings again. "I still can't believe we're in Paris. The City of Love. Can you believe it? What could be better than this?"

I glance around. "Better than this stinky airport? Trust me, I can think of several things. For one, we could be at the Eiffel Tower right now taking in the view of the city while sipping a glass of champagne. Or we could be touring the Louvre Museum and freaking out over how the Mona Lisa stares at us from every angle. There's also the—"

He raises his hands, cutting me off. "Fine, I'll admit we haven't reached the pentacle of perfection yet, but we're getting there. I can feel it."

"It's pinnacle, and don't forget that we're here for a job, not a vacation. We've got nine bodies and no leads. Plus, our escort isn't waiting for us to catch up."

Seth sighs. "Right."

I take his hand and lead us after Pierre. When we step through the doors toward the train to Paris, a strange feeling rises in my gut. I grip Seth's hand tighter as we weave our way through the throng of people.

Pierre maintains a good distance ahead of us, but at least he's not out of sight. As we push forward, the strange feeling intensifies. A sense of I don't know… apprehension?

Cold chills sweep down the entire length of my body as the nightmare of Reagan rears its evil head within my mind once again, doubling down on me. I try and shake it off, but the memory refuses to fade. Drives the fear in me to a new level.

What kinds of evil do you have in store for us, Paris?

CHAPTER THREE

DANK AIR BLASTS MY face and slinks beneath my jacket as I step through the airport terminal doors and out into the wet, late afternoon. Rain-slicked sidewalks shine beneath overhead lights. Pierre pushes ahead through a throng of people waiting for buses and taxis, and Seth and I do our best to keep pace.

Beyond the last taxi sits a white sedan parked next to the curb. Its grille features a silver Peugeot Lion. I'd recognize it anywhere.

A T9 Peugeot 308.

Pierre gestures toward the sedan. "That's us."

"Huh. Not what I was expecting," I say.

The lights flash as Pierre approaches the driver side door. "And what were you expecting? A train ride, perhaps?"

Seth chuckles. "I kinda did."

I elbow Seth right in the gut, and it earns me a scowl. "Certainly not, but I also didn't expect a T9."

Pierre's eyes gleam. "You know your cars, Detective Bergman."

"It's one of her passions," Seth says.

I run my hand along the side of the car. "Definitely not a standard issue police vehicle."

Pierre shrugs and smiles. "I'm old and deserve a touch of comfort, as you Americans say."

"Don't we all." Seth opens the back door for me and then settles into the front passenger seat.

Once secured in our seatbelts, Pierre pulls away from the curb and drives us out of Paris-Charles De Gaulle. Fairly little stands out as I take in my first glimpses of Paris through the backseat window.

"Well, what do you think of our city so far?" I turn and meet Pierre's eyes through the rearview mirror.

"Honestly?" I ask.

He nods.

I stare out the window again. "After falling in love with all the pictures and movies I've seen of Paris, I really want to enjoy your City of Love, but so far it's just another crowded old European city."

"Yes, of course," Pierre says. "The beauty of Paris lies within its center. Given time, I'm certain you'll discover all the magic Paris has to offer, murder aside."

Pierre points out a few landmarks as we drive down dozens of curvy, narrow streets, but he's clearly distracted. After ten months without a single solid lead in his case, it's understandable. In fact, it's almost a requirement at this point. The pressure piled upon his shoulders must rival that of the water the Titanic took on as it sank beneath the frozen ocean.

As we move closer to the center of Paris, the streets begin to squish between old, grimy, multi-level buildings. Most of the buildings feature businesses on their lower levels and apartment or condo living above.

"This is all a drastic change from the wide streets and sprawling, single-story structures that dominate Desert Springs back home," I say.

"I'm certain it is," Pierre says. "Your Desert Springs has a few advantages over my Paris, but I assure you that art and culture aren't among them."

"That's for sure," Seth says. "Unless you count graffiti as art. We've got that in spades."

Pierre glances over at Seth. "Spades?"

"It means we've more than enough graffiti," I say.

"Oh." He nods his head. "Well then, we have graffiti in spades, too."

After driving countless miles, Pierre turns into an old parking structure and heads down two levels before pulling into a parking space. A quick count confirms the level contains about sixty spaces. Only a handful are occupied.

Pierre points toward a nondescript white commercial truck three spaces to our right. "That's us over there."

Us?

For the life of me, I can't figure out why Pierre's brought us here. "What does a truck in a parking lot have to do with the case?"

Pierre smiles at me through the rearview mirror. "Trust me, you'll understand soon enough."

As with the airport, dank, musty air greets me the moment I open my car door. I'd love to know how people live in such an environment. It's like taking a shower and then putting clothes on without toweling off first. I'll never get used to it. Then again, summers back home give the fires of hell a run for its money, so who am I to complain?

The white truck features no discernible decals or markings of any sort, not even on its roll-up back door. A refrigerator unit sits over the top of its cab, fans churning away. Several streaks of deep-blue, red, and black spray paint run down the side of the truck, remnants of graffiti no longer decipherable.

Seth stops a few paces from the truck, turns to Pierre, and raises his arms. "Okay, enough of the Cloak and Dagger stuff. What exactly are we doing here?"

Pierre's expression sours a bit. "As I'm sure you know, investigations sometimes become a bit… how do you say? Dirty?"

"Messy?" I offer.

"Yes, messy." Pierre chuckles. "Some red tapes are hard to cut, if you catch my meaning."

Seth scowls. "I'm afraid I don't."

"Sometimes a body needs to be stashed away for further… processing."

Pierre winks at me. "Understand now?"

Judging by Seth's blank expression, he's still lost, but I'm following Pierre with ease. Somehow, Pierre has managed to keep one of the victims out of the morgue *and* the ground. Given the circumstances, I appreciate the discretion he's affording me and the ability I possess.

I reach over and touch Seth's shoulder. "It's simple, babe. Getting us access to see the body would be difficult enough given that we're foreigners and work for no office with any jurisdiction or authority outside of Desert Springs let alone the US, but getting authorization for us to also examine said body would prove impossible, especially without the presence of a large and unwanted audience."

Pierre nods. "Precisely what I implied."

He presses a button on a secondary key chain fob. The roller door on the back of the truck lurches and then scrolls upward. A blast of cold air greets us, along with a brunette woman and her SIG-Sauer SP 2022 aimed right at us.

Seth grabs my arm and backs us up several steps. "Whoa, what the hell is this?"

"A necessary precaution." Pierre raises his hand, and the woman holsters her weapon, albeit with reluctance. "This is my colleague, Special Agent Thérèse Desmarais."

Thérèse's gaze locks onto Seth, and she bites her lower lip. Drives my fingernails right into the meat of my palms. "Ah, yes, *les Américains.*"

Two seconds flat, and I already hate this Thérèse and her elegant French accent, her beautiful shoulder-length hair, perfect caramel complexion, and piercing amber eyes. Plus, she's dressed to kill in her black boots, denim skinny jeans, pearl V-neck top, and black trench coat. Who in their right mind wears clothes like those while posted inside a refrigerated truck?

No one.

Other than me, that is.

Seth bounds up into the back of the truck. "I'm Detective Seth Ryan." A goofy smile paints his face as he shakes her hand. "But you can just call me

Seth."

Traitor!

Thérèse glances down as though she's shy, but her hand lingers in Seth's for far too long. Admittedly, a fraction of a second would be too long. "A pleasure." Seth's obviously too enamored with her to notice.

We will have words later, Seth Allyn Ryan.

I groan and haul myself up into the back of the truck.

Thérèse steps forward and proffers her hand, but it's her perfume that assaults me first. Sweet. Flowery. Lavenderish. With a hint of cat urine and bile. A nidorous concoction that must've spent decades fermenting in the bowels of some feline before being extracted from its anal glands and bottled. The nauseating stench quickly works its way right down into my empty stomach and gives it a good twist. I'm certain the wretched perfume comes with some sort of posh French name, too.

Eau de chat pipi.

I snicker at my cleverness but immediately feel awkward when I notice all eyes are on me, especially hers.

The right corners of her perfect lips curl upward. "Alice, yes?"

Begrudgingly, I take her hand, expecting it to feel blubbery like a cold, raw chicken thigh, but instead it's warm and soft, and her strong grip surprises me. "Detective Bergman."

"Oh, *formelle*." She smiles, revealing a set of perfect, white teeth. "Please, call me Thérèse."

Several more fitting names come to mind, one being the female name of a dog, but I keep them to myself. "As you wish, Thérèse."

Once Pierre climbs aboard, he presses the button and shuts us inside the back of the truck. Lights buzz and flicker on above us, bringing us out of the darkness. But with the light comes a draught of arctic air. It wraps itself around me and burrows its way beneath my inadequate clothing. I fight off a chill, determined to be as stoic and unaffected by the cold as Thérèse seems to be.

It shouldn't be a competition, and perhaps it's not, but it certainly feels that way. The retched woman has crawled beneath my skin without so much as batting an eyelash. How much more pathetic and insecure could I possibly be?

I shake it off and force myself to focus on my surroundings, which are sparse. At the front end of the ten-foot-long truck bed stand just two items: a padded barstool with stainless-steel legs and a morgue cadaver gurney with a white sheet draped over it. The barstool drops from memory as a silhouette beneath the sheet draws my attention.

Giant feet hang over the end of the gurney, bent awkwardly at the ankles. Given their size, I surmise the victim is male. Tall, too. A standard cadaver gurney is seventy-eight inches in length, so that puts the victim at a minimum of seven feet tall.

"This was the ninth victim to turn up," Pierre says. "He was discovered just off of Rue Lachelier and Boulevard Masséna in the middle of an outdoor basketball court late in the morning on January eighth."

Figures he'd be on a basketball court.

"He *literally* dropped at center court," Thérèse says. "You will see soon enough."

Pierre peels the sheet back, revealing a man of Asian descent and confirming my observations. He positions the sheet just above the man's waist, steps back, and nods at me. "Mr. Li Qiang is all yours, Detective."

A Chinese man.

Everything else inside the truck fades into oblivion as I step up to the gurney and take in the victim. Black hair. Round face. Slight upward slant of the eyes. Thin nose. Plump but not overly large lips. A tuft of hair on his chin. Alive, he would've been quite handsome.

A slash runs perpendicular across the victim's throat. Deep, perfect edges. Likely made with a scalpel or garrote. No detectable bruising of any kind around the wound. A quick check beneath the sheet reveals no bruising or lacerations anywhere else on the front of the body other than a bruise on the top of the victim's right wrist and the incisions made during the autopsy.

No bruised knuckles. No chipped or cracked nails and nothing lodged beneath them. As far as I can tell, the victim didn't put up a fight.

"Only the neck," Thérèse says, as though reading my thoughts. "Several liters of blood drained."

"And the bruising on the wrist?"

Thérèse walks over to the gurney. "The medical examiner's best guess was an insertion point for an IV."

"Pre- or post-mortem?" I ask.

"Hard to tell, but likely post-mortem," Thérèse says. "We've researched several theories as to its purpose, but none have proven to shed light on our investigation." She lifts the victim's head and turns it sideways. "As you can feel right here, the victim suffered post-mortem skull fractures consistent with his head smacking a hard surface with great force."

The fractures aren't obvious to the naked eye, but my gloved fingers easily detect the abnormal concavity of the back of the victim's skull.

"And the cause?" I ask.

"As I said, he literally dropped on the concrete at center court." She lays the victim's head back down. "You'll understand more when we visit the locations of the victims."

"Got it." I refocus on the victim's face. "And who was Mr. Qiang?"

Pierre clears his throat. "A businessman who traded rare commodities for various clients."

"By day." Thérèse's remark draws my attention. She sneers at the dead man and continues, "Three months ago, he faced charges of sex trafficking young women and girls. A truckload of evidence and a key witness had him dead to rights, but both the witness and the evidence disappeared right before the trial was about to begin. The case fell apart, and he walked."

"And then he turns up dead," Seth says. "Can't be coincidence."

Thérèse's cold gaze meets mine. "If you ask me, the man got exactly what he deserved."

Something in her tone makes me think that either the circumstances, the case, or both are personal to her. No matter what the answer, it holds little baring on the corpse lying in front of me.

I stare at Li Qiang and his severed neck for several moments. Given the slight upward angle of the fatal wound and the man's height, he must've been kneeling or lying down when he was killed. Then again, the killer could also be excessively tall. Or maybe they stood on top of something to gain the upper hand. Whatever the circumstances, the killer must've been quick.

You didn't suffer long, did you?

Li Qiang says nothing, but I'll have my answer soon enough.

After positioning the barstool to the left of the man's head, I take a seat. Seth comes to my side and places a hand on my shoulder. I look up at him and stare into his beautiful blue eyes. A soft breath expels the fear and jealousy pent up within me, leaving my heart filled with nothing but love.

How could Thérèse ever be a threat to us?

Seth grimaces. "You sure this is a good idea?"

He always fears. Always doubts. Flawed as he is, it's yet another reason I love him. "It's the only reason I'm here."

"Yeah, I know." He frowns. "It's just… I want you to remember what Isaiah told you about using your *gift*."

I push air through my nostrils and rip off my latex gloves. "Trust me, it's not something I'd ever forget."

He's taken aback, his eyes wide. "Okay, okay. I just want you to be you, you know?"

Seth is the master of digging holes and throwing himself into them. It's almost like he thrives on it.

Or he just likes pissing me off.

"Right, me. Not some blind woman that'll inconvenience your life."

Wow, where did that come from?

Seth withdraws his arm from my shoulders. "That's not what I meant."

"Isn't it?" My mouth speaks as though it has detached itself from my brain. Perhaps it has, and the reason for it stands just a few paces in front of me.

Thérèse.

He sighs and shakes his head. "Look, forget I said anything."

I stare at the body with renewed reluctance. "Already did."

As much as I hate to admit it, Seth isn't wrong. Touching the body might not make me go blind again right away, but it'll certainly push me toward that inevitable fate. Even so, it's not what makes me hesitate.

I know virtually nothing of this man, Li Qiang. For all I know, he could be a Shadow Priest. If so, and if my father is right, entering this man's mind could kill me. Then again, if he's a Centaurian and special like me, I'll experience his death as though it were my own.

But he's not, Alice.

I know this to be true because no birthmark or scar mars the inside of his left wrist. Even so, my hand rises to my neck, and I swallow hard, unprepared to have my head severed from my body. Well, practically severed.

Another thought enters my mind. One I'd never contemplated before.

Does the type of person I touch determine the speed at which my vision deteriorates?

It's a good question, and one I'll have to talk to my father about when I get back home, but it's pointless to think about right now. No matter the answer, I'm here for a single purpose: to bring a serial killer to justice and closure to the victims' families. In order to do that, I must mind tether with this man and find out what he knows.

After several deep breaths, I close my eyes and touch the man's ice-cold shoulder. Seconds tick by, but time doesn't slow as it normally does. No fiery sensation warms my fingertips. Nor do I sense an alien shift within myself. Not a damned thing happens.

My gift has never failed before, and it scares the hell out of me that it has now. Fear and frustration build within my chest. Spread up my neck. Tighten my jaw. My fingers slide off the man's shoulder as I open my eyes and stare at my hand.

What's wrong with me? Am I broken?

I glance back at Seth, shake my head at the question lingering in his eyes, and then focus my gaze on Pierre. "I'm sorry, but this isn't going to work."

Pierre frowns. "*This* as in now, or *this* as in our arrangement?"

Has my time in Paris already ended before it's begun?

I swallow my fear, determined to not let it bother me. But how could it not? Without my gift, I'm useless.

"Here. Now."

Thérèse cocks her head. "Would it help if we left you alone?"

The woman seems to know more about the way I work than I expected, and I don't like it. "Ugh. It's nothing like that."

Seth squeezes my shoulder. "So, what *is* it like, then?"

It's a good question. After a few moments of contemplation, my mind remains blank. "I don't know." I shrug away Seth's hand and hop off the chair.

As I pace next to the gurney, thoughts race through my mind. I voice them without restraint. "Maybe the victim's brain requires blood in order to stay viable for me to tether to it. Or maybe the victim's been dead too long. Or maybe the killer did use drugs on the victim and that destroyed whatever remained of the victim's memories. Or maybe I'm more exhausted from the flight over here than I thought and it's affecting my gift. I just don't know."

"I'm sure it could be any of those things," Pierre says. "The victim's brain certainly lacks blood, and he died—" He takes out his cellphone and looks at it. "—roughly twenty-six-and-a-half days ago. And, as you said, it was a long flight from your Desert Springs."

"Whatever the reason might be, I'm sorry." I sigh. "I wish I had an answer, but I just don't."

Pierre waves his hand. "No, no, you're right. I'm not sure what I was contemplating driving you straight here from the airport. Looking back, I feel the fool."

I know it's not the flight because I'm not tired at all, but Pierre doesn't need to know that. "I would've done the same. In fact, I would have insisted on digging in if you hadn't brought us straight here." Another thought hits me, but I know it's a long shot. "You wouldn't happen to have another body I could examine, would you?"

"I'm afraid we have just the one," Pierre says. "Never mind that right now, though." He gestures toward the back of the truck bed with his arm. "Please allow me to take you to your hotel. We can get started again first thing in the morning. After you've had a chance to rest and acclimate to the time difference."

Thérèse's gaze washes over Seth. Lingers where it shouldn't. "Yes, we want you performing at your peak."

Could she be any more obvious?

Seth seems oblivious to her pass, weaving his fingers together and stretching his arms out in front of himself. "Sounds good to me. I'm thoroughly bushwhacked."

Pierre looks at Seth, his brow deeply furrowed, and his head cocked to one side. "What does this *bush whacked* mean?"

I jump in before Seth has a chance to display his ineptness with vocabulary. "It's North American slang and means he's exhausted."

Pierre frowns, then nods. "I like this bush whacked word." The way he says it, like it's two words instead of one, makes me chuckle. "I will append it to my vocabulary," he says with a final nod.

Seth raises a fist and pumps it in the air. "Score one for the Americans!"

My eyes nearly roll out of my head. "Sometimes, you're such a child."

He shrugs. "As they say, it takes one to know one."

"Seriously? Ugh, where are we? Back in high school?" I shake my head as I walk toward the back of the truck bed and wait as the door slowly rolls upward.

We're not alone.

* * * * *

The young man on the other side of the roll-up door seems as surprised as I am. He tosses a spray paint can on the ground and bolts. As I'm standing there, still processing what just happened, Thérèse leaps off the back of the truck like a total badass. She hardly misses a beat as she hits the concrete, rolls forward over her left shoulder, and pops back onto her feet.

Drawing her weapon, Thérèse takes aim at the fleeing man. *"Continue de courir et je te tire dans le dos!"*

Out of practice, my brain takes several seconds to translate her French back into English.

Keep running and I'll shoot you in the back.

The young man skids to a halt and raises his arms. He turns around, eyes wide. *"Ç'est juste de la peinture. Je jure!"*

Seth joins me at the edge of the truck bed. "What are they saying?"

Weaving my cold fingers around Seth's hot ones brings warmth back into me. "Thérèse threatened to shoot him if he didn't stop running, and he's swearing it's just paint."

Seth frowns. "As opposed to what?"

"I'm guessing his argument is that spray painting a vehicle doesn't warrant being shot in the back."

"Gotcha," Seth says. "Does seem a bit excessive."

Pierre sits down on the edge of the truck bed and hops to the ground. "Let him go, Thérèse. We're done here."

"He's seen us," she growls.

Seth and I share a look of confusion.

What the hell difference does that make?

Pierre shouts at the young man, *"Qu'as-tu vu?"*

"What did you see?" I translate for Seth.

The young man quickly covers his eyes. *"Rien! Je jure!"*

"Nothing! I swear!" I repeat.

"Figured that much." Seth lifts my hand and kisses the back of it.

"Soyez parti," Pierre replies.

The young man turns and runs off, deeper into the parking structure. Thérèse holsters her weapon and returns to the truck, her lip curled into a snarl.

I look up at Seth. "Be gone."

Seth scowls. "That's a bit harsh."

I roll my eyes. "That's what Pierre said to the young man, dork."

Seth grins wryly. "Yeah, I got it."

"Keep it up, smart guy, and you'll be sleeping on the sofa for the foreseeable future."

"Been there, done that." He slashes the air with his free hand. "Totally overrated."

Thérèse dusts off her jacket sleeve and peers up at Seth. "Only if it's done alone."

I handle her pass at Seth easily enough and brush off the wink she gives him afterward, but there's no way I'm allowing Seth's laughter to slide off my back, too. He continues to laugh, right up until I crush his fingers between mine. The ploy works, earning me one of his best glares in weeks, but it glances right off the side of my face as I turn and lock eyes with the devil of Paris.

This woman's gonna be a problem.

CHAPTER FOUR

AFTER COUNTLESS HOURS OF catching Thérèse and Seth in the throes of love through various scenarios and scenery, the first rays of sunlight finally creep into our bedroom suite at the Paris Skyline Hotel and bring me fully awake. Although a figment of my restless mind, Seth's treachery will not go unpunished. I roll over with a fisted hand, but my awkward punch connects with an empty mattress.

Back home, Seth's never out of bed before I am, yet a thorough search of the entire suite confirms he's gone. Returning to the bedroom, I check my phone but have no new messages or calls.

As foolish as it is, my mind immediately targets Thérèse. "If she's somehow involved in his disappearance, I'll find a way to neutralize her for good."

Seth walks into the bedroom, his brow glistening with sweat. "Neutralize who?"

"Where've you been?" I stalk toward him, nails digging into my palms.

"Out for a jog." He pulls off his shirt and wipes himself down with it. "The city's beautiful in the morning."

I struggle to hold onto my anger, but the longer I stare at his bare chest the quicker it diffuses. Abandoning it altogether, I wrap my arms around his waist and press my cheek against his sweaty chest. Nothing in the world smells the way he does, and it drives me mad with desire.

Seth kisses the top of my head. "Brought you some fresh croissants and a piping hot cup of coffee from a bakery just down the street. Trust me when I say they're both beyond amazing."

Grabbing his hand, I drag him toward the bathroom. "Come on, sexy husband. I promise they'll still be good *after* we shower."

We arrive downstairs right at 8am and find two cars awaiting us outside the hotel lobby, the first driven by Pierre and the second by Thérèse. Seth drags us between the two cars and starts to round the bumper of Thérèse's blue Alpine A110.

I grab his arm and yank him around. "Not a chance in hell you're riding with her."

Seth guffaws. "Seriously? You clearly can't stand the woman."

"Good observation, Sherlock." I rise onto my tippy toes and kiss him. "Just get in Pierre's car. We've wasted enough time already."

"Fine, but I thought I was doing you a favor."

"You doing me a favor was the coffee and croissants."

"And the shower? What do you call that?"

"That was me returning you the favor."

"Sure seemed like you got just as much out of it as I did."

Maybe more.

I smile and let myself into Thérèse's car. The luxurious, black Alcantara and leather bucket seat hugs my form as I sink into it. Even though it's a 2019 model, the interior still smells like a new car. Everything about it is beautiful and immaculate, right down to the bright blue stitching on the seats, doors, central console, and steering wheel. The color matches that of the car's exterior.

Goosebumps race up my arms as Thérèse fires up the engine and gives it a few revs. It's the first mid-engine car I've ever been in, and I'm already in love with it. For a moment, I almost forget she's the enemy.

"I can tell by your reaction that we share the same affinity for fast cars."

She smiles, shifts the car into drive, and accelerates right through the stop sign at the end of the street.

I'll be the first to admit the woman reminds me of myself. Too much in fact. And therein lies the problem. If it were only her fashion sense and love of cars that linked us, we'd already be besties, but flirting with Seth crosses an unacceptable line. Now, we'll never be friends.

Thérèse guides the car through traffic with the precision of a Le Mans racer. It's quite impressive and leaves me more relaxed than I ought to be.

"Where are we headed?" I ask, staring out the window at the passing scenery.

"Pierre thought it'd help for you to get a firsthand look at all the places where the bodies have been dumped. He thinks it'll give you a better perspective as to what we're dealing with and why we've failed to make any progress on this case. So, we're headed to the first location now."

"He's not wrong. I studied the pictures he gave me yesterday ad nauseum but gleaned nothing from them. I'm sure having a look for myself will give me a better perspective."

Thérèse glances over at me. "Can I ask you a question?"

I look out the side window again, avoiding eye contact with the woman. "Nothing's stopping you."

"You don't like me, do you?" She turns a sharp corner without breaking. The tires squeal with protest, but the car never misses a beat as it surges forward.

My hand tightens around the door handle, but the reaction has nothing to do with Thérèse's driving. She obviously has no qualms about getting straight to the heart of an issue. It's refreshing, but I won't give her the satisfaction of acknowledging it. I stare straight ahead. "Is it that obvious?"

After a few seconds of glorious silence, she says, "It's because of your husband." She glances over at me again when I don't confirm her suspicion. "I'm right, aren't I?"

I close my eyes and take a deep, calming breath before looking over at her. "I don't like the way you look at him and flirt with him."

She shrugs. "He's attractive. Why would I not flirt with him?"

The folds of my jeans conform to the shapes of my fists. "Because he's my husband." Another deep breath. "How is that not obvious?"

A grin curls her perfect, plump lips. Evil. Sadistic. "You don't trust him."

The sound of my quickening heartbeat fills my ears. Timpani drums pounding out a dark and dramatic moment in my private symphony of rage. She's pushing my buttons, and I know it, yet I can't keep the anger from my voice. "Of course I do."

The front of the car dips as Thérèse brings us to an abrupt stop at a light. She turns and meets my glare with a smile. "Then what's the problem?"

Tension stiffens my jaw. "I don't trust *you.*"

"As they say, it takes two to tango. Even in Paris." The light changes, and Thérèse floors it, pinning me to my seat for a good three-and-a-half seconds before she lets off the gas a bit. The sound of the engine and the smoothness of the ride thrills me, but it's not enough to distract me from our heated conversation.

"Yes," I say, "but you French people seem to know no boundaries when it comes to love."

She laughs. "By love you mean sexual promiscuity."

Heat rises in my cheeks. I turn my attention toward the side window once again and watch the city fly by. "Sure, that too."

A block goes by in silence. It's glorious, but then she starts pressing buttons again. "What do you really know about your husband?"

My jeans are at the mercy of my hands again. "We keep no secrets."

"So you know everything there is to know about him? About his past? I doubt it."

The way she says it—as though she knows something about him that I don't—sends chills down my spine. She can't possibly, yet my gut wrenches at the thought. "No, but Seth's past is irrelevant."

Thérèse chuckles. "Perhaps at first, but something always changes to make it relevant."

She accelerates and weaves between several cars with only inches to spare. If her goal is to scare me, it'll never work. After all, I ride with Seth most of the time, and he exercises no caution when it comes to driving.

After another stint of silence, Thérèse says, "I make it my business to interrogate every lover I have."

"Before or after engaging them?"

"I think you get the most honesty from someone while... engaged." She chuckles again. "It's during these activities that men tend to answer questions honestly. You know, without thinking."

"And that's a technique you use to get your suspects to confess their crimes, right?"

"You're a feisty one, aren't you?"

Admittedly, that was a low dig even for me. "Sorry."

She laughs. "Don't be. I assure you that I only resort to seducing suspects when I've exhausted all other options." The way she says it leaves me wondering if there's truth to it.

I shrug. "Whatever it takes, I guess." I'd do almost anything to solve a case, but there are lines I'd never cross even if I wasn't married to Seth. Sleeping with a suspect would be one of them. Not to mention it could get me suspended or fired.

Thérèse pushes forward with the conversation, "Are you aware of all the women your husband has dated? Does he have an ex-wife? Children? What did he do before he became a detective? Do you know all these things?"

Does anyone?

"No, and as I said before, none of it matters."

"Maybe, maybe not. If he cheated on someone in the past, what's to keep him from doing so again?"

"He *loves* me!"

Button pressed. Well played. I'm starting to think I might be out of my depth and running out of oxygen sparring with this woman.

"Love has nothing to do with cheating," she says.

"He would never hurt me." It sounds more like a plea than a statement of fact. I chide myself.

"I'm sure you're right." Even without her fancy French accent, her condescension would've been obvious. It drips from her lips like drool from a wolf's maw. She continues, "Even so, if Seth were *my* husband, I'd make it my business to know every last detail of his past."

"Yeah, well, he's not your husband," I say.

Perfect response, Alice. Way to stick it to her with vehement patheticism.

"I know."

Thérèse pulls up next to the curb in front of a joint called Renaissance Bar and kills the engine. She then proceeds to place her hand over mine. The strange and likely calculated move throws me for a loop.

"For the record," she says, "Seth and I had a good chat earlier this morning. But I'm sure you already knew that since he tells you everything." She pats my hand, exits the car, and shuts the door before my mind catches up with what she just said.

My teeth grind together, and I snarl.

Why the hell didn't you tell me you saw Thérèse this morning, Seth?

One simple reason stands out, but I refuse to breathe life into it. There's no way in hell I'll give her the upper hand. I get out of the car and slam the door shut. She turns and eyes me across the top of the car. Her smug smile crawls beneath my skin. A parasite laying its eggs.

Moments later, Seth and Pierre pull up behind Thérèse's car. When Seth exits Pierre's car, I greet his boyish smile with a barrage of daggers aimed at his soul. He shrugs and frowns as though he's clueless as to what brought on my assault. Seth's a good detective, so there's no way he can't puzzle together what must've transpired between Thérèse and me on the car ride over. Either way, he'll no longer have the luxury of feigning cluelessness as to the reason my wrath targets him come tonight.

He'd better pray the hotel sofa is comfy.

* * * * *

Pierre points out a section of sidewalk just beyond the front doors of the

Renaissance Bar. "If you recall the photos of the first victim, you'll recognize this spot as the place where the body appeared. As crazy as it sounds, we have a dozen witnesses who attested to it. Several of them were inebriated at the time, but not all. As you can see, there is very little discoloration of the concrete."

Every angle presents the same evidence. Or lack thereof. I look over at Pierre. "The victim was obviously killed somewhere else and then dumped here."

"Right," Pierre says. "This means that the body was drained of blood somewhere else. And just as with Li Qiang and the other victims, our medical examiner found bruising on the top of the right wrist and a punctured vein where an IV line must have been inserted. Although we can't prove it forensically, we're certain the killer used heparin to prevent the blood from coagulating. We also have a theory that propofol was used to sedate the victims."

"Prior to their necks being slashed?" I ask.

"Exactly," Thérèse says. "It would allow the killer to take their time inserting the IV for the heparin."

Seth scratches the back of his head. "And what would they want with all the blood?"

"Satanic ritual, vampirism, blood supply." Thérèse shrugs. "We've yet to form a theory."

Vampirism…

Two years ago, I would've laughed at the mention of vampires or any other supernatural beings, but the Night Mauler changed my perspective on everything. Now, monsters lurk within every shadow and behind every closed door. "Have all the victims had the same blood type?"

"Nope." Pierre continues to stare at the concrete. "We've found nothing to tie any of the victims together. Different ages, races, sexes, eye and hair color, places of work, residential areas, etcetera. Not a single shred of evidence."

"And the killer?" Seth asks. "Hairs, fingerprints, skin underneath a victim's fingernails? Anything?"

"Nothing other than trace amounts of blood on the third victim's clothes, which we cannot be certain belongs to the killer. We are completely in the dark," Thérèse admits.

"How do we proceed?" I ask. The answer's obvious, but none of us are willing to say it aloud.

Seth peers at each of us. "We wait for another body to appear, right?"

Guess I was wrong about not saying it aloud.

Thérèse snorts, but Pierre frowns at Seth. "Perhaps it will come to that, but let's hope not. In the meantime, we'll take you to the locations where the other victims were found."

Seth shakes his head. "What's the point—"

Pierre holds up a hand, cutting Seth off. "Yes, I know. We have very little to show you in the way of evidence, but I assure you that you'll find the last two of our findings quite intriguing." Pierre smiles. "You're already familiar with where we found Li Qiang's body. However, you're unaware of the manner in which it arrived there. In addition to that, the condition of the eighth victim defies everything. I'm certain both findings will shed more light on the reason I asked you to come to Paris. It may also further alter your way of thinking about this case."

Seth and I share a glance. Interest piqued, I say, "Lead on, Pierre."

* * * * *

Pierre and Thérèse take Seth and me on what one might call a tour around central Paris. Each location we visit differs vastly from the previous one, the killer demonstrating little regard as to where the bodies get dumped. By the time we finish walking through the seventh location, Seth looks exhausted. His body still fights the time change. I, on the other hand, am unfazed by the shift.

Serves him right getting up early and meeting with Thérèse and then lying to me about it.

I sigh and try to focus on the case and not Seth's treachery. So far, I've yet to gain insight beyond what Pierre and Thérèse provided us at the onset of our tour, and I'm starting to wonder if I ever will. Then, we arrive at 185 Rue Raymond Losserand.

Hospital Paris Saint-Joseph looms in the background, but the main hospital isn't our destination. Pierre leads us over to an area of new construction in front of Urgences Hôpital Saint Joseph. A three-foot by five-foot section of the recently poured concrete sidewalk is missing. Where it should be sits a hole about four feet deep instead. Yellow police tape surrounds the hole.

Pierre bends down next to the hole and points at it. "This is where we found the eighth victim, Sayda Azar."

"Right." Seth kneels next to Pierre. "She was the one buried chest deep in the concrete, right?"

"Buried isn't the word I'd use for this *veuve noire*." Thérèse hands me a manila folder. "Take a look at the woman's autopsy report. I think you'll find it quite fascinating."

It doesn't take long for me to get to the fascinating part in the report. "Dirt and concrete were found in every part of her body that was beneath the surface." My gaze focuses on the hole. "What the hell?"

Seth rises and snatches the report out of my hands. After scanning it, he frowns. "How is this possible?"

Pierre stands. "We've never seen anything like this before. And as far as I know, no one ever has. It's as though the victim's body and the ground merged—" He weaves his fingers together. "—at a cellular level. It's impossible and incredible."

Everything begins falling into place within my mind.

This is what Jake must've been hinting at when he said the case had a connection to the Shadow Priests.

As I scan the surrounding area, a brutal wave of goosebumps attack, shaking and twisting my shoulders. At first, I'm certain it's just my imagination, but then I can't shake the notion that someone's observing us.

My gaze meets Seth's. A lot can be read from the expressions of a human eye, and I know Seth as well as I know myself. It looks like he's arrived at the same conclusion.

We're likely hunting some sort of Centaurian, and The Shadow Priests are watching us.

Twenty minutes later, we arrive at our final destination: 2 Rue Lachelier. More specifically, a set of three basketball courts just off the road. Several young men and women are playing three on three on the two courts parallel to each other, but the third court that runs perpendicular to the other two sits empty.

Pierre leads us over to the half-court stripe of the empty court and points at its center with his foot. "This is where Li Qiang came to rest."

"Strange way of putting it," Seth says.

Thérèse smiles at Seth as she pulls a tablet out of the shoulder satchel that she brought with her from the car. "It won't be once you see this." After a few taps and swipes, she hands the tablet to Seth.

I move over next to Seth, and he starts the video Thérèse pulled up on the tablet. Over and over, we watch the same event from two different angles. Both show the impossible and leave me questioning everything.

"Now you know why I asked you to come." Pierre smiles faintly when I look up at him.

My mind struggles to wrap itself around what my eyes have seen. "How does a body just appear out of nowhere?"

Seth shakes his head. "It's doctored, right? Bodies don't just fall from the sky."

"We thought the same thing at first." Thérèse reaches out to take the tablet back from Seth. Her fingers touch his and linger there for days. As they do, her eyes meet mine. She's playing a dangerous game, and it's one I'll never let her win.

Seth is mine.

Pierre sighs heavily. "Both videos were inspected forensically and have been determined to be authentic. Or at least they have not been altered by any methods currently known to exist."

"What about the flash just as the body appears?" I ask. "Did they figure out what caused it?"

Thérèse stuffs the tablet back in her satchel. "No idea."

"Huh." My mind returns to the hours of video footage Kenny and I scoured through of the nature preserve while working the Night Mauler case. It gives me an idea. "Can you email me a copy of them?"

Thérèse scowls at me. "Why?"

By God's grace, I resist the urge to answer her slap-worthy tone with the palm of my hand.

"Certainly," Pierre says. Daggers fly from his eyes, pummeling Thérèse into oblivion.

At least I'm not the only one picking up on her hostility.

"You'll have them by the time you get back to your hotel," Thérèse says.

I nod at Pierre. "Thank you."

An hour later, Seth and I crash on the sofa in our hotel room. Naturally, Seth is starving, his stomach rumbling like a distant thunderstorm. The man eats constantly. A teenage boy trapped inside the body of a grown man.

In more ways than one.

A sigh slips from my parted lips. "How about you order us some room service while I give Kenny a call."

Seth jumps up and heads for the small kitchen. "On it."

I pull out my phone and stare at the time. My mind struggles to calculate the difference back home. Finally, I give up.

The phone vibrates in my hand. True to her word, Thérèse has sent me the two videos of Li Qiang falling from the sky. I still don't understand why she reacted the way she did when I requested copies of them. The only thing I can think of is that she's afraid I'll discover something her and the others missed and rub her nose in it.

She deserves much worse.

After forwarding Kenny the videos from the basketball court, I dial his number. He answers on the first ring. "Alice! Kellie and I were just talking about you."

"Oh yeah?" I lie back on the sofa and stare at the ceiling. "Nothing bad I hope."

"Never! You're a rock star to both of us. You know that."

The corner of my lip curls upward. "If you say so."

"I do say so." He laughs. "So, you're in Paris, and you've only been gone for like a day. What's up?"

"Got something I thought you might be able to look into for me."

"Sure."

"I emailed you two video clips."

"Yeah, just saw the email come in."

"It's sensitive. For your eyes only, got it?"

"Of course."

"Good. Do you have a few minutes to look at them now?"

"Yeah… hold on." The sound of a slamming door echoes over the phone. "Sorry about that. The window's open, and the wind caught the door." He grunts. "Okay, I'm at my desk. Playing the first one now."

Twenty seconds roll by. Thirty. The line becomes so quiet that I check it twice to make sure we're still connected. We are. After a full minute, I say, "Well?"

"This is un-freaking-believable."

"Yeah. So, you think you can analyze the videos and verify their authenticity?"

"Already did. These videos are totally legit. Hands down."

"That's what I've been told. Did you notice the flash just as the body appears in the first one?"

"Yup."

"I swear I might've seen something the first time Seth and I watched it. Can you isolate those frames and see if I'm right?"

"On it. Hold on."

"Sure." A few seconds later, my phone vibrates against my ear.

"Sent you a pic. Used some software I've been working on to enhance it."

I pull up the image. It looks like a negative. "What am I supposed to be looking at?"

"After isolating the frame the moment the first part of the body began to appear, I inverted and enhanced it. Then I added some custom filters to it."

"Right, but what am I looking at?"

"Check out the chest region of the body."

It takes several seconds and a lot of squinting before I fully understand what it is I'm looking at. "That's… a hand."

"Yes, and not just any hand."

"A right hand—" My breath catches for a moment. "—and it's missing two fingers!"

"Exactly."

Excitement tightens my chest. "So, it's definitely not the victim's own hand."

"Not a chance. The second video clearly shows that the victim's arms are extended out to his sides."

"That plus the fact that I examined the victim and he wasn't missing any fingers on either hand." I sit up. "Kenny, you're a genius."

"I could get used to hearing that."

"I'm sure you could, and you probably will." My gaze focuses beyond the large hotel window. Central Paris stares right back, its skies cloaked in darkness and its streets bustling with activity beneath a yellowish-orange hue. "Look, I need to wrap my head around what this means."

"Gotcha. When you do, let me know. My mind is blown."

"Will do. Thanks again, and say hello to Kellie for me."

"You're welcome, and I will. Have fun in Paris, and call me if you need anything else."

"You can count on it."

After hanging up, I continue to stare beyond the glass framing the city. A few minutes later, Seth returns with a bottle of wine in a bucket of ice, two long stemmed wine glasses, and a tray piled with croissants, cheeses, and meats. He sets the tray and bucket on the sofa next to me, then sits down.

"Everything okay?" he asks.

"Better than okay." I hand him my phone then snag a piece of cheese off the tray. "As you can see, Kenny's a genius."

Seth squints at the picture on my phone. "And what is it that I'm looking at exactly?"

"It's a hand, Seth." I shove more cheese and several slices of meat into my mouth and talk around it as I chew. "We've got our first lead."

CHAPTER FIVE

AS THE MORNING SUN climbs its way over the eastern horizon, I'm already vying to take on the day. Sleep evaded me most of the night, my mind occupied by a hand with two missing fingers, yet I find myself fully awake. Two cups of coffee and several flaky, buttery croissants likely contribute to my alertness, but the prospect of catching a killer drives me out the door.

I'm itching to find the owner of the three-fingered hand by the time we arrive at Pierre and Thérèse's office, but the feeling doesn't last. Hours later, we're still nowhere close to identifying a suspect.

My mood plummets into the realm of despair and defeat. "How are we supposed to identify a single hand in a city with almost 2.2 million people? It feels like we're attempting the impossible."

"Difficult, yes. Impossible, no." Pierre leans closer to his laptop screen and squints at it. A smile spread across his face. "Believe it or not, I think I've found something."

"To what end?" Thérèse folds her arms. "We're not even certain that this hand exists, are we? It could simply be an artifact in the video or something left over from a previously recorded video or whatever, right?"

Seth, my rugged cowboy, shoots her down without hesitation. "Except that the video is digital. Plus, the hand has been confirmed by both your experts and ours. It's a hand."

Thérèse raised her arms. "Fine. The hand exists, but how will we ever know its significance?"

"Not sure I follow," I say.

She turns and glares at me. "Is the hand's owner responsible for the death of Li Qiang, or were they trying to save his life?"

"Huh." It hadn't occurred to me that there could be more than one explanation as to why the hand rested on Li Qiang's chest. Still, my gut says the hand belongs to the murderer and not some failed savior. "Either way, identifying the person will help lead us to the truth."

"You both realize that the victim's throat was already slit at this point, right?" Seth chuckles. "Seems kinda pointless to try and save someone from falling after they're already dead."

"Ugh." Thérèse pushes herself back from her desk. "You know what the real truth is? Paris—no, the world—is better off without those nine *victims* in it."

The room grows silent, and all eyes turn toward Thérèse, mine included. "What makes you say that?" I ask.

Thérèse stands and scowls at me. "You call yourself a detective, Bergman? Look at the list again." She grabs the pile of case files off her desk and begins tossing them at me. "Li Qiang. Sayda Azar. All nine *victims* were charged with heinous crimes and later acquitted or released. Each of them escaped punishment on some technicality, loss of damning evidence, or the death of a key witness. All nine of them!"

Pierre scowls at her. "That's enough, Thérèse."

She huffs and sits back down. "If you ask me, this killer has done the world a favor."

Despite loathing her and the passes she makes at Seth, I can't help but feel we share some sort of kindred spirit. So many who are guilty escape their punishment, and it burns me every time it happens. Especially if it's because of something I did or forgot to do.

Seth shakes his head. "Vigilantes circumvent the law and often fail to process all the facts before acting. They get it wrong almost as often as they get it right." He turns to Pierre. "You said you think you have something?"

"Well, I'm glad someone was listening." He adjusts his glasses, then stares at his monitor. "After searching the database for people with priors that also have missing fingers and through hospital records for people with multi-finger amputations, I've come up with a list of three possible suspects."

"Three is far better than 2.2 million," Seth says. "Good job narrowing it down."

Thérèse pipes up. "We should also reinterview all of Li Qiang's known associates. See if any of them have missing fingers or if any of them know anyone who does."

After gathering up the case files Thérèse threw at me, I stack them neatly on the corner of her desk. With a smile, I say to her, "I thought you weren't on board with the missing fingers angle."

She shrugs. "As with everything else pertaining to this case, it's likely a dead-end. But we've got nothing else to go on at the moment, so we might as well be thorough."

"Remember, it's the right hand we're interested in. Moreover, if they're not missing a middle finger and pinky, then they aren't our suspect." Pierre stands, grabs several printouts off the printer, then snatches his jacket off the back of his chair. "Seth, you're with me. We'll go check out the first two suspects." He hands one of the printouts to me, then points at me and Thérèse with two fingers. "The two of you will go have a chat with Li Qiang's family and associates and then check out this third suspect."

My gaze meets Seth's. I'm in a no-win situation. As much as I dislike Thérèse and would rather work with just about anyone else on the planet, there's no way I'd ever leave him alone with her. My trust in Seth remains solid, but a she-devil like Thérèse has many tools in her seduction chest that could break the will of any man regardless of his strength and willpower.

I will not let you be broken, my love.

Thérèse snatches the printout from my hand and stares at it for several seconds before looking toward Pierre. "A woman?"

He turns and scowls. "We must follow all leads to their end no matter how unlikely they may be."

"Yes, I understand, but do you really think a woman is capable of overpowering and murdering nine people?" Thérèse asks.

Pierre crosses his arms, and his scowl deepens. *"Le mal ne connaît pas de genre."* He peers over at Seth. "Evil knows no gender."

Seth nods as I stare at the back of Thérèse's head and smirk.

No doubt about that.

"Amende." Thérèse turns and shoves the printout into my chest. "Let's go." She doesn't wait for a response before storming out of the office.

I snatch up the printout just before it hits the floor. A middle-aged woman stares up at me from the piece of paper. She looks harmless enough, but experience has taught me to never judge a suspect by their appearance. Killers come in all sorts of packages. A quick glance through the hospital report leaves me with as many questions as answers. The specifics of the woman's injuries are vague, not listing the exact fingers lost, but it does give the reported reason for them: a culinary accident.

Good with knives.

The thought makes me chuckle. How good could she possibly be when she managed to chop off not one but two of her own fingers? The answer is obvious.

Not good at all.

Seth kisses my cheek. "Good luck, and be careful. Associates of a Chinese mobster won't take kindly to you poking around in their business."

"I know." I fold up the printout and shove it into my back pocket. "You be careful, too." I glance at Pierre. "Both of you."

Pierre nods. After kissing Seth one last time, I exit the office and chase down Thérèse.

* * * * *

After two hours of fruitless interviews with some of Li Qiang's previous associates, Thérèse and I turn our sights on Laurette Rapace, the culinary amputee. A light drizzle adds to the day's depressing mood as the lead on Ms. Rapace takes us into the 14th arrondissement and down a tree-lined street. Winter does the neighborhood no favors, the trees stripped of their leaves and transformed into ominous, bony beasts ready to stab anyone who draws too close.

Blackish-green doors with twisted, black wrought iron over painted windowpanes greet us at the front of the building. As with most of Paris, the doors have seen better days, both cracked, chipped, and scuffed from top to bottom.

The stench of urine fills my nasal cavity the moment we set foot inside the doors and carries with me as we traverse the long, dark hallway stretching toward the back of the building. Stains, both fresh and browned with age line the walls and soil the dense, dirty carpets. No amount of cleaning would ever reveal the building's original color palate.

A stairway at the end of the hallway leads to the upper-level apartments. The black, metal handrail droops from the wall, threatening to dislodge itself completely with the slightest touch. Safety concerns aside, the handrail sports more stains than the carpets and walls do, some so recent that they still glisten beneath the pale overhead lights.

I steer clear of the handrail as we traverse the metal stairs. Thérèse does the same, sticking to the middle of the treads. Given Ms. Rapace's address and the numbering of the second-floor apartments, we surmise she lives on the third floor, so we ascend the second flight of stairs.

Somehow, the top floor manages to surpass the first two floors with its disgustingness. Ratty carpets squish beneath my boots, wet with God knows what, and the rank odor surpasses that of a rotting corpse. How anyone could live in these conditions surpasses my understanding.

After locating apartment B314, Thérèse gives the door a hard rap. The door creaks and groans as it swings inward several inches. Unsurprisingly, no light spills through the open door. Thérèse glances at me as she draws her SIG-Sauer SP 2022. Her eyes say stay behind me.

She eases the door open a bit farther with her foot. *"Bonjour? C'est la police."*

No response comes from the awaiting darkness, but the muffled sound of shattering glass emits from deep within the apartment. We share a look, then Thérèse switches on a flashlight and moves inside. I follow close behind, unarmed and without flashlight.

The source of the darkness becomes obvious the moment I set foot inside the door: columns of stacked boxes and papers fill the apartment, floor to ceiling. We've stepped into a maze reminiscent of the one I encountered in the offices at Dunharrow Storage back in Desert Springs. I half-expect Reagan to be lurking around one of the next turns, collapsed over a pile of papers and snoring with the volume of a foghorn. Nevertheless, silence reigns over the deep shadows.

Thérèse calls for the woman as she leads us farther into the deadly hellscape. "Laurette Rapace?"

Around three more corners, we come face-to-face with the source who produced the shattered glass sound. A woman matching Laurette Rapace's photo stands with her back to a kitchen sink, eyes wild. She clutches a long shard of glass in her hand. The window behind the sink is broken, its shards littered across the green Formica countertop and all over the concrete floor. The shards sparkle as Thérèse's flashlight beam passes over them.

The woman squints into the light, her pupils little more than pinpoints. She waves the shard wildly at Thérèse. *"Approche plus près, et je te coupe-coupe-coupe!"* Blood drips from her hand. Splatters on the paper-lined floor.

"We're not here to hurt you," I say.

The woman freezes as her gaze locks on me. *"Américaine?"*

"Yes." I squeeze in next to Thérèse. "My name is Alice."

I take a step toward the woman, and she points the bloody shard at my face. "Perhaps your French ain't so good, *Alice.* As I told your friend, come closer, and I'll cut-cut-cut!"

"Put the glass shard down, or I'll put a bullet through your skull," Thérèse growls. *"Comprendre?"*

The woman stands defiant, her eyes narrowed. She spits at us. Or at least at Thérèse.

"You are Laurette Rapace, are you not?" I say, trying my best to diffuse the tension.

The woman nods. Still clutches the shard. Her eyes dart back and forth between Thérèse and me. "State your business and be gone." She huffs. "As you can see, I'm busy-busy-busy. Like a bee." She makes a buzzing sound with her lips.

Busy doing what?

I share a glance with Thérèse as Laurette continues to bleed all over the floor. She's clearly oblivious of her injury.

Thérèse says, "Where were you on the morning of January 8th?"

Laurette's eyes narrow as she scratches the side of her nose with the shard, leaving a streak of blood. "Might ask you the samie-same-same."

Thérèse lowers her weapon and points her flashlight at the ceiling. "The quicker you answer our questions, the sooner we'll leave you alone."

Laurette cocks her head and stares up at the water-stained ceiling. She taps her chin with the shard. "A Wednesday, was it? Yes, yes, yes." A smile cracks her lips. "Wednesdays are for the birds. Birdie-bird-birds. Tweet-tweet-tweet, you see? Just like today." She whistles loudly.

Thérèse glares at the woman. "Are you mad?"

Laurette shrugs. "Depends who you ask. White coats say yes-yes-yes. Birdie-bird-birds say noooo. Pills make it right as rain, especially on a rainy rain day." She takes a deep breath, then licks her lips. "Mmmm. Can almost taste it, can't you? Drippity-drip-drip-drip."

"Taste the stench of this place?" Thérèse nods. "Absolutely."

The woman has no tact. How does she function as a detective?

I slide my hands into my jacket pockets and inch forward. "You feed the birds every Wednesday morning, right?"

Laurette grins and rocks her head side to side. "Tick-tock, tick-tock. Just like a clock-clock. Never miss a single day. No way, no way."

Although fairly certain she's not our killer, I still want to see her hand.

She's held it behind her back the entire time we've stood here. Admittedly, it raises my suspicion.

"One last question, or rather request," I say to her. "Could you show us your hand?"

Laurette raises the glass shard in her left hand and twists her wrist. "See what you see. Fine by me."

"The other hand," Thérèse says.

Laurette looks over her shoulder and frowns. "Five to three. Nothing to see."

"One quick glance, and we'll be on our way," I say. "I promise."

The woman taps her cheek with the flat side of the shard, then nods. "One quick view. But only for you." She sticks her tongue out at Thérèse, then motions me forward.

"Agreed," I say.

Thérèse touches my arm, but I shrug her off. The potential danger Laurette presents isn't lost on me, my racing pulse proof of my awareness. However, we can't leave without knowing for certain that she's not our killer, and forcing the woman to do anything against her will might prove fatal for one or more of us.

I step in front of Thérèse, blocking her view of Laurette. "Show me."

Laurette closes her eyes and winces as she pulls her arm from behind her back. "Five to three. Five to three. No more cutting veggies for me."

I stare at the hand with two missing fingers: pinky and ring finger.

It's not her.

An instant later, she thrusts her arm behind her back again. In that same instant, something pokes my belly. Hard enough to take notice but not hard enough to penetrate my layers of clothing. A quick glance confirms the shard presses against my stomach. Laurette glares at me. Eyes glassy with tears.

"It's time to go," I say to Thérèse. "She's not the one we're looking for."

"You're certain?"

I nod, my eyes still locked with Laurette's. "We're done here."

"Come again, it goes in," Laurette snarls. "Drippity-drip-drip, like the rainy rain."

"Understood." I back away, then follow Thérèse out of the apartment.

Once outside, I breathe a bit easier, both from the fresher air and the easing tension in my gut.

Thérèse grabs my arm and pulls me around to face her. Anger creases her brow. "Pull something like that again, and I'll send you packing."

I rip my arm from her grasp. "What the hell's your problem? I just saved your life in there."

"No, you didn't. What you almost did was get yourself killed, and you put my life at risk in the process."

"Wow, you're delusional. That woman would've attacked you if I hadn't intervened."

"Perhaps, and I would've put her down," she snarls.

"Put her down?" I can't believe she just said that. "Laurette's a human being, Thérèse, not some sort of rabid animal."

"Did you not see that place? She lives in a cesspool of filth. And there was nothing sane in her eyes or her actions." Thérèse forces air through her nose. "Next time, you let me handle the interrogations, Bergman. Understood? This isn't America, and you're nothing more than a visitor here."

"You're right, but you're forgetting two important things."

"And what are those?"

"First, I'm here at Pierre's request, not yours. And second, I'm the only reason you have any leads at all." I yank my jacket down over my hips. "You should be thanking me."

Thérèse scowls. "Don't get ahead of yourself. This case is far from solving itself."

I pull my phone out of my pocket and discover I've missed several calls and texts from both Pierre and Seth. Checking the latest text message makes me smile. "Maybe, and maybe not. Seth says they have a suspect in custody."

Thérèse's expression darkens. "A suspect does not make a killer. And even if it is our killer, we still have no proof." She walks over to her car and opens the door. "Well, don't just stand there with your phone in your face.

Let's go have a look at this potential killer."

* * * * *

Jean-Luc Cartier sits back in one of the interrogation room chairs, arms crossed over his barrel chest. Satanic tattoos cover the better part of his arms: several pentagrams, a bearded goat's head, rivers of blood flowing from sacrificial altars, decapitated bodies. Imagery that looks like it came straight from the covers of Slayer albums from the 90s.

Beads of sweat glisten on the top of the man's bald scalp. Pierre or Thérèse must've turned up the room temperature to fluster him. Sometimes the tactic works, but Jean-Luc looks to be right at home in the heat.

Prepping for an afterlife in hell.

Seth and I sit back and watch Pierre and Thérèse interrogate the man through the two-way glass in the adjoining room. It's not the first time I've watched an interrogation this way, but it is the first time I've been banned from an interrogation room altogether, and it feels strange.

Before rendering us voyeurs, Pierre cited many rules and regulations that prevent Seth and me from participating in the interrogation, a lack of French citizenship at the top of the list. It sucks, but some rules should never be broken. If it were me sitting in Jean-Luc's chair, I definitely wouldn't want some foreigner interrogating me, either.

As the interview proceeds, I translate the conversation into English for Seth's benefit. It's better than having to get him up to speed later.

Pierre slides a photo across the table, toward Jean-Luc. "Do you know him?" he asks.

Jean-Luc hardly glances at the photo of Li Qiang. "Nope."

"Take another look," Pierre insists, tapping the photo.

"Don't need to." The man cracks his knuckles. "Don't associate with his type."

Thérèse leans forward. "And what type is that? Chinese?"

Jean-Luc smiles at Thérèse, revealing a mouthful of filed teeth. "The type that gets themselves killed."

"So, you do know him." Pierre scribbles something onto a pad of paper.

"Said I didn't."

"No?" Thérèse says. "We never mentioned that he was dead."

Jean-Luc stares at Thérèse for several seconds, then grins. "Listen, pretty thing. No one brings a man like me in unless there's a dead body." He winks at her. "Having said that, you never would've found the body if I'd had anything to do with it."

Thérèse leans even farther over the table. "Are you wanting to confess something?"

"Maybe I am." He grins again. "You've stirred the devil in me. Come by my place tonight. Alone."

"Over my dead body," Pierre growls.

Jean-Luc shrugs. "It could be arranged."

Thérèse lunges from her chair, grabs Jean-Luc by the front of his shirt and pulls him toward her. I wish I could see the expression on her face right now.

"Are you threatening the life of an officer?" she asks.

Jean-Luc casually unfolds his arms and raises his left hand, unfazed by her aggression. "Hold up, pretty thing. The suggestion was *his*, not mine."

My heart races as my eyes lock onto the inside of the man's left wrist. The two-way glass smacks against my forehead, my mind oblivious to the fact that I'd left my seat until that instant. Everyone in the room turns and stares at the two-way glass, but the only thing I care about is what's on Jean-Luc's wrist. Sinewy scars bulge beneath lines and curves and circles of multi-colored ink. The tattoo distorts what lies beneath, and I'm certain it's not by accident.

Is he like me?

The question ripples through my mind and sets off a chain reaction of additional thoughts surrounding the case. The video of Li Qiang plays over in my mind. A hand against his chest.

Pushing or pulling? Foe or friend? Killer or savior? Human or… Centaurian?

The word *Centaurian* elicits many feelings within me, none of them good.

No matter how hard I strive, my mind refuses to believe another world exists. If ever I related to a character in the Bible, it would be doubting Thomas. I would've insisted on seeing Jesus's wounds, too.

Admittedly, I *am* different, but most people are, right? It's our differences that make each of us unique. That make us human. Besides, there are plenty of mediums in the world who converse with the dead. Are all of them from another world, too?

Not a chance.

Seth touches my arm and rips me out of the world within my head. "Come on. The interrogation's over."

I stare through the two-way glass. Into an empty room. "What happened? Did they charge him?"

"For having two missing fingers?" Seth scoffs. "I don't think so."

Pierre opens the door and walks in. His soured face draws my attention. "That one's a real piece of work, as you Americans say."

"It's him, Pierre." I smack my palm with my fist. "I can feel it."

"As highly as I value your keen senses, I'm afraid we have nothing to hold him on." Pierre frowns. "Furthermore, he has a solid alibi for the majority of the murders."

Seth scowls. "Oh yeah? How solid?"

Pierre eyes Seth. "Solid. Jean-Luc was serving time for racketeering and extortion until just a few months ago."

"Serving time?" It doesn't make sense. I saw the mark on his wrist. I'm certain of it.

"Yes. And as part of his probation, he's been wearing an ankle monitor with GPS." Pierre holds up his hand, stopping me from arguing with him. "We checked the data. He hasn't been anywhere near the murder sites."

"And his wrist?" I look at Seth for backup. "You saw it, right? The mark hidden beneath the ink?"

He nods. "Yeah, I did."

Pierre nods. "I know what you're thinking, but the man has matching scars on both wrists. It's some sort of satanic ritual mutilation. I've seen it dozens of times before."

Frustration creeps into my voice. "But his fingers were a match, too, right? Pinky and middle finger."

"A match to a fuzzy image," Thérèse says as she enters the room and stands next to Pierre. "For all we know, those other two fingers could be folded under and not missing at all."

Rage boils beneath my skin as I glare daggers at Thérèse. "What's your problem? Do you not want to catch this killer, or do you just hate the fact that I've made more progress in two days than you have in ten months?"

Thérèse glowers at me. "Is that what you call this wild goose chase? The way I see it, we're no better off than we were before you arrived. In fact, I'm still unclear as to why you're even here."

"Unlike you, I bring value to the investigation," I say.

"And what value might that be?" She scoffs. "Your supposed *gift* that doesn't even work?"

"Maybe it didn't work for me yesterday, but at least I'm still a good detective. You're tactless and reckless."

"Enough!" Thérèse roars.

My hand jumps to my hip. "Oh, I'm sorry. I didn't realize you were so sensitive to hearing the truth. Next time, I'll say earmuffs first so you can cover your ears."

"You b—"

Pierre grabs hold of Thérèse's arm and squeezes it. "Take a step back and breathe, Thérèse." He looks at me. The displeasure in his gaze drives guilt into my chest. "I think it's time we all get some air and maybe some food. It's been a long day."

"Good idea," Seth says. "I know I'm not at my best when I'm hungry and tired." The shot's directed at me, and it stings.

Thérèse shrugs off Pierre's hand and takes a deep breath. "You all go ahead without me. I'll stay here and finish the interview write-up."

"Very well," Pierre says. "I'll drive Seth and Alice back to their hotel."

"Fine." Thérèse turns and leaves the room.

Pierre sighs loudly. "As I'm sure you know, this job can be... trying at times."

"No need to tell me," Seth says.

"I'm certain that's true." Pierre gestures toward the door with his arm. "Shall we?"

CHAPTER SIX

A BUZZ FROM MY back pocket pulls my thoughts away from the rain-soaked streets of Paris and the mysteries that lie buried beneath their surface.

Switching my glass of Auxey-Duresses Rouge to my other hand, I fish my phone out and answer it as I walk toward the kitchen. "Hello?"

"Make sure you're alone."

Distortion cloaks the caller's voice. Reminds me of the killer in the movie *Scream*. Checking the caller ID provides no help as to who I'm speaking with, the number unknown.

Immediately, I'm put on edge. Stand frozen between the living area and the kitchen.

"Who is this?" I demand, heat rising into my cheeks even as an unwarranted chill shrugs my shoulders.

"This isn't a game, Alice." Hostility in the caller's voice oozes through the phone, and hearing my name ratchets up the tension further.

"No?" I swallow a lump in my throat. "Then why are you hiding your identity?"

The three-foot gap between the curtains on the opposite side of the room draws my attention. Moments before the call, I stood at that very gap, taking in the beautiful, turbulent night sky hanging over Paris through the twenty-seventh-floor window of my hotel room. Now, the curtain gap feels too wide. The floor too high. A fall inevitable.

An inexplicable dizziness settles upon me as the room begins carouseling round and round. As it picks up speed, I shift my gaze toward the crystal stemware glass situated between my fingers and resting on my palm. Its crimson liquid sloshes about.

I stagger over to the sofa and crash upon it, the sound of shattering glass at my feet barely audible. "Did… did you drug me?" I ask, the phone still smashed against my cheek.

"Yes, Alice. Your reputation warrants it."

"My reputation?" The sofa's ice-cold leather leeches what little warmth remains in my bones as I sink farther into its plush exterior. My hand shakes violently, making it difficult to hang onto the phone. "What did you give me?"

"Are you alone or not?" Anger flares in the distorted voice.

Of course I'm alone, but instinct tells me to lie. "No."

After a brief pause, the caller says, "You're lying to me, Alice. I can hear it in your voice. Tell me the truth. You're alone, aren't you?"

Numbness radiates out from my core and settles in my arms and legs, paralyzing me.

What the hell is happening?

"Answer me," the caller growls.

Words scratch along the back of my parched throat and plummet off the end of my tongue. "I am alone, but I won't be for long. My husband will be back from the gym soon."

"Another lie, I'm sure, but I will make this quick."

The phone falls from my hand and skitters across the floor. Hot tears leak from the corners of my eyes and roll down my cheeks. Fear courses through my veins and screams in my mind, yet each breath pours from my lungs without hindrance. Pulse remains slow. Steady.

Must be a sedative in the drugs.

Heavy footfall sounds on the tile floor. Comes from the direction of the bedroom, not the suite entrance. No amount of effort lifts my heavy head from the sofa as the demon approaches.

"Good evening, Alice."

My breath catches.

I know that voice.

"Reagan?" His name pathetically squeaks from my lips.

The bald-headed man steps around the far end of the sofa and faces me. He holds a gold FNX-45 Tactical FDE equipped with a silencer in his left hand. Levels the gun's barrel at my head. A smile cracks his lips.

"It's been far too long, my redheaded dame." The way he says it— lustfully, yet with a tinge of malice—draws bile into my throat. I choke it back down even as his hunter-green eyes travel the length of my body, pausing both times they encounter my chest.

Although paralyzed, my mind remains sharp. "You came through the mirror in the bedroom?"

"Naturally." Reagan's gaze scans the large room. "Quite the setup." He walks over to the large windows and draws the curtains open. Emits a whistle from his lips. "And a view of the Eiffel Tower, too. They must be paying you a handsome sum to afford such a grand suite."

The tips of my fingers begin to tingle. With a great deal of effort, I manage to wiggle two of them.

Whatever he drugged me with must be wearing off already.

It doesn't make any sense, and I can only come up with two explanations as to why. Either he's not planning on staying long, or he's going to kill me. Not wanting to die, I'm praying the first explanation is the case.

I stare up at the troughed ceiling, still unable to move my head. "What do you want, Reagan?"

He returns to the center of the living room and stares intently at me before speaking. "I've been to Paris a few times, but always on business, like this evening. One of these days, I'll have to make this place a romantic vacation destination. City of Love and all that, am I right?"

Something with his tone always gets under my skin. Irritates me. "Are you here to kill me or just talk me to death?" I ask.

Reagan tsks at me with his tongue. His gun wags with each sound. "Naivety doesn't suit you, Alice. We both know you can't be killed so easily." He looks down at the gun in his hand. "This weapon ensures my protection, nothing more."

What is it with these Shadow Priests thinking I'm some sort of immortal god?

If only.

More tingling prickles my arms and legs as they begin to awaken. I fight the need to shake my limbs and force myself to remain still. "Out with it, Reagan. What do you want?"

"Right down to business with you, isn't it?" He shakes his head, then licks his chapped lips. "Remember that kiss we shared?" His eyes close for a few seconds as he groans aloud. "Oh, what a moment that was."

I slip my arm off the front of the sofa, pretending it's still numb. My fingers locate a shard of glass, and I palm it before he notices. "That kiss was stolen, not shared."

He chuckles. "Perhaps, but you enjoyed it."

The memory repulses me, but perhaps I can use it to my advantage. "Did I?"

Reagan moves toward me, a crooked grin upon his lips. "No woman can resist my charm, not even you." He sweeps away shards of glass with his foot, then kneels next to the sofa and aims his gun at the underside of my chin. "You know I'm not the man you met at the storage place, right?"

My eyes meet his. "No?"

"Bill was simply a persona I used to throw you off, and it worked perfectly, I might add." Malice twists his features. "I assure you, I'm a far more cunning foe than you can imagine. Now, drop the piece of glass, or I'll put a bullet right into your pretty little skull."

"Fine." The shard drops from my open palm.

His features soften as he frowns and cocks his head. "I wonder how long it would take for you to recover if I did shoot you in the head."

I stiffen.

Forever.

A swarm of scenarios of how to turn the tables on Reagan bombard me. Under normal circumstances, I could easily outmaneuver and subdue him, but I'm not sure how sluggish the drugs have made me. Despite his delusions about those like me, one wrong move could easily end my life.

I take a deep breath, then focus on his gaze. "How about we concentrate on why you're here and not on what shooting me might accomplish. Sound good?"

Reagan reaches over and moves a strand of hair from my cheek. The backs of his fingers scrape across my face, sending a repulsive chill down my spine. "One day, I'll punch your card to the afterlife. If the afterlife exists, that is. For now, let's talk about the case you're working on here in Paris."

I feign ignorance. "The case?"

"I know that you and your worthless husband are assisting the French Police with their string of murders, so fill me in on the details."

"Why do you care about it?" I ask, honestly perplexed.

Reagan glares at me. "In case you haven't noticed, I'm the one holding the gun. So stop asking questions and answer me."

He's obviously kept tabs on the investigation, so there's no point in lying about it. "I'm sure you've seen the news. Nine bodies, no leads."

"Yes, but we both know the news stations only report what's been fed to them." He presses the barrel against the underside of my chin and snarls. "Tell me everything they're not saying. I want every last detail."

I close my eyes, my heart now racing. "You've wasted a trip."

"I might not be able to kill you while you can still see, but I sure as hell can hurt you. Lie to me again, and we'll find out just how much pain you can withstand before passing out."

I glare at him. "I'm not lying."

He sighs. "You think I don't know about the body in the refrigerator truck?"

My body turns cold.

He has someone on the inside?

Of course, it makes sense. The Shadow Priests are everywhere. Thoughts fly through my mind as to who the leak might be. One person in particular surfaces.

Thérèse.

She's been cold and vindictive from the beginning, but I just can't see her being a member of the Shadow Priests. Then, another thought strikes me.

The spray paint guy.

It's the most likely answer. Or at least the only one I can think of off the top of my head. My suspect list is quite short.

After hesitating long enough to get full feeling back into my arms, I say, "You know about Li Qiang?"

"Yes, but what I don't know is what he told you," Reagan says.

So then it must be the spray paint guy.

"Not much, considering he's dead and all that."

Reagan stands up. Aims his gun at the left side of my chest. His finger moves over the trigger. "We know you can talk to the dead, Alice. So, tell me what I want to know before I stop your heart."

"Nothing." I groan. "Look, I'm not sure what happened with Li Qiang. When I touched him, I got nothing. Satisfied?"

Reagan glares at me, his eyes calculating. "I believe you, but why?"

"Why do you believe me? How should I know?"

He frowns, then shakes his head. "No, not that. Why didn't he talk to you?" The gun dips downward as his finger slides away from the trigger.

At the same time, the sofa presses against me. Head to toe. Yet a haze still lingers within my mind. I need to buy a few more minutes.

I squint at him. "How the hell am I supposed to know?"

Reagan cocks his head to the side. "Has it happened before?"

"No, but I've never tried to mind tether with someone who's been dead for several weeks, either."

"Mind tether. That's an interesting way of putting it." He nods slowly. "Yes, I like it. Anyway, you had a limited window of opportunity. His brain must've deteriorated too far for you to probe it."

Reagan's insight into my ability is astounding and disturbing. It makes me wonder how he knows so much.

How many like me has he killed?

I push the thought aside and nod. "Yeah. That's as good an explanation as any."

Reagan cocks his head again. "What else? What made you look into Jean-Luc Cartier?"

My gut wrenches again. "How do you know about that?"

He points his gun right at my face. "Just answer the question, Alice."

"Fine. Our suspect is missing two fingers on his right hand."

"And how do you know this?"

"Surveillance footage of Li Qiang. You can see the hand on his chest when he appears above the basketball court." I sigh. "Look, that's all I know so far."

Reagan eyes me for a long time. "Very well."

"I shared my notes with you, so why don't you share yours with me? What do *you* know?"

"Nice try, Alice." Reagan grins. "I'm afraid the knowledge sharing is a one-way street, and you're headed in the wrong direction." He reaches into his pocket and retrieves a business card. "Any leads, you call this number." He tosses the card down, and it lands on my stomach.

I ignore the card and stare him in the eye. "And if I don't?"

"You know how this works, Alice. It won't be you that gets the bullet."

Heat envelops my neck and crawls up my face. "No one threatens my family. You just signed your death warrant, Reagan."

His right eyebrow rises. "Did I?"

I grunt and pack all my strength into a swift kick to the side of his left knee. It pops. Crunches. Reagan roars as he twists and falls backward.

A sick thud echoes as his head smacks and bounces off the tile floor. His gun skitters across the slick tiles and comes to a rest a dozen feet across the room.

Not wasting a moment, I explode off the sofa and land on my feet. Glass crunches underneath my shoes. Then, the night rushes at me from every direction. Suffocates me.

Pain rips through my knees. A cold, hard surface rises up and smacks me in the face. Drives the wind from my lungs. My head pulses with pain as I spin out of control in a growing sea of darkness.

Reagan will not win.

I push myself up onto my hands and knees and shake my head. The darkness recedes, if only a little, but the pain intensifies. Burns through my kneecaps, all the way to the backs of my knees. I grit my teeth and growl.

Through spotted vision I locate Reagan's golden gun. Just as I'm about to go for it, Reagan's meaty fingers wrap around my ankle. He pulls me to the floor. The blow drives the breath from my lungs again. I kick hard with my free leg but connect with nothing.

Reagan grabs my other foot and begins reeling me back toward him. The bastard is far stronger than I could've ever imagined, his iron grip impossible to break free from.

The darkness in my vision recedes farther as I slide backward across the floor. Then, a sharp object bites into my arm. I spot the glass shard, now glistening with crimson.

Shard in hand, I twist around and stab at Reagan's arms. The shard finds purchase and burrows into his right forearm.

"Ugh," he groans.

Reagan's grip fails, and I surge forward on hands and knees. Fire burns in my knees, but I keep crawling until I reach the gun at the far side of the room.

By the time I grab the gun and turn around, Reagan's up on his feet and hobbling toward the bedroom.

The mirror!

I pull myself up and stumble after him. "Stop, or I'll shoot you in the back!"

Despite his mangled knee, Reagan manages to move even faster. Through the bedroom door. He glances back a few paces before reaching the full-length mirror attached to the bathroom door. I squeeze off a round, knowing it's too late to prevent his escape.

Bang!

Reagan twists to his right as the bullet rips into the back of his left shoulder.

Crack!

The bathroom door explodes inward. Glass shatters and rains down on the tile floor.

Crash!

Reagan and the door hit the floor and slide to a stop with a loud screech. Blood soaks his shirt where I shot him.

Standing just inside the bedroom door, I say, "Make a move, and it'll be the last thing you do." Reagan groans but doesn't move.

In the corner of the bedroom next to the desk stands a floor lamp. After tucking the gun inside the waistband of my jeans, I unplug the lamp, stand on its base, and yank on the cord as hard as I can. It takes several more yanks before the cord finally rips out of its base.

Two minutes later, Reagan lies on his stomach with his hands bound behind his back. The cord loops around his belt several times to secure his hands even better.

Stepping back, I retrieve the gun from my waistband and point it at him. "On your feet."

Reagan glares at me from the corner of his eye. "You busted my knee, stabbed my forearm with a piece of glass, shot me in the shoulder, and then tied my hands behind my back. Just how the hell do you expect me to stand up on my own?"

Admittedly, he has a good point. "Fine. You can just lie there."

"I'll bleed out."

I scoff. "Stop being a baby. I didn't hit anything vital. Besides, the wounds have already coagulated."

"Maybe so, but what about an infection? You need to clean them all out before sepsis sets in."

"Not a chance in hell, Reagan. You're the one who drugged me and invaded my hotel suite. You should've thought about the consequences *before* you made such a stupid decision. With any luck, you'll die of infection."

A loud knock rattles the hotel suite door. "Mr. And Mrs. Ryan? This is Claude from hotel security. Are you in there?"

"Keep quiet and don't move," I growl at Reagan, then back toward the bedroom door, keeping my eyes on him. "Yes?"

"Is everything okay in there?"

"Yes, I just stepped out of the shower. Did you need something?"

"The guest staying in the room beneath yours said that he heard several loud bangs that sounded like they came from your suite."

"Loud bangs? That's strange. I didn't hear anything while I was in the shower."

"You're certain everything's okay in there?"

"Yes, of course. I'd let you in, but I'm not decent and my husband is out."

"No problem. I'm glad you're okay. If you need any assistance, please don't hesitate to call."

"Thank you."

Reagan flops around on the door and manages to flip himself over onto his back. A sizable crimson stain soils the left side of his white T-shirt, centered around a bullet-shaped hole. He groans as he works his way into a sitting position. Unlike the blithering man I knew as Bill, Reagan remains calm and collected, his eyes trained on me and the golden gun.

"What do you want from me?" he asks.

I return to the bathroom doorway. "Answers."

"And what makes you think I'll talk?"

"Simple. If you tell me everything I want to know, you'll keep breathing. Otherwise, I'll put a bullet through your heart and extract the answers from your lifeless corpse."

He scooches over to the vanity and leans against it. Then, he closes his eyes. "Trust me, you wouldn't wanna see the things tossing around inside my head."

"I'm sure you're right." I click the magazine release and verify there are

13 more rounds, plus the round already chambered. Shoving it back in, I take aim again. "So, let's make a deal. You answer each question truthfully, and I won't make life worse for you. Each time you lie or refuse to answer, you'll receive another bullet. Understood?"

Reagan nods. "Yeah, but that sounds risky. Another shot, and security will be back."

"You let me worry about that." I retrieve the chair tucked beneath the bedroom desk and place it just outside the bathroom before settling down on it. "At Dunharrow Storage a few years back you were on the phone. You mentioned someone named Morgan while talking about the Shadow Mirror. Who is Morgan, and where can I find them?"

Reagan's eyes open. He winces as he shifts his weight. It's the first time I've seen him truly in pain, and the better part of me enjoys watching him suffer. He sighs loudly, and his gaze turns toward the ceiling.

Silence hangs in the air for several seconds and it seems like I'll need to encourage him to talk, but then he finally does. "I've known Morgan most of my life. We grew up together in SoCal and became instant best friends the day we met. Morgan's a straight ace, but I've always had a knack for finding and getting into trouble. Way over my head at times. But Morgan's always there to rescue me no matter the situation. Without her, I would've died a hundred times over."

Morgan's a woman?

The revelation shocks me. Leaves me with a question I never thought I'd be asking, but I can't quell my curiosity. "The two of you are lovers?"

Reagan shakes his head. "God, no. She's far outside my league. A universe away." His eyes meet mine. "Like you, but not. She's *all* human. Understandable. Relatable. Smartest woman I know. No offense."

"None taken. You don't know me." I lean forward in the chair, my elbows on my thighs and the gun aimed at his midsection. "So, Morgan's the head of the Shadow Priests?"

He chuckles, then grimaces. "You really understand nothing of us, do you?"

"How could I? Even in death, The Braille Killer refused to divulge much of anything."

"The Braille Killer." Reagan scoffs. "He knew nothing of us but the lies we fed him. He was a loose cannon and couldn't be trusted with our secrets, but his obsession with you gave us an advantage. A way to test the waters without getting wet, so to speak."

"I don't follow."

"Each of your kind possess a uniqueness that must be tested. It's the only way we've survived for so long, and the only way we'll win the war."

"War? That's what you think this is?"

"What else would you call it? Your kind invaded our planet and continue to corrupt our sacred gene pool with your vile spawn. How could such an atrocity be anything other than an act of war?"

"Sacred gene pool?" I shake my head. "Listen to yourself, Reagan. I'm no different than you. Sure, I use far more of my brain than you ever could, but that doesn't make me your enemy. That just makes me smarter. You attack those who are like me, *unprovoked*, and dare call us evil? You're a hypocrite."

"Call me what you like, but it doesn't change the facts. You were born blind, yet now you see. One might call your transformation a miracle if they were delusional, but we both know the truth. Taking lives restores your sight and grants you immortality. And you're just one of many with anti-human abilities." His brow furrows. "Like that thing I killed in the valley. It sure as hell wasn't human and deserved to be put down."

"And you'd put me down, too?"

"Admittedly, you're easy on the eyes, but I wouldn't hesitate, given the chance. The world must be cleansed."

I've never wanted to pull a trigger more than I do right now, but I'm not a psychotic killer like Reagan. Instead, I circle the conversation back to the beginning. "If Morgan isn't the head of the Shadow Priests, then who is?"

Reagan laughs. "We aren't Freemasons, Alice. There is no hierarchy to our organization. Each of us possesses both power and independence over every aspect of our lives. Yes, several of us work together toward a common goal, but there's no head you can sever that will bring us down. You watch too many movies."

"Fine. So, what about the Shadow Mirror? Who controls it, and where can I find it?"

Malice flashes in his eyes. "Even if I knew, and I don't, I'd never tell you."

I shake my head. "You really do have a small brain inside that head of yours, don't you?"

He glares at me. "What's that supposed to mean?"

"It means that you're a liar, Reagan. You wouldn't be in my hotel suite right now if you didn't know where the Shadow Mirror was located." I rise from the chair and stand over him. Point the muzzle at his crotch. Pull back the slide. "Last chance. Where's the mirror? Where did you take it after I found it in the storage unit?"

Reagan sneers. "'*Found it*' is a funny choice of words."

The recoil is minimal, but the bang echoes between the marble floor and walls like a cannon. Without the suppressor, it would've been deafening.

Reagan yells a slew of profanities as his pant leg blossoms with blood. A crimson pool spreads over the door and across the floor beneath him.

"I warned you, Reagan. Lie to me again, and the next one will force you to pee in a bag the rest of your life."

Reagan grimaces and says something inaudible.

"You need to speak up. Where's the mirror?"

"It. Never. Left," he manages. His chest heaves with labored breathing.

The hotel phone rings, but I ignore it. "As you know, I watched a video recording from the storage facility. It was you talking on the phone to Russell. You said that the mirror had been moved."

"Lied." He wheezes. "To throw you. Off," he gasps.

"It's Morgan who controls the mirror, isn't it?"

Reagan stares up at me with defiance, his eyes glossy with unfallen tears. "Touch a hair on her head, and I'll bury you in hell."

"Bold words for—"

Hairs on my nape rise as the electronic lock on the hotel suite door moans and disengages.

I glare down at Reagan. "Don't make a noise, understood?" He nods.

After sliding the gun into my waistband and covering it with my shirt, I head out of the bedroom suite, closing the door behind me. Seth and two hotel security guards enter the unit just as I turn around.

"Alice!" Seth says. "Are you okay?"

One look into his eyes, and a flood of emotions overwhelms me. Weakens my legs. I lean against the wall as tears streak down my face. All I can do is nod.

Seth's eyes scan the room. Stop when they take in the shattered glass and burgundy liquid splattered across the living room floor.

"Are you alone, Ma'am?" asks one of the security guards. His French accent is thick.

I nod again, still unable to form words. Seth walks over and wraps his arms around me. "Another nightmare?"

"Yes," I whisper.

He pulls back. Eyes my waist, then searches my eyes.

"Please make them leave," I say.

Seth nods, releases me, then turns toward the security guards. "Everything's okay here. My wife suffers from vivid nightmares, especially when she's left alone. She must've thought she was about to be attacked, hence the broken glass and wine all over the floor." He glances over his shoulder at me. "Isn't that right, honey?" I give him a soft nod, and he says, "We'll get it cleaned up."

The second security guard doesn't look convinced with Seth's explanation. "Several guests reported hearing what sounded like multiple gunshots. A shattered glass wouldn't have been heard nor mistaken as a gunshot." I recognize his voice from earlier.

Claude.

Seth shrugs. "Agreed, so whatever they heard obviously didn't come from this suite."

"Perhaps not, but we'd feel better searching the suite anyway," Claude says.

"I'm sure you would," Seth says, "but it's unnecessary." He pulls a business card from his wallet and hands it to Claude. "As you can see, I'm a police officer from the US. So is my wife. If she says nothing happened in here, then nothing happened here. Understood?"

Claude doesn't look convinced. I wipe my eyes and tuck strands of hair behind my ears before eying the young man. "Claude, right?"

He nods. "Yes, ma'am."

"As my husband explained, I have vivid nightmares. Sometimes, they come when I'm awake, as it did earlier. I thought I saw someone peering at me through the balcony door and it startled me. I dropped my glass of wine and it shattered. I feel so foolish."

Claude looks at the first security guard and the older man shrugs then nods. Claude hands the business card back to Seth. "Very well. However, if any further loud noises are reported, we will insist on a thorough search of your suite."

Seth glances at me. "It won't come to that."

The first security guard nods, then he and Claude turn and exit the suite. Seth locks the door behind them, then turns around and stares at me. "I'm guessing you have a good explanation as to why there's wine and glass shards all over the floor, but more importantly why you have a gun tucked inside your waistband."

I chew on my nail and motion toward the bedroom door with my head, avoiding eye contact. It takes everything I have to keep tears from falling again, but then our eyes meet. For some reason, Seth has a way of sieving emotions out of me. Tears streak my cheeks and drip on the floor.

Seth crosses over to me and places a hand on my shoulder. "No matter what's happened, everything will be okay."

I wipe my face with my T-shirt. "No, it won't."

He opens the bedroom door. Stands there in silence for what feels like an eternity, his hand still grasping the door lever. Then, his head slowly shakes. "Ugh. We need to call Thérèse."

Anger and fear collide inside my chest. Struggle for dominance. "You can't do that," I groan.

He looks at me, his beautiful eyes full of sympathy and questions. "It's either her or Pierre, and I'm fairly certain Pierre will be less understanding of whatever—" He sweeps his arm into the bedroom. "—*this* is."

As much as I hate it, he's right. Thérèse is a rogue and more like me than I'll ever admit. With a deep sigh, I nod, hand him the gun from my waistband, then retreat to the sofa.

After Seth makes the call to Thérèse, he drags Reagan out of the bathroom and bedroom and into the middle of the living room, leaving a bloody trail across the suite floors. Reagan lies back on the floor and groans, his clothes soaked in blood and his skin ashen.

I glare down at Reagan. "Why did you bring him in here, Seth?"

Seth heads into the kitchen. "Bathroom mirror."

Well, that makes sense.

He washes his hands in the kitchen sink, then comes back and settles on the sofa next to me. After staring at Reagan for a long time, he says, "I think it's time you tell me everything that happened."

CHAPTER SEVEN

THÉRÈSE ARRIVES AT OUR hotel suite a little after midnight. Seth greets her at the door and immediately begins explaining the situation with Reagan to her. She doesn't even bat an eyelash when he tells her that Reagan entered the suite through the bedroom mirror. Either she misunderstands what he means by it, or she's witnessed other strange and unexplainable things in her career beyond our current case.

After Seth walks her through the entire encounter, they return to the living room. She crosses her arms and glares daggers at Reagan—a spiteful look she normally reserves for me. Feels good not being on the receiving end for a change.

"I can tell you're French Police," Reagan says to Thérèse. "Take me into custody. Better yet, how about a hospital? I've been shot twice, you know." His face looks pale, but none of his wounds are life-threatening.

At least not yet.

Thérèse sneers. "Tonight, I'm more of a concerned citizen."

She turns and stares at me as though she's noticing me for the first time. There's something different about her tonight, her usual disdain for me virtually nonexistent. She pulls a syringe filled with a clear substance out of her jacket pocket and offers it to me.

With reluctance, I take the syringe from her and hold it up toward the ceiling as thought the ambient glow of the recessed lights will magically reveal its contents. "What's this?"

"Sodium thiopental," Thérèse says.

"Truth serum?" Seth scowls. "Do I even want to know why you just happen to be carrying that in your pocket?"

"You told me over the phone that you needed answers from this *pig*," she says, gesturing toward Reagan with her head.

"You thoroughly insult me," Reagan huffs. "I'm the only one in the room that's *not* in law enforcement."

"Shut up, Reagan." I hand the syringe back to Thérèse. "From everything I've read, it's known to be ineffective."

She nods. "On some people, yes. Isn't it worth a shot, though?"

Seth chuckles. "Yeah, I see what you did there."

Thérèse cocks her head and frowns at Seth. "And what is it that you saw me do?"

"Never mind Seth." I perch on the edge of the sofa. "Go ahead and give the serum to Reagan."

Reagan rolls his eyes. "You're wasting your time."

Thérèse crouches next to him. "Stay still." A wicked smile curls her lips. "I've never done this before."

Reagan closes his eyes as she bleeds the needle and then stabs it into his right thigh. Surprisingly, he doesn't even flinch. Then again, I'm sure a needle prick fails to fire the nerves after already being shot twice.

Thérèse stands back up and smiles at me. "You'll need to give it a few minutes to work its way into his bloodstream." Her gaze rises above my head. Seth's standing directly behind me and the sofa. "Alice is right, you know. Once you've retrieved whatever information you need, killing him will make this situation far easier to deal with."

"I'm right here," Reagan groans. "You know I can hear you, right?"

Thérèse draws her weapon and points it at Reagan's chest. "One more word, and this discussion will be over."

I'm starting to like this woman more and more, yet the thought of us ever being friends makes my stomach do flips. She's still my enemy where Seth's concerned, and that's all that will ever matter.

Seth walks around the sofa and pushes Thérèse's arm down. "The discussion *is* over."

Thérèse eyes me and raises her right eyebrow. "Is it?"

"Yes," Seth says with firmness and finality in his voice. He walks over to the floor-to-ceiling windows and parts the drapes with his hand. "We're in the City of Love, for God's sake. No one dies tonight, understood?"

"Fine." Thérèse holsters her gun. "I need to make a few calls and arrange transportation for our *friend*." She retreats into the bedroom and closes the door behind her.

Reagan sighs. "Thank you, Mr. Ryan."

Seth releases the drapes, and they fall back into place. Then, he turns and faces the two of us again. To Reagan he says, "You're damn right you'd better say thank you. As worthless as you are, I just saved your life. You'd better be thanking God that you didn't hurt Alice, too. If you had, I would've killed you myself."

Reagan shrugs slightly, then winces. "Wow, that smarts." He looks up at me. "Think you could do me a solid and untie my hands? It's not like I could just walk out of here."

"Do you a solid?" I can't believe the nerve of this man. "Not a snowball's chance in hell."

"Besides, we know you wouldn't need to walk out of here," Seth says. "You'd just need to get to another mirror."

Reagan shakes his head. "Trust me, it doesn't work like that."

"No?" I lean closer. "Then how *does* it work?"

Reagan frowns, then sniffs the air and wrinkles his nose. "Why does it smell like garlic in here?" He scowls at me. "Is that you?"

Seth walks over and smacks the back of Reagan's head. "That's the serum, you idiot. Now, stop stalling and answer Alice's question."

Reagan exhales, then starts spewing information. "The Shadow Mirror can only be tethered to one location at a time. One mirror. That same mirror must be used to return." He looks at me, then rolls his eyes. "You destroyed the mirror, severing the connection and stranding me here. Understand?"

I stare hard at him, but it's impossible to tell if he's lying or not. "Is that so?"

He snarls, "Yes, Alice. And that wasn't nice of you."

Seth scratches the back of his neck. "Somehow, I think that actually makes sense." He kneels next to Reagan. "What bothers me is why you came here in the first place."

Reagan's gaze focuses on me and turns frigid. "I'm always watching you, Alice. Waiting patiently for my chance to end your life. But then a unique opportunity presented itself. A case so bizarre that only one of *your* kind could be behind the killings."

"That's why you came?" Seth asks. "You're hunting the killer?"

Subconsciously, I already knew this, yet it still hits me like a revelation.

"Yes." Reagan scrunches his eyes. "Ugh. Why do I feel so compelled to tell you both everything? It's like you've suddenly become my best friends, and I'm confiding in you. I can't focus my mind long enough to lie."

"That's good." I sit back on the sofa. "While you're still so forthcoming, you can answer another question, too. Since you just came through the mirror today, who's been here this past week?"

"An informant, and they've been here for months."

"Not good enough, Reagan. Give me a name and description."

He shakes his head. "Not possible."

"Are you asking for another bullet?"

Reagan grimaces. "No. It's not possible because I've had no contact with them. I came here because of you. Because I realized you were here in Paris when I searched for you using the Shadow Mirror."

Another question arises in my mind. "Speaking of the Shadow Mirror again, is it true that you can't just track anyone with it?"

"Yes," Reagan says.

Even though the Braille Killer gave me the same answer, it still stuns me to hear it confirmed.

"Elaborate," Seth says.

Reagan gestures at me with his head. "Works only on her kind. And children." He groans. Struggles to keep from saying anything else.

"How?" Reagan doesn't answer, so I stretch out my leg and press my foot against his bullet-wounded thigh. "Answer me, or I'll stand up and make you scream."

He winces. "Okay, okay. We use DNA. Hair. Skin. Blood. We need something physical from the person in order to track them."

"And how about what you told me earlier about the mirror. Was that true?"

He glares at me. Defiant. I rise off the sofa and apply more force to his wounded leg.

Reagan grunts. Face turns several shades redder. But he remains silent.

I grind the heel of my boot into his leg. "Trust me, the pain will only get worse if you keep refusing to answer me."

Tears streak Reagan's face, and he starts hyperventilating.

"Alice—"

"No, Seth. I will not relent. This is far too important." I set my jaw and place my entire weight on Reagan's leg.

Reagan screams. Nods wildly as he writhes on the floor. Then, his body falls limp.

I step back and assess. Regan's chest slowly rises.

Still alive. Too bad.

Fresh blood soils the left side of his pants, and a small amount pools beneath his leg. More blood covers the sole of my boot, leaving a partial print on the tile when I step back. I wipe most of the blood off my boot with a portion of his shirt that isn't already saturated with blood, but upon closer inspection it proves it'll require a good scrubbing later. Blood remains in the crevices of the logo stamped into the bottom of its heel.

Seth walks over and sits on the sofa. He pulls on his hair and sighs. "I guess this explains the nightmares you've been having, right?"

My mind remains focused on the things Reagan revealed to us, so I fail to follow Seth's logic. "Why would it? I commune with the dead, Seth. Not see the future."

"Yeah, I know, but that doesn't mean that you weren't consciously aware of him watching you." He grimaces. "Us."

"Subconsciously, and maybe I was." The more I think about it, the more sense it begins to make.

Seth looks down at Reagan and scowls. "You think he ever watched us having sex?"

Chills race down my spine. "Ugh! I don't even want to think about what he might've seen us doing."

"Sorry I brought it up." He rubs his eyes. "So anyway, what did Reagan tell you about the mirror earlier? You didn't mention anything to me about it before."

"He said it remains at Dunharrow Storage."

Seth gasps. "Seriously? It's been there all this time?"

"Yeah, apparently. Speaking of which, I need to call Rico and let him know." I rise from the sofa and pull my phone out of my back pocket.

Seth nods, then closes his eyes and leans into the sofa. "I'll be right here if you need me."

* * * * *

The hotel corridor sits in silence as I pace back and forth in front of the door to my suite. Two passes along the corridor's entire length confirm that a single mirror hangs from its walls, at the far end by the elevators. It's a good distance from me, yet it still unsettles me every time I face it. I'm half-tempted to go over and shatter the damned thing.

A deep breath calms my nerves a little, but it's Rico's face staring up at me from my phone's contact list that vanquishes my fear. I tap his face and lean against one of the corridor walls while I wait for it to connect. After several rings, the line clicks.

"Hello, you've reached Rico's Cane Shoppe."

"Rico, it's Alice," I say.

"I'm sorry I'm unable to take your call right now, but if you—" I end the call and rest my head against the wall.

Dammit, Rico. Where are you?

The business card he gave me several years ago still sits in my wallet. I pull it out of my wallet, punch in the number listed on it, and wait. The line picks up on the first ring.

"Steven's VCR Repair. How can we help get your tape rolling?" Not even Jake's deep, Texas drawl can distract me right now.

"Jake, I don't have time for this charade."

"You're speaking with Steven—"

"You're not listening to me, Jake. This is Detective Alice Bergman. I have sensitive information for Mirador."

Three distinct clicks sound in my ear, followed by a slew of dial-up modem sounds from the nineties. Then, perfect silence ushers in. After several seconds, I check to see if I'm still connected and confirm the seconds are still increasing on the call time.

"Alice?" Again, the voice sounds like Jake's. Now, I'm totally confused.

"Is this Jake Barnes?"

"The one and only, darlin'." His smile beams through his words. "Steven said you have some sensitive information for me."

I'm still too confused to understand what's happening. "Huh?"

"Ah, I see." Jake laughs. "You just told him that so you could talk to me, didn't you?"

"Wait a minute. You're not Steven?"

Jake chuckles. "We both get that a lot, but no. He's my older brother. Does VCR repairs, just as he says."

I'm not sure how there's still a market for VCR repair, but it's the last thing that matters right now. "I'm still confused. Why did Rico give me your brother's business card?"

"It's the only way we have to get a secure line going. Anyway, you've reached the right place, am I right?"

I pull my phone away from my ear and glance at it. "Yeah, but my end isn't secure. I'm still going through my carrier's towers."

"Sure you are, but the line's now encrypted, end-to-end. Trust me, it's untraceable and unbreakable. And that means a lot coming from a cowboy who breaks wild mustangs." He chuckles. "Seriously, though, this call cannot be tapped or intercepted. Anyway, you mind doing me a favor?"

"After all you've done for me? Name it."

"I've switched us over to a video call, so how about you pull that phone away from your cheek so I can get a good look at your beautiful face. It's been far too long."

Heat rises in my cheeks. "You know I'm married, Jake. Happily."

"Yeah, I know, but that don't mean another man can't admire your beauty from afar. After all, a woman needs to know now and again that she's still got it."

I smile. "Is that right?"

"Scout's honor."

I pull the phone away from my face and stare at the screen. Jake's two gold-capped teeth gleam beneath the shadow of his black cowboy hat. "So, you were a boy scout?"

Jake's smile widens. "Never said that, darlin', but it sure is good to see your face."

"I'd say likewise, but I'd be lying."

He jerks his head back and grimaces. "Ouch! That stings somethin' fierce."

I laugh. "I swear, it's not as bad as it sounded. Raise that cowboy hat of yours up so that I can get a better look at your face."

"Oh, I see. How about I do you one better?" Jake reaches up and removes his hat. "There we go, darlin'. Just let me know when you got what you need." He winks at me.

Thick, brown eyebrows hover above a pair of deep-set hazel eyes. A scar graces the bridge of his narrow nose and runs beneath his left eye—a story

I'll be sure to ask about another time. Shallow creases extend from the corners of his mouth and eyes, and a good three days' worth of silvery-brown stubble covers his cheeks, jaw, and neck. Gold caps aside, he has his mother's smile.

"Not bad, cowboy. Not bad at all," I say.

Jake winks again, then returns his hat to his head. "A bit rough around the edges these days, but I still get noticed now and again."

"I'm sure the ladies fall all over you at your shindigs and watering holes."

"That they do." He tips his hat toward the screen. "Now, what's this I hear about sensitive information you have for me?"

"First off, I captured Reagan."

"That's the little twirp I shot in the canyon, right?"

"The same one."

"Good deal. You put him down?"

"Trust me, I contemplated it, but Seth wouldn't hear of it." I wave my hand. "Anyway, with a bit of coercion, Reagan admitted that the Shadow Mirror never left Dunharrow Storage."

Jake leans back and shakes his head. "Well, I'll be danged. And you're certain that snake wasn't lyin'?"

"Positive. Look, the place needs to be monitored twenty-four seven and searched top to bottom. We can't let that mirror slip through our fingers."

"Already on it." He clears his throat. "Look, it's been fun, darlin', but I need to get movin'. Desert Springs is a several-hour drive from where I'm at."

"Understood. Keep me posted, Jake."

"When I know, you'll know. Promise."

My screen goes dark, and Jake's gone. I close my eyes and lean my head against the wall. "God, please let them find that mirror."

Back inside the suite, Seth's already gathered up the few belongings we have.

"What's going on?" I ask, staring at the bags.

"Given the state of this place, we're switching rooms."

I look around. "In the middle of the night?"

"You still wanna sleep in here after what happened?"

"Not really, but—"

"But nothing. Thérèse has already made the arrangements. Just one floor up and one room over. Same beautiful view. No blood."

"It's the mirrors I'm worried about."

"I knew you would be, so they're being removed as we speak."

"Good." My gaze travels beyond the sofa. "And what about Reagan?"

"His wounds will be dressed, and then he'll be booked. Simple as that."

It all sounds too perfect. "And how will we explain all the damage we've done in here? You know Pierre won't get his deposit back."

"Again, Thérèse has it handled. Something about a cleanup crew. In an hour or so, it'll look like nothing ever happened. And please don't ask or argue with me about it."

I raise my hands. "No arguments here. At this point, I just want to lie down somewhere comfortable and have you hold me until I fall asleep."

Seth smiles. "Now that I can do." He takes my hand and leads us out of the suite.

* * * * *

Sometime later, I find myself alone in bed. The curtains are drawn wide, displaying Paris and all its glory. The far horizon glows with the beginnings of a new day. Somewhere deeper within the hotel suite, I hear Seth's voice. Can't quite make out what he's saying, but it's obvious by his tone that he's unhappy with whoever's on the other end of the conversation.

Quiet as a mouse, I slip out of bed, don a silk bathrobe, and sneak into the living room. Seth's sitting at the dining room table in his underwear with his back to me.

"…that wasn't our agreement, and you know it. You owed me, and now we're even. Call me again, and I will burn you, Frankie. Understand? … *Nyet. Do svidaniya.*" Seth slams his phone down on the table and sighs.

My mind spirals out of control with thoughts and questions about what I just overheard.

Who is Frankie? Why would Seth want to burn them? And since when does Seth know Russian?

My conversation with Thérèse comes rushing back to the forefront of my mind. Smacks me across the back of the head like a two-by-four.

"If Seth were my husband, I'd make it my business to know every last detail of his past," she'd said.

Maybe she's right.

After waiting a full minute to compose myself, I approach Seth. Louder than before so that he can hear me coming. "Everything okay, babe?"

Seth turns in the chair. "Yeah, of course. I was just listening to a bit of news. Did I wake you?"

My feet stall in the middle of the living room. Pulse drums my ears. I'm gobsmacked that he just lied to me without so much as a blink.

I feign a yawn and swallow hard before answering. "Nope. Just woke up and found myself alone in bed, so I came to find you."

"Oh, I see." He stands and walks over to me. Takes my hand. "Come on, we still have an hour or so before we need to be up."

Confusion and anger cause me to resist when he tries to pull me toward the bedroom. "I'm already awake now."

And I want to know who Frankie is.

Seth kisses my forehead. My cheek. Then, his warm breath caresses my ear. He whispers, "Yes, Mrs. Ryan, but I never said anything about us sleeping."

"Oh." A soft nibble on my earlobe melts away the anger and draws butterflies up from my stomach, showering me with goosebumps from head to toe. "Mr. Ryan," I moan. My shoulders shudder.

He ushers me back into the bedroom and lays me down on the bed. Although I wouldn't want to be anywhere else right now, my mind refuses to let go of the partial conversation I overheard. A sinking feeling that there's so much more to the man I call my husband than I ever thought weighs me down and prevents me from fully engaging in the moment.

But I want to engage. *Need* to. I've missed his touch for far too long. Even if it's only been a few days since we last made love.

I close my eyes and bargain with myself to let go just for a little while.

For the love of God, we're in Paris. Please, Alice, stop being the detective for twenty minutes and give me this moment with my husband. If you do, I promise I'll check his call history when he showers. I'll get to the bottom of everything. I swear it.

When I open my eyes, Seth's staring down at me. Head cocked to one side, concern creases his brow. "You okay?"

I reach up, wrap my hands around the back of his neck, and smile. "Never better, my love." The lie slips right through my lips, almost convincing even me. But my thoughts don't lie.

Frankie… Are you a man or a woman?

＊ ＊ ＊ ＊ ＊

Seth's whistling streams through the open bathroom door as the shower bursts to life. I wait a minute, then head for the long dresser across the bedroom. His cellphone's sitting there. Begs for its call history to be accessed.

Of all the nefarious things I've done in my life, few have left my stomach twisted in knots as badly as what I'm about to do now. I should confront him about it instead of sneaking behind his back, but he lied to me first. Or at least he wasn't forthright about the phone call.

But I lied to him, too.

Guilt bubbles in the pit of my stomach and tightens my chest as I grab his phone and punch in the screen lock code. The phone angrily buzzes in my hand. "Invalid Access Code" it warns.

Each breath becomes shallower. Almost leaves me gasping for air.

Sweat drips from my armpits as I enter the code again.

Bzzzz!!

"Dammit, Seth," I whisper. "When did you change your code?"

Palms damp, I close my eyes. Envision Seth pressing the numbers. Then, it hits me. I've put my own code in twice.

"Stupid, Alice. Real stupid."

The third time—with Seth's code and not mine—it finally unlocks. With a few taps the call history displays, but there's another problem. Apparently, Seth's already deleted the call.

My heart aches with betrayal as I close the call history and lock the phone. I set it back down on the dresser and return to the bed. Every thought that enters my mind sends me farther down into a raging tempest as I pull the covers up to my shoulders.

Bitterness threatens to consume me, but I refuse to give into it. Doing so would drive Seth right into Thérèse's arms, and I'll never let that happen. No, I will take this in stride. Compartmentalize it like a case.

What's going on, Seth? What are you hiding from me?

I may know nothing about what he's hiding, but I'm a good detective for a reason. I'll never stop searching for the truth, and I'll get to it no matter where it leads me.

I must.

CHAPTER EIGHT

THE HOTEL PHONE ON the nightstand next to the bed rings with urgency, pulling me from a dream where I'm in pursuit of a suspect while driving a black Lamborghini with a yellow bat symbol on its hood. I'm willing to roll over and ignore the phone, but Seth apparently isn't. He reaches over me and picks up the receiver. I sniff his armpit as it passes by and softly moan. He always smells so good.

"Yeah?" Seth's voice croaks.

I can't hear the person on the other end of the phone call, but I'm certain something's up when Seth stiffens.

Frankie?

It's a ridiculous thought. Whoever Frankie might be, they're certainly not stupid enough to call Seth on a hotel phone. Nor would they have the number to do so.

"Thanks, Pierre. We'll get over there as soon as we can." Seth returns the phone receiver to its cradle, kisses me, then throws the covers off the end of the bed. "Time to get that sexy body of yours moving, babe. We've got a tenth victim."

All thoughts of Frankie evaporate in an instant.

Tenth victim.

A groan escapes from my lips when I finally glance at the clock. "Ugh. You do realize that it's three twelve in the morning on Valentine's Day, right?" I sock him in the stomach playfully. "You sure know how to dig yourself a hole, Mr. Ryan."

"Back off, Tyson. This one's on Pierre, not me." He slides off the bed and heads into the adjoining bathroom. "He said an Uber will be waiting for us outside the hotel lobby in five minutes."

After ten days and nothing but dead ends, I should be happy we have a new victim. Well, not happy for the victim but happy that their death might lead to capturing this killer. Nevertheless, three in the morning is still three in the morning, and I really need my beauty sleep. I stare up at the ceiling and sigh.

Stop whining and get up, Alice.

Twenty-three minutes later, our Uber driver drops us off at a location just two miles from the hotel. Several police cars have the street cordoned off, and yellow crime scene tape surrounds the sidewalk and front entrance of a small protestant church. Thérèse and Pierre await us just behind the police line.

It's been five days since the whole Reagan incident, and it's now a bit awkward being around Pierre since we kept the entire thing from him. I can't help feeling like we betrayed his trust even though he may never find out about it. After a brief greeting, Thérèse escorts Seth and me over to the front of the church.

A male victim lies on his side across the three short steps leading up to a pair of blue doors. Medium build. Blond hair cropped short. Shaven face. Manicured nails. A black overcoat. White, collared shirt sans tie. Black slacks. Black Italian leather shoes. A gold Rolex watch on his right wrist and a platinum band on his left ring finger.

I glance back at the surrounding neighborhood. Not a single nice car lines the street, and there's graffiti and trash everywhere my eyes focus. "I'm guessing he's not from around here."

Thérèse checks her notepad. "According to the victim's ID, his name is René Edelmann. Forty-eight years old." She points toward a man wearing a black suit with a white shirt being interviewed by two uniformed officers. "That's Thomas Moulin, the pastor of this church. He discovered the body on the steps when he was about to leave for the night." She checks her phone. "That was about an hour ago. He bent down to check the victim for a pulse, and that's when he noticed the slit across the man's throat. He called it in right after that."

Pierre walks over, a grim look on his face as he stares down at the victim. "I was really hoping our investigation wouldn't come down to this." He sighs heavily, then looks over at me. "Give me five minutes, and I'll have the area cleared of personnel so that you can do what I brought you here to do without having an audience present."

I nod. "Appreciate it, Pierre."

Seth kneels next to the victim as he snaps on a pair of latex gloves. "Take a look at the victim's shoes. The bottoms are covered in some sort of yellowish dust."

Kneeling next to Seth, I examine the shoes myself. Sure enough, a yellow film coats the bottoms of them. The toes are scuffed, too. Based on the victim's overall appearance, the scuffs must've happened right before, during, or after his death.

"Limestone dust," Thérèse confirms.

I glance up at her. "From the catacombs?"

"We locals call the catacombs *les k'tas*, but yes."

Seth stands. "What about the other victims? Were their shoes covered in limestone dust, too?"

"Yes," Thérèse says, "but that's quite common around here."

Every last detail of the case files Pierre gave me are ingrained into my photographic memory. Not one of them mentioned anything about limestone dust. I peer up at Thérèse and scowl. "I don't understand. Why wasn't that detail mentioned on any of the reports?"

"An oversight, I'm sure," she admits. "For the record, there are literally miles and miles of catacombs beneath Paris, most of which have never been explored. At least not legally. Because of this, it would be impossible to track down a specific location in the catacombs even if a crime does take place somewhere down there."

"Sounds like a perfect place to commit murder," Seth says, then kneels next to me again.

Thérèse touches Seth's shoulder and smiles down at him. "It would be my first choice, too, but I'd leave the body down there. No body, no crime."

Seth chuckles. "We think alike."

Every last atom in my body begs me to lash out at the vile woman for daring to lay her hand on Seth, but instead I clear my mind and focus my gaze on the victim's face. It's the only thing that matters right now.

Who were you, René Edelmann?

Soon, I'll hopefully find out.

If my gift works…

Pierre returns and stands next to Thérèse. "It's your time to shine, Alice." He offers a weary smile when I glance up at him. "For the love of God, please find something we can use to nail this bastard."

I nod curtly. "I'll do everything I can."

Pierre and Thérèse back away from the front steps of the church, leaving Seth and me alone with the victim. I swallow hard, my stomach pretzeled.

Seth strokes my back. "You've got this, babe."

I glance over at him. "And if it doesn't work again?"

He smiles, then kisses the top of my head. "Trust me, it will."

At least one of us has confidence.

I take a deep breath, ease it from my lungs, then stare at the victim. "Show me."

The sounds of Paris fade into the distance as I reach down and touch René Edelmann's hand. Despite the frigid night, his flesh remains warm against my cold fingers. Time itself halts as my pulse slows to a crawl. A familiar fire burns my skin, and that strange, alien shift occurs within me once again. Never have I been so happy to feel so strange. Then, just as Slavik Garin's hand had done to me so many months ago, René's hand grabs mine and pulls me into his world.

* * * * *

René smashes the empty bottle of Spirytus vodka on a large, white boulder half-buried in the dirt. The 192 proof liquid burns as it continues to settle in the pit of his stomach, its hellish aftertaste fire in his throat. It doesn't take long before he needs to relieve himself. It never does.

He unzips his trousers and urinates on a small bouquet of dead lilies next to the large boulder, saturating them and the ground. Once he finishes, he zips up and spits on the ground. "It's more than you deserve, Natasha." He spits again, then stares into the distance.

A barren field, miles wide and several miles deep, separates him from a lone, two-story structure with a pitched roof. Five giant white letters painted across the side of the roof seem to glow in the moonlight. ROUGE. It's the name his father went by and the name of his father's barn-building company.

Had everything gone as planned, René would've married Natasha in that cursed building. Instead, she met her end not far from its double doors. Now, tears fill his eyes, and his chest aches just looking at the damned barn.

"I would've given you the world, Natasha, but you had to cross me." His hands curl into fists at his sides, and he stomps the ground. "Ugh! Why did you do this to me?"

"She did nothing to you, René, and you know it."

René turns, and his pulse quickens. He doesn't recognize the manly voice or the tall figure cloaked in darkness that it emanated from. The figure walks with an odd, jerky gait as he slowly approaches. Almost stumbles forward with each step as though something's wrong with his feet or legs.

Five paces away, the man stops and lowers the hood of his black cloak. Green eyes shine in the pale moonlight, but René's gaze focuses on the man's slightly misshapen head and distorted features.

Does he not have a nose?

René can't be sure. Perhaps it is merely a trick of light and shadow or the effects of the alcohol surging through his veins.

Must be the vodka.

He points at the man with an unsteady hand, his finger almost wagging. "Who the hell are you?" he growls.

"Who I am is irrelevant." The man proffers an empty hand with two missing fingers. "All you need know is that I am here to relieve you of your miserable existence. Come, take my hand."

René eyes the man's hand for several moments. Wills his vision to hold steady as he searches for any sort of weapon, but the man refuses to stay in focus. He detects none but knows himself to be unreliable given his current physical and mental state.

Today hasn't been his best day. Each consecutive anniversary of Natasha's death hits him harder. A sledgehammer to the chest. But it's not guilt. How could it be? Her actions left him no choice.

René forces his mind to refocus on the nameless man. The outstretched hand. Fear grows within his gut as his gaze rises to meet the stranger's eyes once again. It envelops him. Leaves him breathless like nothing he's ever felt before.

He takes an unsteady step backward. "You're trespassing. Leave this place, or I'll put you in the ground, too."

The man does not heed his warning. Instead, he draws closer. Far too close, his outstretched hand just a foot or so away. "You'll feel little more than a slight jolt."

"The hell I will." René leans forward and swats at the man's hand. Almost misses altogether given his inebriated state. But their fingers touch. Only for an instant. But it's evidently enough as René experiences the jolt that the man said would come. Reminds him of a time when he touched a live electrical wire as it rockets up his arm and spreads throughout his entire body.

He looks down. Watches pieces of himself disintegrate into oblivion.

Impossible.

"My God! What is this?" he asks. "What have you done to me?"

"Only what's necessary," the man says, his face etched with sorrow. "And God has nothing to do with it."

René screams, more out of fear than pain, but the sound remains within his mind, never getting a chance to pierce his lips. Darkness closes in around him, snuffing out the moonlight as the night sky and the entire countryside begin to fade. Then, an unexplainable force pulls him backward and into perfect darkness.

* * * * *

Two blue doors materialize out of the darkness as I gasp for air.

Seth's at my side, his arm tight around my shoulder and his hand on my waist. "Are you okay?"

"Yeah, I think so." I take a deep breath and allow the world around me to settle. "Thankfully, it worked this time, and the victim wasn't a Shadow Priest."

Thérèse returns. Her eyes narrow as she stares down at me. "And what exactly is a Shadow Priest?"

Waving her off, I say, "It's not important." My eyes meet Seth's intense gaze. "I saw the killer's face, and it certainly wasn't Jean-Luc. Plus, I think I might know where the victim was killed."

Thérèse scoffs. "I've worked with psychics and mediums in the past who were absolutely certain of what they saw, too, yet none of their information proved accurate or useful." She crosses her arms, and her eyes narrow. "How can you be so certain of what you think you saw?"

Rage boils in my veins. "I don't *think* I saw anything."

I'm about to explode off the ground and tackle Thérèse to the ground when Pierre steps into our little circle around the victim. His genuine smile brings my anger down to a simmer and saves me from a potential lawsuit.

Pierre gives me a wink, then addresses Thérèse. "As you know, Detective Bergman is neither a psychic nor a medium. Admittedly, her unique talent exceeds my understanding, but her past results stand on their own merit. If she says she saw our killer, you'd be wise to believe her."

Thérèse nods, but she's clearly perturbed about something. After more than ten months without any leads in the case other than the hand on Li Qiang's chest, I would've thought she'd be ecstatic. But then the truth of her supposed skepticism hits me. A smile cracks my lips.

She's jealous of me.

I shrug Seth's arm off my shoulders and pull myself up. The church and its blue doors teeter-totter in front of me, and my legs begin to tingle with fatigue, leaving me unstable. Thérèse grabs my arm and steadies me before I face-plant right into the victim.

"Are you sure you're alright?" A hint of concern blossoms in her voice. Either she's an exceptional actor or she's a little more human than I give her credit for. I'm definitely leaning toward exceptional actor.

I nod and instantly realize I've made a poor choice. Thérèse's hand becomes my anchor as I latch onto it with my other hand. Nausea brews in the pit of my stomach, and bile sets fire to my chest as it rises into my throat. I close my eyes for a few moments and take a deep breath, staving off the urge to purge myself and contaminate the entire scene.

It wouldn't be the first time if I did.

My fingers leave behind red imprints as I peel them away from Thérèse's hand. "I'm okay now. Just a bit lightheaded."

Pierre eyes me, his brow wrinkled with concern. "You're a ghost, Alice." He pulls out a clear baggie from within his jacket pocket. It contains some sort of homemade granola bar. He offers the bag to me. "Here, eat this. It'll give you a quick energy boost."

My mind leaps into the past and conjures up the disgusting stuff Rico gave me after I first used my white cane, Esther, and depleted my energy. With reluctance, I accept Pierre's offering. "Thank you."

When the seal on the bag breaks, it releases a vulgar scent that burns my nostrils. Without additional help, the granola bar's garlicky smell could ward off a coven of vampires. Even Vlad himself would have a hard time fighting its pungent odor.

After an initial hesitance, I lift the granola bar to my lips and sink my teeth into the dense bar. The vile taste hits my tongue instantaneously and clings to my lips like a dirty diaper. Wet, garlicky cardboard with faint notes of dillweed, cilantro, onion, and honey.

The more I chew, the worse the taste becomes, bombarding my tastebuds with a symphony of nastiness. It takes every ounce of my willpower to force it down without gagging or spitting it back out. My entire body quivers.

Dear God…

Pierre claps his hands. "You are indeed a strong-willed woman, Detective Bergman. Most who have tried my bars spat them out. I assure you the bars are an acquired taste, much like escargot."

"I just don't get the whole acquired taste thing," Seth says. "If I don't like something on the first try, why the hell would I ever try it again?"

"I agree," Thérèse says. "There are far too many food options in the world to bother with ones that are—" Her nose wrinkles. "—*méchante*."

Seth's laughter cranks my head around and narrows my eyes.

Did he actually understand her, or is he just stoking her ego?

His laughter subsides when his gaze meets mine. Creases form across his brow. "What?"

"Nothing," I huff.

"I might not understand French," Seth says, "but that doesn't mean I didn't get the gist of what Thérèse was saying."

"*Méchante* means nasty," Thérèse says.

Seth nods at Thérèse and gestures toward her with his hand. "Exactly. Your facial expression said everything I needed to know."

"Whatever." I push everything from my mind and concentrate on what I witnessed through the victim's eyes. "Pierre, we need to visit the property of René Edelmann's father. It's an expansive farm with a large, barn-type structure."

Pierre nods once. "This property is where the victim was killed?"

I shrug. "I think it might be, but I'm not certain. Either way, there's something buried there that you'll definitely want to see."

"Very good." He turns to Thérèse. "Make the call and get us an address."

"On it." Thérèse steps around the body and brushes shoulders with Seth as she descends the stairs. The two of them share a brief glance before she struts away from the scene. Angry thunderclouds build in my mind once again and threaten to unleash their fury upon Seth, but he's not the one to blame.

This is my fault, Seth. I should've come to Paris alone.

CHAPTER NINE

PIERRE AND I SPEND most of the hour-and-a-half-long drive to the Edelmann property south of Paris in utter silence. Despite my apprehensions toward Seth riding with Holly Homewrecker, Pierre had insisted on the pairing.

In hindsight, I realize Pierre is a wise man and far more perceptive than I've given him credit for thus far. After the brushed shoulder incident on the church steps, I might've snapped and attacked her on the car ride over, potentially causing an accident and killing one or both of us in the process.

And I still might.

In the distance, a large structure rises above the horizon. It matches what I saw in my vision perfectly. Leaning forward in the seat, I point in its direction. "That's the place."

Pierre nods. "Right you are."

He turns down a long, dirt access road that slowly curves toward the two-story, red-walled structure. Giant, white letters stretch across the side of the pitched tin roof.

"Rouge," I say, more to myself than anything.

Pierre pulls the car up next to Thérèse's car. It's empty, so she and Seth must be exploring the property already. As I reach for the door handle, Pierre touches my other wrist. Concern bleeds from his eyes when I turn and meet his gaze.

"What?" The word barks from my lips with a snap.

"You should know that she only does it because it bothers you," he says.

I know exactly what he's talking about, yet I can't accept that it's so obvious. It must come from his own lips. "Does what?"

He withdraws his hand and leans back in his seat. "Flirts with your husband."

There. It's out. A living, breathing fact. But I don't feel any better. In fact, it's somehow worse.

I rub my palm on my jeans. "If Seth didn't enjoy it, I wouldn't care at all."

Pierre frowns at me. "Are you so different from him? Have you never appreciated another man's complements or enjoyed the stare of a stranger from across a room?"

A tinge of guilt rises from my gut as Jake's face materializes in my mind. Pierre's not wrong.

He continues, "You're a beautiful woman, Detective Bergman. I assure you, Seth is a very lucky man."

His bluntness smacks me right in the face. Sends droves of blood into my cheeks and forces my gaze downward. "I… yes…" I shrug. "Thank you?"

Pierre grips the steering wheel. "In my experience, and I'll admit I've had a lot over the years, nothing drives a man into the arms of another woman faster than jealousy and scorn. It works both ways, mind you. You'll be best served ignoring Thérèse. Once she realizes you're no longer participating in her game, she'll back off. After all, she enjoys the thrill of making you jealous far more than the thought of stealing your husband."

I glance over at Pierre. "You think so?"

"I know so. Thérèse has a history of doing it to many people, myself included." He pats my shoulder halfheartedly. "Do yourself a favor and turn up the heat when you're alone with Seth. Show him how much you love and appreciate him. It's all any of us crazy humans ever want, and it'll keep him faithful."

My eyes follow Seth through the car windshield as he exits the massive building in front of us. "You're far wiser than your years, Pierre."

"There's no need to patronize me, Alice. I'm well aware of the years I've tucked under my belt. Do yourself and that husband of yours a favor and just consider the wisdom I've imparted upon you."

I nod curtly. "Thank you. I will."

The frigid morning air blasts my face and fills the car when I throw the door open. It's far colder out here in the countryside than it had been in the city, and it chills me to the bone within seconds of exiting the car. Zipping up my jacket helps a little, but my hands still feel like ice in my pockets.

Pierre makes his way around the car. "You said that you have something to show me?"

I glance over my shoulder and toward the barren field before giving Pierre a nod. "Yeah. Got a shovel?"

He grins. "Of course. I make sure I'm always prepared for anything and everything."

Pierre fetches a shovel from the trunk of his car. "Lead the way, Detective Bergman."

Seth and Thérèse join us as we trek across the field.

"What are we looking for out here?" Seth asks.

"We're not *looking* for anything." I point ahead at a large, out of place, white boulder protruding from the ground. "See that rock? That's where we're headed."

We arrive at the white boulder, and Seth immediately crouches down and picks up a dead bouquet of lilies lying next to it.

"Dear God!" Seth tosses the bouquet back down. He shakes his arms, shoulders, and head. "Ugh! Those flowers smell like piss and vodka."

"Well, they should," I say with a snicker. "René Edelmann just watered them last night."

Pierre and Thérèse bust up laughing.

Seth glares at me as he wipes his hand on his jeans. "You could've warned me not to pick them up."

I shrug. "You didn't give me a chance to."

Seth huffs. "Why are we out here, anyway?"

"This is the spot where the victim was killed… or at least abducted."

Thérèse's eyes scan the ground. "There's broken glass everywhere, but I don't see any blood, drag marks, or anything else other than some partial footprints."

As much as I hate to admit it, Thérèse is right. The ground literally sparkles all around us, but there's no sign of a struggle.

What the hell happened to you out here, Mr. Edelmann?

Pierre frowns at me. "You're certain this is the right spot?"

The encounter between the victim and the cloaked man plays back in my head. "Yes, but I'm not exactly sure what happened here last night."

Thérèse scowls at me. "You've led us out here on a wild goose chase? Ugh! Why are you wasting our time?"

Seth cuts in before I have a chance to level her. "First off, Alice never wastes time when it comes to an investigation. If she says that something happened here, then it did. Second, you need to get down from that pedestal you've put yourself on. You've had ten months to crack this case and nothing to show for it, so get over yourself. It's pathetic."

My stomach flutters with excitement as Thérèse's face turns bright red.

Damn straight!

Pierre thrusts the spaded end of the shovel into the ground between Thérèse and Seth. "Enough. Both of you." His gaze meets mine, the soft edge gone. "You said there was something to show me. Now's the time to do so."

I circle the white boulder. "We need to dig around or beneath this thing."

Thérèse's eyes scan the ground again. "For what? A murder weapon or something?" For once, there's no condescension in her tone.

"Not a what but a who," I say.

Seth scratches the back of his neck. "Okay, now I'm really confused. We already have the victim's body, so who are we going to find here?"

"As it turns out, our victim has a victim of his own," I say.

Thérèse's eyes widen as she stares at the ground. "Edelmann's fiancée is buried here?"

I nod. "Natasha. I'm certain he buried her here. That's why he left the bouquet of lilies next to the boulder and smashed all the vodka bottles. He loved her, but he thought that she had betrayed him, so he killed her."

"Then we dig," Pierre says. He pushes the shovel handle toward Seth and offers a slight grin. "As you might've guessed, my digging days are over."

Two hours later and far deeper than I would've imagined, Seth unearths what looks like the corner of a blue tarp. From here, it takes another fifteen minutes to unbury the rest of it.

Twine binds the tarp together in several places, and the shape it's taken on leaves no doubt as to what lies within its folds. Once exhumed, Pierre pulls out a pocketknife, kneels next to the tarp, and cuts the twine. The folds of the tarp slide apart, revealing the remains of a brunette. The right side of her skull looks like it's been crushed.

Pierre sits back on his heels and sighs. "It's her, alright. Natasha Baird." He points at the remains of her left hand. "I recognize that engagement ring from her missing persons file."

Thérèse clenches her fist and smiles. "I knew that bastard was guilty."

Pierre stands and faces me. "This solves one open case, and I'm truly appreciative of it, but I'm not sure how it helps with ours."

"I think I do, and it goes back to what Thérèse said before." My mind files back through all the notes on the previous nine victims, quickly verifying what I'm about to say. "Finding Natasha's body speaks to the pattern of how our killer chooses his victims. Each of them were charged with heinous crimes but never convicted. I think that says something very important about our killer."

Pierre nods slowly. "Yes, a vigilante."

"And someone who keeps current with the news," Seth adds.

"Yes, to both, and I know exactly what he looks like," I say.

Thérèse crosses her arms. "Can you describe him for me?"

It's a strange request. Not the request itself but in the way she asks. It's as though she knows something about the killer and has kept it to herself and seeks confirmation one way or the other about it from me. Then again, I'm probably reading too much into it.

"I'll do better than that," I say. "I'll draw you a picture."

"I can sit you down with a sketch artist," Pierre offers. "We've got several who are exceptional."

"No need for that," Seth says, a hint of pride in his voice. "As you might not know, Alice has a photographic memory. She's developed a unique way to basically transfer an image from her mind onto a piece of paper. She's kind of like a human photocopier."

I'm not sure if I'm prouder of Seth's understanding of what I can do or the fact that he actually said photographic and not photogenic.

Guess he learns after all.

Thérèse eyes me. "You remember everything?"

"Basically, yes. That is if I've committed it to memory. For instance, I don't remember every building we've passed in Paris, nor do I remember every face I've seen. However, I can keep track of it if needed."

"Remarkable," Pierre says. "Let's head back to my car. I have a sketch pad and pencil in the trunk." He looks over at Thérèse and points back at the corpse lying on the tarp. "Call this in and see that it gets taken care of."

She nods and pulls out her phone, but the look in her eyes tells me that she's unhappy with something about the situation. There are only two things I can think of that might've soured her mood. Either it's being ordered around by Pierre or the fact that I solved a case no one else had been able to for several years. I'm positive it's the latter.

And I'll solve this other one, too.

Back at Pierre's car, I settle into the passenger seat and stare at the blank sheet of paper sitting in my lap. The pencil sits between my fingers, ready to reveal the killer. Eyes open, I conjure the man's disfigured face in my mind and project it onto the sheet of paper. To anyone watching, the sheet remains blank, but I see every last detail. Every nuance. Scars and wrinkles and freckles.

As the pencil moves in my hand, the killer begins taking shape and comes to life. Ten minutes later, I revel in what I've drawn. The killer's face stares up at me from the page. Leaves my flesh prickled. I half expect him to breathe, talk, or wink at me, yet he never moves.

After snapping a picture of the drawing with my phone, I exit the car and head over to Pierre and Seth.

I proffer the sketch to Pierre. "This is your man. Our killer."

Pierre takes the sketch from me and studies it for several minutes before looking back up. A smile parts his lips, and his head shakes. "You are indeed a remarkable woman. If I didn't know better, I might've mistaken this for a black-and-white photo."

"Told you she was good." Seth beams ear-to-ear as he places his arm around me and squeezes.

Pierre calls Thérèse over and hands her the sketch. The instant her eyes meet the paper, I swear I glimpse a spark of recognition in them, but it fades just as quickly. The longer her gaze lingers on the drawing, the less certain I become of what I thought I saw.

She hands the sketch back to Pierre. "I'll admit that the quality of the sketch is impeccable. However, the man looks like some creature from a horror movie rather than one from real life."

Pierre eyes the sketch again, then nods. "Maybe so, but that doesn't mean it's not accurate. We'll run it through our databases and get it out to all the news outlets. If this man exists, someone must know him."

Thérèse crosses her arms, a move she's employing at an increasing rate. "You're certain that's our best option, Pierre? Posting a caricature on national news?"

"Caricature?" Seth guffaws. "Am I missing something?"

She shoots him a glare that could melt a planet right out of existence. "I'm not one who takes kindly to looking foolish." She points at the sketch still in Pierre's possession. "No one could possibly look like that."

"And yet he does," I say.

The focus of Thérèse's glare turns against Pierre. "You be sure and leave my name out of everything. I still have a career ahead of me." She turns and storms off toward the boulder and the exhumed body.

Pierre sighs. "You must forgive her. As confident as she may seem, she's quite vulnerable. Several months ago, a reporter interviewed her about the case. The vile woman twisted Thérèse's words and made her look foolish and incompetent. She's been upset over it ever since."

Too bad I missed that.

Seth nods. "Been there before, and it sucks."

I've been there before, too, and it indeed sucks. But I still would've loved to watch Thérèse squirm.

* * * * *

Back at the hotel, I text a picture of the killer's sketch to Kenny and then call him. He answers on the second ring.

"Hey, Alice! Was wondering when I'd hear from you again. What's with that creep show dude you sent me?"

"Well, that's what our killer looks like."

"Are you for real? Whoa. That dude's got a totally messed-up head." He chuckles. "Must've been dropped way too many times as a child."

I smirk. "Right? Anyway, I was wondering if you could do me a favor."

"Whatever it is, I'm your guy. You know that."

"And I appreciate you more than you'll ever know. Anyway…" I'm always reluctant to ask Kenny to do anything that's not entirely above board, and I'm starting to think that I shouldn't now, so I change the subject. "I was wondering if you could check on my parents sometime this week. I haven't heard from them in a while, and I'm worried about them."

Wow, that was lame.

"Um, yeah, sure. Not a problem. Isaiah's always got a great story to tell, and your mom's cooking never lets me down."

"Great. Thanks, Kenny. I appreciate it." Silence hangs on the line for several seconds before I continue. "Look, it's late here. I should probably let you go so I can get some sleep."

"Yeah, of course. And don't worry about anything. I'll also do that thing you called about but refuse to ask of me."

"I'm not sure what you're—"

"Yes, you are. I'm scouring videos from all across Paris as we speak. Once I get a hit, and you know I will, I'll give you a buzz." The drumming of his fingers on some hard surface echoes through the phone. "Given the excessive amount of historical data I'll need to go through, plus all the new data generated every second… it might take me a week or so to produce some good leads for you."

As much as I fear him getting caught accessing private video feeds across Paris, I know there's no other way to accomplish the task. Done through proper channels, the search warrants alone could take months to issue. Not only that, but many of the feeds would be inaccessible simply because they would remain unknown to us.

He's our best and only option.

"Kenny… be careful."

"Always am. Besides, I never leave a trace. You know that."

"So far." I sigh loudly. "Every time I call you, I put you right in the crosshairs of danger. I swear it's not my intention, Kenny, but how often can it happen before there can be no other conclusion?"

"Don't even sweat it, Alice. You taught me to be fearless years ago, remember?"

"I know what you're referring to, but you've still got Kellie to think about. Don't get me wrong, I know you think about her every moment of your life, but I'd never forgive myself if something happened to you because of me. She would suffer for it more than anyone else."

"I don't disagree, but the world needs heroes like you. And you need nerdy sidekicks like me to help you save the world. It is what it is, and I will never regret helping you."

There's nothing I can say that would stop him now, and if I'm being honest with myself, I wouldn't allow myself to do so anyway given the stakes. After all, Kenny's likely the only person in the world capable of tracking down this killer. He's not just talented with computers but has an actual gift with technology. A gift like mine, signified by the mark on the inside of his left wrist.

"I know. Love ya, kid." My voice tremors.

Kenny laughs. "Love ya back. Hey, say hi to Seth for me."

"Will do." I smile. "Give all my love to Kellie. Oh, and my parents when you see them."

"Always, Alice. Catch ya on the flip side."

After hanging up, I sink back into the sofa cushions and close my eyes. For the first time since arriving in Paris, it feels like we might have a fighting chance in cracking this case.

God, I hope so.

"Everything good back home?" Seth asks.

He's leaning over me when I open my eyes. "Yeah. When did you get back from the gym?"

"A few minutes ago." He kisses my forehead. "I'm about to go hop in the shower."

The word shower acts like a trigger word, reminding me of the phone call Seth hid from me.

Frankie... How had I forgotten?

Seth grins. "Wanna join me?"

My eyes study his neck. Bare chest. Ripped muscles glistening with sweat. All the stress and tiredness I've been carrying around Paris begins to melt away. Even when I'm angry with him, he's irresistible. Pulse racing, I reach up and cradle his sweaty face in my hands and pull his upside-down lips against mine. We stay lip-locked for what feels like a glorious eternity before he pulls away.

Light twinkles in his beautiful, blue eyes. "Well?"

I take his hand and kiss the back of it. "Never thought you'd ask. You go get it heated up, and I'll come join you."

"What could be more important than us getting naked in the shower?"

"I forgot to ask Kenny to check on my parents." It's a small little white lie, yet it still makes me feel like crap.

"Alright, but don't take too long. We'll need as much hot water as possible."

Depending on what I find, you might already be in hot water.

"Won't be but a minute. Promise."

Seth heads for the bedroom, and I call Kenny back.

Kenny answers immediately. "Hey, didn't expect to hear from you so soon. No results yet."

"Yeah, I understand, but that's not why I called back. There's something else I need to ask of you. Top secret classified stuff, understood?"

"Name it. Lips are sealed."

"This past Sunday, February ninth, Seth either called someone or got a call from someone. It was around six in the morning Paris time. You think you can track it down for me?"

"I won't ask why, but do you have the number?"

"No. He deleted it from his call history."

"Oh." There's a brief pause, then, "Oh! I see. Right. You want me to figure out *who* he was talking to." He breathes heavily. "It might take some time to get you a number. If you're lucky, maybe a location, too."

"Good. Will it help knowing that Seth was talking to someone named Frankie and in Russian?"

"Whoa…"

"Yeah, I know. It could be nothing." My gut says it's an impossibility, but I can't voice that to myself let alone Kenny. "Anyway, track it when you can. And whatever you do, don't text me or leave me a voicemail about it. Only a call. Got it?"

"Roger that. Whatever I find will be for your ears only."

"Thanks, Kenny. I owe you big."

He snickers. "Yeah, I know."

After ending the call, I walk into the bedroom and strip out of my clothes. Seth's whistling a tune to some 80s rock song in the shower, but I can't place it.

Inside the bathroom, steam fills the small space. I head into it and into Seth's awaiting arms in the shower. There's still no other place I'd want to be, yet I can't help but mull over what Kenny might discover. As stupid as it is, there's one thought that keeps circling my brain, and it sticks out beyond all my other thoughts.

God, I hope Frankie's a man.

CHAPTER TEN

TEN VICTIMS. COUNTLESS ASSOCIATIONS. Three weeks we've spent re-interviewing everyone who could be tracked down, utilizing my sketch of the killer to find a connection. Yet we yielded nothing.

Zero. Zilch. Zip. Nada.

Despite the inebriated state of René Edelmann on the night he was killed or abducted, I'm certain of what I saw, and it's frustrating to say the least. The odds none of the people we interviewed knew the killer are astronomically high. And to top it off, every single call from the hotline given out by the news outlets and papers have led to dead ends. It one hundred percent sucks.

As the sun begins to slip beyond the western horizon of Paris, I sit on the edge of a concrete fountain not far from the Louvre. Seth's gone to grab us a couple of hotdogs wrapped in flaky croissants from one of the street vendors.

Normally, I'd be salivating with anticipation, but our lack of progress on the case has suppressed my appetite. Don't get me wrong, I'll still eat the hotdog and enjoy it, but not with as much enthusiasm as I normally might.

My phone rings in my pocket. Caller ID says it's Kenny.

God, I hope he has some good news.

I answer it. "Hello?"

"Hey Alice, it's Kenny." Dejection rings in his voice, but I try not to read too much into it.

"Yeah, I know," I say. "Your number's programmed into my phone."

He chuckles. "Oh, right." After clearing his throat, he continues. "So, I've gone over the footage of every last camera I could find, but your killer seems to be a ghost."

"Damn." I grind my teeth.

"Yeah, it's weird. It's almost as if he has the ability to avoid every camera in the entire city."

Avoiding all surveillance isn't in the realm of possibility these days, but I have no explanation that makes sense. "I was really hoping you had some good news for me."

"Yeah, me too. I'm sorry."

"No, no. It's not your fault, Kenny. You did a great job. I really appreciate it."

Kenny sighs. "I just wish I could've helped with this."

"Yeah, it sucks, but you've done more for me over the years than I ever should've asked of you." After a brief pause, I say, "Speaking of which, what about the other matter we discussed?"

"Still working on it. Got a few feelers out. Shouldn't be too much longer."

"Good. Keep me posted."

"Yeah, I definitely will."

Kenny hangs up, leaving me feeling lost and alone. I stare at the sketch and retrace every detail from the encounter René had with the killer, but nothing new comes to mind.

Just who the hell are you?

A young woman in soiled, torn jeans and a grimy gray sweatshirt glances my way as she walks by. It's the third time she's done so. Even in my current frame of mind, I'd never forget her stringy hair held back with a dirty, purple bandanna. She stops, likely sensing me watching her. Then, she circles back and stops a few feet in front of me. Stares in my direction but not directly at me. Says nothing.

A rank odor surrounds her. One of the many homeless who wander the streets of Paris, she's likely not bathed in months. I can't help but wonder what drove her to homelessness. She can't be more than twenty or so.

"Can I help you?" I ask in French.

She shakes her head, then turns to leave.

"I'm Alice." I stand and proffer my hand, but she just stares at it when she turns back. "Anyway, what made you decide to come over here?"

She glances at the sketch in my hands, then looks around cautiously. Finally, her brown eyes meet mine. "Darcy. Just Darcy."

"That's a beautiful name, Darcy."

She half smiles. "Pretty, like your hair." Her eyes linger on the sketch again. "Seen him before."

My pulse spikes. I turn the sketch around and show it to her. "This man?"

Darcy nods, then cautiously looks around again. She motions for me to follow her, then heads around the backside of the fountain. Nestled in the crook of two tall buildings, we're now a little more shielded from view.

"What's wrong?" I ask.

"Not right in the head, you know. Talks to himself." She squeezes her eyes shut and shakes her head. "Dark, dark thoughts no one should ever speak aloud."

Chills race down my arms. "Do you know where I can find this man?"

Darcy trembles. Nods. Opens her eyes. They're glossy with tears.

I reach for her shoulder, and she flinches. "Don't know me," she whispers.

I pull my hand back. "I'm sorry, Darcy. You're right. I shouldn't have done that."

She nods. Lower lip quivers. "No one touches."

There's no way I could ever imagine what she's gone through, but it tears me up inside just thinking about it. "Of course." I hold up the sketch again. "Anything at all will help."

"Don't know where right now," she says, "but know where he sleeps."

"Is it close by?"

Darcy shakes her head. "Far north. A… uh…" She holds the sides of her head and grimaces. After a few seconds, she looks at me. "Train station?"

"Transit station?" I ask, remembering several of them on the map.

She nods. "Yes. Transit station. Always there. Used to sleep there too. But scares me. Scares us all."

"Do you know his name?"

"Sometimes Trace. Sometimes Moonshine." She shudders. "I don't like it when he's not Trace."

Seth comes around the far side of the fountain, hotdogs in hand. "There you are."

Darcy backs into the far corner. I hold up my hand and signal Seth to halt. He does even though his face scrunches with confusion.

"It's okay, Darcy," I say. "This is my husband, Seth. He's one of the good guys, too." I take one of the hotdogs from him and hold it out toward her. "Take this. You've earned it."

Darcy eyes Seth then the hotdog. She reaches out, snatches it from my hand, then runs off.

Seth scowls. "What was that all about?"

His scowl deepens when I snatch the second hotdog from him and take a big bite out of it before handing it back. It tastes glorious, especially with the ketchup, mustard, and relish. I'm tempted to steal the rest of it, but that would be downright mean.

Instead, I grab Seth's hand and tug on his arm. "Come on, I think I know where we can find our killer."

* * * * *

Late that evening, Seth, Thérèse, and I, along with a large handful of French Police, stand just outside one of the transit stations in northern Paris. All of us face Pierre and await final instructions. A feeling of unease hangs in the air and unsettles my stomach.

For the first time since arriving in Paris, Pierre has opted to arm Seth and me with SIG Sauer Pro SP 2022s. Seth's right at home with the gun, just like he is with any weapon, but the piece isn't what I'm accustomed to and feels a bit awkward in my hands. It still gives me a sense of security, though.

Pierre holds up a printout for everyone to see, lit up with a flashlight. "As I stated in the briefing," he says in French, "Trace Moonshine is our target. We do not know if he's our killer, but keep in mind that he suffers from a brain disorder. Because of this, consider him to be dangerous and easily agitated. And, as I said before, the goal is to capture him alive if possible. Under no circumstances should you take a head shot unless the situation warrants it and no other option remains. Am I clear?"

"*Cristal,*" the police officers say in unison, even as they look at each other with a bit of confusion.

None of them know anything about my gift, and Pierre's assured me that it will stay that way. The only thing they've been told is that Seth and I were brought in to assist with the case.

Pierre nods curtly. "Good. Let's move out and keep alert. This is a big place. He could be hiding anywhere."

"*Oui monsieur,*" they echo. The police officers begin spreading out as they enter through the front of the transit station.

Seth and I follow Thérèse and Pierre through the station building and out to the platforms. Given the hour and poor lighting, it's hard to tell the number of platforms and trains sitting on the tracks. My guess is at least twenty trains, but there are probably more. Plenty of places for a man to hide, even one of Trace Moonshine's size.

Pierre leads us straight to the center platform and motions for Seth and Thérèse to take the left train while we take the one on the right. Pierre enters the first car while I continue along the platform, scanning the gaps between the platform and the parked train. It's a small and an unlikely place to hide, but those are often the places men like Trace choose.

Bang!

The gunshot echoes across the transit station platforms like a cannon, startling me and making it impossible to know which direction it came from. Pierre ducks his head outside one of the train car doors. I shake my head, understanding his unspoken question of what happened.

"*Policier à terre,*" comes a voice over the hand radio. "*Je répète, officier à terre. Tir ami.*"

Friendly fire?

My stomach lurches.

Damn.

Moments later, something darts between shadows toward the end of the platform, moving from my right to my left. At this distance, it could've been anything, yet somehow, I'm certain it's the man we're after.

Pulse racing, I mash down the button on the hand radio. "Suspect just crossed the north end of platform eight, heading west."

Pierre joins me on the platform, and we begin heading toward the far end.

"I'm on platform seven," Thérèse says over the radio. "Didn't see anyone pass my way."

I glance at Pierre, a twinge of fear lodged in my throat. "Well then, he's either under or on one of those two trains," I say, pointing to my left. "Likely the one Seth's on."

Pierre nods. "You continue to the end of the platform, and I'll get on this first train. One way or another, we'll catch him."

"Okay."

He grabs my arm as I'm about to walk off. "Alice, be careful. If this is our guy, he's already killed at least ten people."

"Understood. Watch yourself, too." I take off toward the north, my eyes peeled and my heart slamming against my ribcage.

The shadows deepen as I reach the far end of the platform, the moon ducking behind a bank of ominous clouds. The wind picks up and lightning flashes across the sky, obliterating the shadows. In that bright instant, it's obvious no one lurks down on the tracks.

Another flash comes as I turn back south. Shadows scatter for another moment, but then one appears that I swear hadn't been there before.

My gaze rises toward the first train on my right. Continues upward until I see the man standing atop it. He looks down at me, but shadows obscure his face.

Thunder rumbles. Shakes me from the inside out. Comes from within me as much as it does from the rapidly expanding air around the path of the lightning bolts.

The lightning acts as a switch, causing rain to begin falling from the sky. Sheets of it pour down, driven by a westerly wind. The drops sting as they pelt my face. Drench me and blur my eyes. By the time I wipe my face and raise my weapon, the shadow man is gone.

"Dammit!"

Circling back toward the end of the platform again, I catch a glimpse of him entering the last train car.

I smash down the button on the radio. "He's headed your way, Pierre!" Holstering my gun, I leap onto the end deck of the train car with abandon, never once thinking about how slick its metal surface might be.

My first foot sticks the landing, but the second slides right out from under me. Somehow, I manage to wrap my arm around the metal handrail before performing splits I might not walk away from. The move slows my fall but doesn't keep me from hitting the deck as I twist around.

Air bursts from my lungs as the steel plate drives into my chest. It takes a few moments for me to recover and find my feet again. When I finally do, I burst through the train car door and into the dining carriage, my SP 2022 leading the charge.

In the middle of the car stands a man cloaked in shadows. The same one I spotted on top of the train. But he's not alone. Pierre hangs awkwardly from the crook of the man's arm. From where I stand, it's impossible to know if Pierre is dead or just knocked unconscious.

God, let him be alive.

Seth stands at the opposite end of the car, his weapon trained on the suspect. "Gently lay the man down and step away from him," Seth says. I can barely hear him over the thunderous rain drumming the metal roof and pelting the windows.

The suspect strikes the side of his own head with the heel of his palm.

"Look what you've done to us, Moonshine."

Between the deep shadows, pounding rain, and the evidential agony distorting his voice, it's impossible for me to be certain that this man is the same one I saw with René in the field at the Edelmann property.

"Release the man," I say in French.

"I told you to stay out of it," the man growls, "but you never listen, do you?"

A second voice. Distinctly different from the first one he used.

What's happening?

I take a step toward the man. "I'm listening now."

The man glances my direction, but I still can't get a good look at his face because he's wearing a hoodie. "This is between us," he growls.

"She's only trying to help," says the man in his first voice.

"You think I care, Trace?" says the second voice. "They're on to us, and there's only one way to be free."

"I don't want to die, Moonshine," he whimpers.

"What's done is done." The man raises his free arm toward me. Points something at me. A knife, a gun, or perhaps just his hand. I can't tell, nor do I have a clean shot.

Lightning flashes in quick succession outside the car windows. A strobe light of magnificent power.

Crash! Bang!

At first, the sounds seem to reach my ears in reverse, but then several additional bright flashes reveal the truth. Shards of glass and the left side of the suspect's head expand forward, spraying the opposite wall of the dining car. Through two sets of rain-soaked windows I spot Thérèse. She stands inside the train car parallel to us, her gun still aimed at the suspect.

Pierre and the man drop to the car floor with a *thud*. Seth and I reach the two of them simultaneously. Pierre groans when Seth shines a flashlight in his face. The other man lies still, blood pooling beneath his mangled head.

"He wasn't armed." I look up at Seth, anger simmering just beneath the surface. "She did it on purpose, you know."

"If you're talking about Thérèse saving Pierre's life, then I agree." He grunts as he bends down and rolls Trace Moonshine off of Pierre.

"I'm not, and you know it," I growl.

"First of all, think about what you're saying. The man held Pierre in his grasp. A body shot could've passed through him and struck Pierre. She took the only viable shot."

"Why are you defending her?"

"I'm not. I'm just stating the obvious." He eyes me. "You gonna help me make sure Pierre's okay, or are you just going to sit there and argue?"

"Fine."

Other than a lump on the back of his head, Pierre looks to be unharmed. His pulse remains strong even though he hasn't woken up yet.

I reach up and touch Seth's arm. "Look, Thérèse might've taken the only possible shot, but that's not what concerns me the most."

He scowls. "Then what does?"

There's no point in beating around the bush, so I don't. "I don't think this is our killer."

"You don't think so?" He sighs when I shake my head. "Why not?"

"Well for starters, Trace isn't missing any fingers."

Seth looks over at Trace. "He's wearing gloves, Alice."

He moves around to the other side of the body and kneels next to it. With a grunt, he pulls off Trace's right glove. Sure enough, the man is missing two fingers.

My heart sinks, but only for a moment. "Okay, so he's missing the correct fingers. But that still doesn't make him our killer."

Seth shakes his head. "How much proof do you need?"

"Trace and the man who stood in that field with René Edelmann shared few similarities. For one, the man in the field had a hard time walking. Trace moved easily."

"You're certain of that?" he asks.

"Positive."

"A simple touch of Trace's hand could confirm it, right?"

I'm shocked at his suggestion given his earlier concerns about me going blind. I take my flashlight and shine it right at Trace's head. Or what's left of it. "Perhaps you didn't notice the missing part of his head, but I did. Thérèse sprayed his gray matter all over this car."

Seth shrugs. "Maybe, but are you certain that your ability requires the brain to be intact?"

Frustration gets the better of me. "How the hell would I know, Seth? It's not like my ability came with an instruction manual."

Seth raises his hands. "Okay. Look, I get it. I know you're frustrated right now. It's understandable, but at least we're all still alive."

I stare at the bloody mess highlighted by my flashlight beam. "Trace isn't. Not even a little bit."

Pierre groans, then opens his eyes. He reaches for the back of his head. "What happened?"

"The suspect somehow got the jump on you," Seth says.

He rubs the back of his head and grimaces. "I walked through the car door and just blacked out."

"It's over."

All three of us look up at Thérèse who's now standing behind Seth. Rain soaked and flattened hair, she still looks good. It pisses me off even more.

"Is it?" I shout. It's not even sort of a question.

"Look at the facts," she bites back. "I saved Pierre's life and eliminated the threat with a single shot. That's over in my book."

"Ugh." I point at Trace Moonshine with my flashlight again. "We don't know anything about this man, and now we might never know if he was our killer thanks to you."

Pierre glances over his shoulder and grimaces. "You certainly made a mess of his head, Thérèse."

"And you'll live to see another day," she snarls.

There's no point arguing about it now, so I change the subject. "All three of you need to move back from Trace. There's still a slim chance I can glean something of value."

Thérèse eyes Trace and wrinkles her nose. "Be my guest."

Seth stands and helps Pierre to his feet. Then, the three of them retreat to the far end of the car, leaving me alone with Trace. After witnessing the conversation he had with himself, I'm hesitant to touch him. The man clearly suffered from dissociative identity disorder, schizophrenia, or some other kind of brain issue along those lines. The thought of suffering from such a condition sends me spiraling down a rabbit hole of questions.

If I can still connect with him, how will it work? Will I be able to see through each personality or be relegated to whichever one was last present? If his mind is fractured, as it certainly seems, could it trap me inside? Will it fracture my own mind? Or will it kill me?

A call to my father right now would ease my mind, but he never had a rulebook that explained our mutual gift, either. No, there's only one path forward: touch the man and see what happens.

My pulse races as I reach over and lift Trace Moonshine's shirtsleeve. He bears no marks or scars on his left wrist.

He's not like me.

But what does that mean? If he is our killer, then how did he do it? How did he transport the bodies and make them appear out of nothing? No answer readily comes to mind.

Guess there's only one way to find out.

After a long, deep breath, I touch the back of Trace's hand.

Fire fills me. Sparks and tingles just beneath my skin. Then comes the alien shift. Strange, yet invigorating.

Trace's hand twists around and latches onto mine. Then, everything I've grown to expect when mind tethering changes.

The world splits in two. Fractured, like a mirror.

Pierre hangs limp in Moonshine's arm, his weight little more than a sack of potatoes. Across from Moonshine—on the opposite side of the fracture—stands Trace. The same man, yet not. Trace looks younger. Years younger. And scrawny. Not deathly so, but certainly malnourished.

The two men argue, just as they had in the dining car several minutes earlier. But this time, I see them both.

Their exchange repeats over and over. A broken record.

All the hairs on my arms stand on end as though charged with gobs of static electricity. Then, a blinding light flashes in my vision and leaves me seeing spots of blue, red, and white. Searing pain bursts behind my temples.

A few seconds later, an unexplainable force yanks me backward. The fracture mends itself and leaves me heaving in the dining car, crouched over the body of Trace Moonshine.

"Alice?" Seth rushes forward. "Are you okay?"

Even though I can't seem to put it into words, something within me feels a bit off. The longer I sit here, the more I realize that I'm far from okay. The edges of everything look tattered, and it scares the hell out of me. Admitting it though, especially in front of Thérèse and Pierre, isn't an option I'm willing to exercise.

I rub my temples, hoping the issue goes away. "Yeah, I think so."

"Good, because you scared the hell out of me. I've never seen you jerk back so hard before."

"Did you get anything from him?" Thérèse asks. She's now standing next to Seth.

I glare up at her, knowing it's her fault. "Looks like we're at a dead end with this one."

CHAPTER ELEVEN

IT'S BEEN TWO DAYS since Thérèse cratered the left side of Trace Moonshine's head. Two days for me to lie back and overanalyze every last detail. No matter how many times I replay the events that day, they make no sense.

For starters, why did the Darcy girl single me out at the fountain and choose to talk to me? I've never been in the public eye with this case, so was it just a lucky coincidence that she came up to me, or did someone pay her to do it? If someone paid her, then why? What purpose would it serve?

To throw the investigation off.

It makes perfect sense, so who would want to do that other than the real killer? My brow furrows as my mind comes up empty.

No one.

Unlike the man from René's memory, Trace moved without physical impediment.

Just as I told Seth.

Even though Trace suffered subconjunctival hemorrhaging in his eye, I'm certain his iris color differed from that of the killer's. In addition to those discrepancies, he bore no mark on his left wrist, either. In my book, that's evidence enough to prove without a doubt that Trace and the man from René's memory are two different people.

They must be.

Like Reagan, I'm certain the killer must be someone different. Special, like me, but not. A Centaurian if I'm to believe Rico and my father. Between the Night Mauler case and this one, I'm almost there. Almost ready to believe in other worlds and things beyond imagination.

Almost.

No matter what I believe about Centauria or any other world for that matter, it has no bearing on this case. Every detail feels off about it. The puzzle pieces required to solve it exist, but they remain upside-down, turned over, and without a picture to follow.

So, what can I do to flip them over?

Bursts of vibrations pull me out of my head. Kenny's calling, so I answer it. "Hey, bud, what's up?"

"Are you alone?" he asks.

Gooseflesh envelops me. "Hold on."

Rising from my lounge chair on our hotel suite balcony, I stick my head through the open door. Seth's prepping dinner in the kitchen, his back toward the living room and me. I ease the door shut and sit back down.

A lump the size of Jupiter rises in my throat as I start imagining all the horrific things Kenny might tell me. Frankie's the mother of Seth's children and looking for money. Or she's a beautiful Russian woman from his past who wants him back now that he's off the market. Or perhaps it's the name he uses for Thérèse when they're together behind my back like they were weeks ago.

The last thought stings far more than it should. I shake it and the rest of them from my head and clear my throat before speaking. "Yeah, I'm alone. What have you got for me?"

"Geesh, I'm not really sure where to start."

"How about with Frankie? What do you know about her?" I'm hedging my bets that Frankie's a female and praying she's not.

"Well, for starters, Frankie would make a very ugly woman. I mean *really* ugly."

Oh thank you, God!

I reel my excitement in before speaking again. "Okay, so Frankie's a man. That's a relief. Do you know his full name?"

"I scoured the dark web for traces of him and kept coming back to a single name. Frankie Stravinsky. He's got ties back to the KGB from decades ago."

KGB? Why would Seth have anything to do with someone like that?

"You're sure about that?" My voice cracks.

"Yeah," Kenny says. "Get this. His nickname is *The Cleaner*. Apparently, he takes care of cleaning up messes for mafias and drug cartels all across the world."

"What kinds of messes?"

"You know, the kind that need to be silenced. He's famous for leaving no traces behind. Like ever. He disappears all kinds of people."

I turn in my chair and stare through the window at a man I obviously know nothing about.

Who's the man I married?

The question rips a hole in my chest and stabs me repeatedly. How could I have been so complacent knowing nothing about Seth's past?

"Anything else?" I ask.

"Don't be mad at me..." Kenny sighs loudly.

"What is it?" I demand, my heart now hammering.

"After discovering Frankie's identity, I decided to do a bit of digging on Seth, too."

No matter how hard I try, my jaw muscles refuse to move. And my tongue clings to the bottom of my mouth, a dead fish in a sea of sand.

Kenny continues, "I'm not sure what it means, but Seth Ryan didn't exist ten years ago."

"You're certain of that?"

"Trust me, I had to dive deep on this one. It's not surprising no one ever knew because it's hidden so well. If I hadn't been looking for a discrepancy, I never would've found the anomalies in the data. Whoever created his fake identity did a great job. I'm sure that's why he's passed every background check, but they weren't me. They forgot to change the original dates on all the fake entries." He sighs. "Anyway, I'm really sorry, Alice."

Tears streak my face. Blur the balcony and the city beyond its edge. I dig my nails into my palms, but it doesn't keep the tears from flowing. The phone slips from my hand. Clatters on the balcony floor tile.

God, why do you hate me?

* * * * *

The balcony door slides open as I lay in the chair crying my eyes out. I make no effort to wipe my face. It would be a pointless effort now.

Life is pointless.

"Alice, dinner's about—" His tone switches immediately. "—my God, what happened?" He kneels next to my lounger and touches my arm.

I jerk my arm away. "Don't touch me."

"Okay, I'm sorry." He picks my phone up of the floor. "Who were you talking to?"

"It doesn't matter." I take a deep breath and suck a string of snot back up my nose. It's likely the most unattractive thing I've ever done in front of Seth, but I don't give a damn. I turn and glare at him. He's fuzzy around the edges, likely due to my wet, bloodshot eyes. "I know everything."

He leans back on his heels and frowns. "Am I supposed to understand what that means?"

"Damn right you should." After a moment of brooding, I say, "I know about Frankie."

Seth sighs heavily. "I had a feeling you heard part of my conversation the other morning."

"I know who he is, too." I wipe my eyes and stare at the Eiffel Tower, but it remains out of focus.

"I'm not sure you do," Seth says.

"A hitman for the mafia. Ex-KGB. Need I go on?"

"Yes, he's certainly those things, but there's a lot more." Seth settles down on the floor. "Look, I lied to you when I said Thérèse was taking care of the situation with Reagan."

Anger boils up, replacing the hurt I feel within. If I could glare holes right through him, I would. "You had Reagan killed after you refused to let me kill him, didn't you?"

"No, Alice." He shakes his head. "God, no. I would never do that. You know me."

Never have I heard such a poor choice of words. Then again, I should expect it from Seth. "Do I?"

"Look, Alice, I knew Frankie from way back. He owed me a favor, so I had him send some of his people to the hotel to clean up the mess you made."

My hands ball into fists. "You say it as though any of it was my fault."

"That's not what I meant." Seth huffs. "Look, if you were to go down to the old suite, you'd find no evidence that a struggle ever happened." He cocks his head, his brow furrowed. "Trust me, Reagan's very much alive."

"How can I believe you, Seth? How can I ever believe anything you ever tell me again?"

"I don't understand what's going on here." He pushes his hair back with his hand. "Look, the only reason I didn't say anything about Frankie was because I was protecting you and didn't want you involved. He's a dangerous man, Alice. The kind you wish you'd never met."

"Protecting me?" The floodgates of wrath burst wide open. "Is that why you've been lying to me for years? Tell me, husband. Just who the hell are you because you're sure not a man named Seth Ryan!"

He leans back and closes his eyes. "I knew this day would come."

"And what day is that? The one where you throw me off a balcony and claim it's suicide?"

Seth's eyes pop open. He shakes his head and looks at me with disgust. "What's wrong with you? You know I'd never harm a hair on your head. You're my world, Alice."

"Am I? You sure have a funny way of showing it."

He rises from the floor and proffers his hand. "Come inside with me, and

I'll tell you everything over dinner."

"I don't want you touching me right now."

Maybe never again.

"Fine." Seth sets my phone on the floor then walks over to the door before looking back at me. "Dinner's ready. I'll be at the table. Just let me know when you're ready to listen." He turns and goes inside.

The evening sky smolders with fiery clouds of reds, pinks, oranges, and yellows. It's strikingly beautiful and sours my mood further. I stand up and shoot two birds at Paris. The gestures do nothing to lighten my mood.

"City of *Broken* Love is more like it."

* * * * *

An untouched portion of chicken and rice with a side of greens sits on the plate in front of me. To its left, a plate of buttery croissants and strawberry jam. On its right, a decadent slice of cheesecake dripping with caramel and fudge. Seth—or whoever the hell the man sitting across from me really is— prepared the main course but bought the croissants and cheesecake from one of the restaurants in the hotel lobby.

The only thing missing from the spread he placed in front of me is the wine in my glass. I've downed four full glasses while we've sat in silence. Even though my head's been swimming on my shoulders for the last hour or so, I would've drunk four more glasses by now if he hadn't taken the bottle away.

Admittedly, I don't hold my liquor well on good days, but tonight I'm wrecked. Sure, there are several factors contributing to my current state of mind, the primary ones being the blue-eyed impostor sitting across from me and me drinking on an empty stomach, but there's far more to it. More than the heartache. More than the betrayal.

My mind feels muddied. Weighed down by some unknown force. Its effects shred the edges of my vision and shoot pulses of pain through my eyes and into the back of my skull when I concentrate on anything for very long.

During these episodes, I lose memories, and I'm unable to form cohesive thoughts.

The man across the table from me—the stranger I gave my heart to and vowed to love for eternity—has always known what to do or say in these situations, but I can no longer rely on him. He's broken the trust I stupidly thought we shared, and I will not allow myself to be vulnerable with him ever again.

Seth's eyes brim with sorrow as he stares down at an empty plate. I almost feel sorry for him, my heart still tethered to the man I thought I knew. But my mind knows better. Knows the liar. The betrayer.

I'm done with the silence and want answers. Words slur from my drunken lips, "Sssspill it out."

Our gazes meet, but only for a moment before I cast my eyes back on the plate of cold food in front of me. Allowing him to gaze into my eyes and touch my very soul would be too much for me to bear. I'm not sure if I'll ever allow our eyes to meet again.

"Promise me that you'll allow me to tell you everything before you jump to any conclusions and make judgments about what you hear. Can you do that?"

Already judged you, Mr. Not Seth.

I nod and quickly discover it's not the right move. The entire dining room dips and sways and twists before me. Closing my eyes does little to stabilize my equilibrium, nor does it quell the storm brewing in the pit of my stomach.

The croissant falls to pieces when I smash it into the dish of strawberry jam. On the second try. A line of jam drops follow my hand across the table, all the way to my mouth. The croissant barely gets a chew before I swallow it down and reach for another.

Seth stares at me, jaw loose and eyes wide, as I stuff my mouth with another croissant and then dig my fingers into the cheesecake. What he thinks of me no longer matters. I scoop the cheesecake into my mouth and lick the caramel and fudge from my fingers.

"Talk already." Bits of cheesecake spew from my mouth.

Seth exhales loudly and leans on the table with his elbows. "I don't know if you'll remember any of this tomorrow, but here it goes. I was born Klaus Sebastian Rein in East Germany a few years before the fall of the wall. I never knew my father, and my mother died when I was four. My sister Alana and I were thrown into the foster care system where we bounced around from family to family for two years before a Russian couple living in Poland took us in."

"Frankie?" I ask before stuffing another handful of cheesecake into my mouth.

"No, but they were associates of Frankie's. The only reason they adopted us was to use us for smuggling guns and drugs across the borders of France, Germany, Poland, and several other European countries. I learned a great deal about the underbelly of society and could move in and out of any circles by the time I was twelve. At that point, Frankie saw potential in me and took me under his wing. Working for him drove a wedge between Alana and me, but I didn't care. She wanted out, but I wanted the world Frankie presented to me.

"At fourteen, I took the fall for a brutal murder Frankie had committed in Romania. It cost me four years of my life, but it also gave me time to think about everything. Frankie never once visited me in detention, nor did my adoptive parents, but Alana came every week. Her doing so saved my life in more ways than one. Once I was released, she and I acquired new identities and fled to the United States.

"The day we landed in Atlanta, we vowed to never look back and never tell anyone the truth of our past. Somehow, we wound up in Desert Springs with just enough money to rent a studio apartment for a few months. Given my background in the criminal underworld, I applied at the police academy and quickly made my mark.

"Alana got her GED and went to nursing school. She didn't enjoy the desert heat and wanted to be somewhere where she could utilize her ICU skills, so she moved to Seattle. Six years later, she found out she had stage four colon cancer. A few months after that, she was gone. I buried myself in work after her death, and you know the rest of the story."

"So, your sister did die from cancer. Glad that part wasn't a lie." My eyes widen as Seth shakes his head. "My God, that's not what I meant. I'm not glad your sister died. Not at all. Trust me, it sounded better in my head."

Seth broods. "I never lied to you, Alice. I just didn't divulge my past. You know there's a difference."

Whether or not intended, the dig reopens several wounds. How many lies did I tell him before coming clean about my past?

Too many to remember.

Seth sits up straight and continues, "I never planned on reconnecting with Frankie, but then everything happened with you and Reagan. I made the first call to Frankie after Thérèse broke down. She could easily take care of Reagan, but she didn't know what to do about the mess and feared what Pierre would say when he found out. Neither of us wanted that to happen, so I called Frankie."

My head swims a little less as the croissants and cheesecake work to counterbalance the gobs of wine in my system. "And the other morning?"

"The call you overheard was Frankie trying to lure me back in with some sort of guilt trip. The bastard acted as though I owed him something. What he didn't realize was I had kept proof of the murder he'd committed all those years ago, and I told him as much."

"And that's when you told him that he had owed you and now you were even."

He nods. "Yes."

"I still don't get it, though. If you had proof that Frankie committed the murder, then why did you take the fall? Or better yet, why did you keep the proof if you worshiped him?"

"After everything I'd been through in my life, I had learned to never trust anyone, no matter how nice they might seem. Frankie had always been good to me and promised to reward me when I served out my sentence, but he also taught me that having leverage over someone meant more than anything else. You could control someone with the right leverage. I wasn't sure if I'd ever need leverage over Frankie but knew it couldn't hurt. And I'm glad I kept it, too."

Seth leans back in his chair and sighs. "That's the truth. Every last bit of it. Now you know everything there is to know about me."

A weight greater than that of the Eiffel Tower begins lifting from my shoulders and unburdens my aching heart. I stand up, stumble around the dining room table, and fall into Seth's arms.

"I'm sorry I kept all that from you," he says.

"I believe you, Seth, and I forgive you," I say between sobs, "but I'm still going to check your story out."

"I understand." He strokes my hair and kisses my forehead. "Make sure you tell Kenny to search for Nikolay Ivanov. That's the name my adoptive parents gave me."

After wiping my face on Seth's shirt—an amalgamation of snot, caramel, fudge, and strawberry jam—I pull back and gaze into his eyes. "So, how many languages do you speak?"

"Half a dozen, or so. Why?"

"You know French, don't you?" He laughs, and I sock him in the arm. "You've been pretending to not understand anything this entire trip!"

"I know, and it's been tough, but I didn't want to explain all this."

"You're a damn good liar."

"Years of practice, but I'm not so sure that's a good thing."

"It isn't." Another thought strikes me. "And what about all the times you use the wrong words? Have you been faking that, too?"

His face scrunches up. "Hey, that's not fair. Just because I speak many languages doesn't make me an expert in all of them. Remember, English isn't my native language."

The truth of it blows my mind.

Seth cradles me in his arms and stands. "I think it's time we get you into the shower. You're a mess."

I smear caramel on his cheek with my finger and grin. "Not so hot yourself, Mr. Ryan. Or is it *Herr* Rein? Ivanov?"

"Keep it up, and you'll have to sleep off your hangover alone."

I wrap my arms around his neck and lean my head against his shoulder. "Never."

CHAPTER TWELVE

IT'S FRIDAY EVENING AND the beginning of what looks to be a blustery weekend in Paris. The rain has poured relentlessly all day, darkening the skies, soaking the streets, and hampering my mood.

For once, I'd love to have a romantic dinner with Seth at one of the Eiffel Tower restaurants, but fate rears its ugly head again. Much to my chagrin, Thérèse invited us and Pierre over to her apartment for dinner. I loathe the thought of attending, but both Seth and Pierre insisted.

As usual, Pierre picks us up from the hotel and drives us over to Thérèse's apartment somewhere on the west side of Paris. We pull up in front of an unremarkable building and head up to the fourth floor. The place is far from posh and a bit of a letdown if I'm being honest. I expected more from her.

Thérèse answers the door not long after Pierre knocks. Hair up and sporting a miniskirt, she's more beautiful than ever. Her shapely, tanned legs draw the eye, and I can only imagine where Seth's are looking right now. I refuse to check.

Although Thérèse made an impression, the entrance to her apartment falls flat. Yellowish white linoleum floors with brown, intertwining diamonds greet us at the door. The floors continue into the small, galley kitchen to the left. Grayish-beige, pressed wood cabinets hang from the ceiling and sit beneath yellow Formica countertops that look like they came straight out of the sixties. A pass-through window from the kitchen overlooks a small dining room.

Blonde wood flooring flows throughout the rest of the apartment from the entry, but the lack of area or throw rugs leaves it looking cold, unfinished, and uninviting. To the right of the entry sits the living room. Calling the area sparsely decorated would be too kind.

A single brown leather recliner sits in the corner of the room, next to a floor lamp with a brown shade affixed to it. Next to the recliner stands a metal TV tray, and a small pile of books sit atop it. Not a single piece of art hangs from any of the walls. No bookshelves. No TV or stand. Nothing else occupies the room.

In the dining room, a decrepit fixture hangs from the ceiling by a brass chain. Beneath the fixture sit four folding chairs around a square card table with a black top. Two doors lie beyond the dining room, one to a common bathroom and the other to what must be Thérèse's bedroom.

"I know it's not much," Thérèse says, "but I'm rarely ever here."

"No need to explain," Seth says. "Alice and I are the same way." I smile at Seth.

Liar.

Pierre raises his nose and sniffs the air. "Something smells delicious."

Thérèse retreats into the kitchen. "*Bœuf bourguignon,* and I admit I didn't cook any of it. All the food came from a little place down the street from here. Unfortunately, my cooking skills rival that of my decorating skills."

At least she's honest about something.

"Please, take a seat at the table, and I'll serve us food and wine," she says.

Once we're all settled around the table with full bowls, plates, and glasses, Pierre slides his chair back from the table, stands, then raises his glass. "I'd like to propose a toast."

Thérèse, Seth, and I join him in standing. His gaze meets mine, and he smiles. I'm not sure what he's about to say, but I'm prepared for anything.

"To Detective Bergman," Pierre says. "She singlehandedly broke the case wide open and led us to our killer."

"To Alice," Seth and Thérèse say, both of them smiling.

I lower my glass. "Come on, guys. We all know it isn't true."

"Isn't it, though?" Thérèse asks. "You're the one who identified the killer through the memories of René Edelmann. Then, you found a young woman who led us right to Trace Moonshine."

I look to Pierre. "Those are both true statements, but I still don't think Trace is our killer."

Pierre grins. "As you know, we recovered the murder weapon from some of Trace's belongings. Not only did the garrote have his fingerprints on its handles, but its blade also had trace amounts of René's blood still on it. As you know, it doesn't get much better than that, especially after the year Thérèse and I have had trying to hunt him. And he was also missing the correct fingers."

"I—"

Pierre raises his finger in the air. "Hold on, Alice. I'm not quite done. I know what you're going to say. Trace didn't look exactly like your sketch, but that's understandable. If you recall, René Edelmann was inebriated when you joined his mind. His condition likely skewed what you saw through his eyes."

"I get all that, Pierre, but don't you think it's too perfect?" I ask.

Thérèse scowls. "How so?"

I place my glass on the table and cross my arms. "The evidence wraps Trace up all nicely with a bow, but there are still too many issues. First, he doesn't fit the profile of our killer. Second, we still have no clue as to where the murders took place or what purpose he had for draining his victims' blood. Third, the man I saw in the field with René Edelmann moved with an impediment and Trace Moonshine moved without issue. Fourth, how do you explain the bodies appearing out of thin air all across Paris?"

"To answer the fourth, he was different, like you," Thérèse says.

"No." I pull up my sleeve and bear my left wrist. "See this mark?" I point at the mark I've had on the inside of my left wrist since I hit puberty.

Thérèse nods. "I do."

"Good. A mark like this is how you know whether or not someone is different. Trace Moonshine bore no such mark."

Seth chimes in. "I have another thought." He takes a sip of wine from his glass, then puts it down. "You might not want to hear this, Pierre, but what if Trace Moonshine was working with someone else?"

Pierre's expression sours. "An accomplice? Please don't say that."

Seth nods. "It covers all the issues Alice has brought up."

Pierre sits down, his face pale and his mood flattened. He takes a sip of his wine. "God, I hope you're wrong."

I study Seth for a moment, then sit back down. "He is. Not necessarily on the part about there being two people involved but in the assumption that Trace Moonshine could be one of them. I heard him talking on that train. There's no way he could possibly work with someone else with his mental issues."

Thérèse empties her glass in one long swig, then returns to her chair. Her eyes narrow as she stares across the table at me. "I have another thought for you to contemplate, Detective Bergman."

"Oh yeah? I'd love to hear it."

"I've read many studies about schizophrenia and other disorders of the mind. There are many well-documented cases where a subject physically changes with each personality. Everything from eye color to allergies to physical maladies and disabilities. What if Trace Moonshine was one such person? If so, wouldn't it be possible that he might only exhibit the mark while controlled by a specific personality? It could also explain why he physically moved differently."

Mind blown. Literally. Why I hadn't thought of it eludes me. I hate and admire her simultaneously.

Well played, Thérèse.

The more I think about it, the more fascinated I become at how she and I mirror each other in so many ways. Almost like sisters. But our likeness is also one of the catalysts to our explosive relationship.

Finally, I say, "I concede."

Thérèse smiles and leans back in her chair. "It's settled, then. We celebrate the end of a case and make an announcement to the world in the morning."

Dinner and the rest of the evening play out without further conflict or excitement. At Pierre's first yawn, we say our goodbyes to Thérèse, and then Pierre drives us back to our hotel.

Back inside our suite, I head straight for the sofa and collapse into it. Seth heads for the shower. The man takes more showers than I can keep track of.

As I lie there, my mind circles around what Thérèse said regarding Trace Moonshine. I want to believe she's right and head back home on Monday, but my gut and my brain say it isn't true. The more I study the scenes in my mind, the more convinced I become that Trace and the man who stood in that field with René Edelmann cannot be the same person.

This isn't over, but how can I prove it?

* * * * *

Three in the morning, and I've yet to fall asleep and stay that way for more than ten minutes at a time. Every time I do, another thought jerks me awake. This instance, my mind is focused on the last ten killings and more specifically on the times of death.

The dates and times are scattered across the calendar without rhyme or reason. At least not upon first glance. But then a pattern emerges from the chaos.

I reach over and shake Seth. "Hey, are you awake?"

Seth groans. "Guess I am now."

"Good." I switch on the nightstand lamp and sit up.

Seth rolls over and squints at me. "Now, I really am, but the question as to why I should be remains."

"There's a pattern to the killings, Seth. They're not random."

"Meaning what? They're all connected? We determined the killer was a vigilante."

"No, I'm talking about the dates. There's a pattern. One month, five days, and several hours between each killing."

He sits up and rubs his eyes, now more alert. "Show me."

I grab a pen and a pad of paper from the nightstand drawer and write out the ten dates. "Here, take a look."

March 25th, 2019, Sunday 00:00-03:00
April 30th, 2019, Tuesday 18:00-21:00
June 6th, 2019, Thursday 01:00-04:00
July 11th, 2019, Thursday 20:00-23:00
August 17th, 2019, Saturday 04:00-07:00
September 22nd, 2019, Sunday 19:00-22:00
October 28th, 2019, Monday 00:00-03:00
December 2nd, 2019, Monday 19:00-22:00
January 8th, 2020, Wednesday 05:00-08:00
February 13th, 2020, Thursday 22:00-01:00

Seth studies the list for several minutes before looking back up. "Many of these dates are thirty-six days apart, but three of them are thirty-seven days apart. There's also two that are thirty-five. I hate to ask, but where's the pattern?"

"The pattern isn't the number of days between killings but an exact month on the calendar plus five days and several hours. You see it now?"

He squints at the paper like the answer's hidden just beneath its surface and begins to nod. "Yeah, I can see it now. Add an extra day when it switches from night to morning, right?"

I reach over and fuss his hair. "Exactly."

"Okay, so you've discovered that the killer had a pattern. But what's the significance if we've already captured him?"

"Look at the last date."

"A month ago today. So?"

"Ugh! What I'm saying is that another body might turn up Thursday morning."

"If Trace *isn't* the killer."

"Yes, of course."

"So, what then? We just hang around Paris for another week and pray another body doesn't drop out of nowhere?"

"Now you're getting it." I grab my phone off the nightstand. "I need to tell Pierre not to make his announcement later this morning. If for no other reason than caution, that is."

Seth frowns. "He's not gonna like that."

"I know, but he'll like it even less if he announces to the world that he's caught the killer only to have another body show up a few days later."

He scratches the back of his neck. "I know you're right about warning him, and you're rarely wrong about your hunches, but I hope you're wrong this time."

"Never, Seth. I'm never wrong." I press my finger into his rock-hard abs and grin. "About anything. Don't forget the agreement clause in the contract you signed before marrying me."

"Yes, of course. The 'Alice is never wrong' prenup." He rolls his eyes and shakes his head. "Worst mistake of my life."

I gasp. "Marrying me?"

"No, signing that stupid agreement."

"Well, you're lucky you did. Otherwise, I might've bailed on you."

"I'm sure you would've." He leans over and kisses me.

After several more glorious kisses, I push him away. "Anyway, I'll send Pierre a text message now."

Seth shrugs, then lays back down. "You wake him up, and it's on you."

"I don't, and it's on you next week."

"Fine. Send the text."

* * * * *

The next morning, I've got a text message waiting for me from Pierre. Turns out he's just as reluctant to close the case as I am. It wasn't just the discovery of the killer's pattern but also something I said at Thérèse's last night. Too many perfect bows.

Damn straight.

Seth's already out of bed, and I can hear the TV going in the living room, but it's turned down too low for me to make anything out. "Seth, what are you doing?"

"Watching the local news. Some girl jumped off a building earlier this morning. Happened just east of here."

The covers are snuggly and warm, and I don't want to abandon them, but death always piques my interest, especially when it involves some sort of unnatural causes. With great effort, I force myself out of bed, slip on a pair of hotel slippers, and make my way into the living room.

A picture of the jumper remains on screen while the reporter continues to talk, but her words fade into oblivion. My stomach lurches.

"Seth, that's the girl from the fountain. That's Darcy."

He cocks his head at the screen. "Are you sure?"

"She certainly doesn't look homeless in that picture, but yeah, I'm one hundred percent positive."

"Says her name is Hanna, not Darcy."

"Yeah, I see that." I sit down on the edge of the sofa, still fixated on the girl. "She must've lied to me."

"About her name?"

"Not just that, but about all of it."

Seth turns and eyes me. "Okay, now *you're* taking a big leap."

"Am I? I was about to go looking for her today to verify her story and she turns up dead. To me, that's not a leap. Someone obviously didn't want her talking to me again."

He reaches over and rubs the top of my hand. "She jumped off a building, babe. It's not a conspiracy."

"I don't think she was suicidal."

"You met her for like five minutes and she lied to you about who she was. How could you possibly make that determination?"

"It might not make sense to you, but I have."

"Fine. Let's say she wasn't suicidal the other day but then found out that what she told you led to Trance Moonshine's death. Guilt can lead to suicide, right?"

"It's *Trace* Moonshine, and you're right about the damage guilt can do, but I saw the fear in her eyes when she spoke about him. There's no way she faked that raw emotion." I sit back on the sofa and take a deep breath. "Not only that, but too many coincidences are impossible. That's what you taught me, remember?"

Seth frowns. "Did I? Sounds way too smart."

I punch him in the leg. "Seriously, we need to let Pierre know. It might be nothing—"

"But it might not be," he finishes. "Got it."

After dialing Pierre's number, I put it on speakerphone so Seth can hear it too.

Pierre picks up immediately. "Good morning, Detective Bergman. You received my text?"

I glance at Seth. "I did, but that's not why I'm calling."

"You sound concerned. What is it?"

"Remember the girl that I got the information from regarding Trace Moonshine?"

"Yes, of course. A homeless girl outside the Louvre if memory serves me."

"That's what I thought, but now I'm not so sure. Her picture is all over the news. She's dead, Pierre. They say she committed suicide."

"The same girl? And you don't believe it?"

"Not for a second. Confirming it one way or another would set my mind at ease."

"I understand, and I'm inclined to agree, but getting you access to the body would be difficult right now. How about I look into the case and see if anything seems off about it. If there is, I'll bring you in. If not, then we'll chalk it up to tragic coincidence and move on. Sound good?"

"I can live with that, Pierre. Thank you."

"Anything for you, Alice. And I mean that sincerely."

When I end the call, Seth glares at me and shakes his head.

"What?"

"You know what."

"I can't help it, Seth. God gave me this ability for a reason."

"Oh, so now you believe in God. Only when it's convenient, right?"

"I'll admit that my relationship with God is complicated, but that's irrelevant. A girl's dead, Seth. There's nothing convenient at all about that."

"I know, but you've been using your ability a lot lately." He scrunches his eyes and bows his head. "It's just that I…"

"Look, I don't want to go blind any more than you want to live with a blind woman. I get it. But caution isn't me, and you know it. That's one of the things you love about me, right?"

He nods. "Okay, but you need to tell me if anything starts to change."

My mind reels back to the brief moments inside Trace Moonshine's head. "Well, there was something, but I'm not sure what to make of it."

Seth sighs. "I knew there was something off with you the other day when we were at the transit station. Am I right?"

This time, I nod. "I only saw a few seconds, but it was different again. I was still me. Watching him talk to himself in the dining car. But he… wasn't alone."

"Right. Pierre and I were there, too."

"Yes, but that's not what I mean. There was a split in my vision. Like a mirror cracked from top to bottom. Trace Moonshine stood on both sides of the crack, facing each other. But what was even stranger was that Trace and Moonshine were two distinct people."

"Wait a minute. You're saying that you saw two people there?"

"Yes, I mean, not like what you're thinking. Trace and Moonshine are the same person, but they didn't possess the same traits. They were two halves of a whole."

"This is madness." He points a finger at me. "I forbid you from touching another body until we get you figured out. Understood?"

"It doesn't work that way, Seth. Things only get figured out by doing them, not by sitting back and worrying."

Seth's hand balls into a fist. "No more."

"And when I'm right and another body turns up? What then?"

"We'll discuss it *if* or *when* it happens, and not before then."

"Okay." I can't believe I just agreed to his terms, but he is my husband and I love him. I pull myself up off the sofa. "I'm going to go take a shower, and then you're going to take me somewhere with piles of croissants."

Seth smiles. "And coffee. I know just the place."

CHAPTER THIRTEEN

THURSDAY COMES AND GOES without producing another body, and it devastates my pride. I've never been so disappointed about being wrong before, especially when my being right would've meant someone else had been killed.

The more I think about it, the more disappointed I become with myself. Trace Moonshine must've been the killer. All the physical evidence pointed to him, yet I tried to ignore it.

For what? To save face with Thérèse?

I know it's true, but I still refuse to accept it. The woman's been under my skin the entire time I've been in Paris. She's a parasite, and I'll be glad when I'm rid of her for good.

"You got everything packed?" Seth asks.

"Everything but my pride."

He squeezes my shoulder. "You'll be back on top in no time."

I gasp. "You're a naughty little monkey, Mr. Ryan."

Seth laughs. "That's not what I meant."

"Well, that's too bad. Guess the flight back to the states will be a boring one."

The hotel phone rings, and I answer it. "Hello?"

"Mrs. Ryan, your car has arrived."

"Very good. Thank you." I hang up and look at Seth. "Guess it's time to blow this joint."

"Can't say I'm sorry to leave this place."

"Me, neither."

Downstairs, a limousine awaits us outside the hotel lobby. Pierre and Thérèse are waiting for us inside.

"What's this?" I ask as I climb inside.

"I thought it would be nice to send you guys off in style," Thérèse says.

Seth climbs in behind me. "This was your idea, Thérèse?"

She smiles at him. "It was."

He rubs his hands together. "I feel like a celebrity, now."

"Don't get used to it," I say.

Just as we arrive at the airport, Pierre gets a call. He steps away while the limo driver unloads our bags from the trunk. Somehow, we've managed to double our luggage while staying here. According to my phone, we've still got plenty of time to catch our flight, so we wait for Pierre to return so that we can say our final goodbyes.

Pierre hangs up and walks over to us, his expression grimmer than I can ever remember. "We've got another body."

I thrust my fist in the air. "Yes! I wasn't wrong!"

Pierre, Thérèse, and Seth all look at me as though I've lost my mind. Perhaps I have, but I don't care. They're just lucky I don't break out in a little dance right in front of Thérèse to rub it in.

I feign embarrassment. "Oh my goodness, did I just do that?"

Seth shakes his head. "Not your best moment, Alice."

Thérèse crosses her arms and scowls at me. "I cannot believe you would celebrate someone's death in such a manner."

And you really wouldn't believe what I'm thinking right now.

Pierre gestures toward the open limo door while the driver returns our luggage to the trunk. "All of you, back in the car. We've got another body to examine."

"And a killer to catch," Seth says.

I squeeze his hand. "Exactly."

Thérèse says nothing else before crawling back into the car, and it puts a smile on my face.

Sucks to be wrong, doesn't it?

* * * * *

To say we get some strange looks pulling up to the crime scene in a limousine would be an understatement. I'm certain it's a first for everyone involved.

Pierre exits the car first and engages with one of the many police officers on scene. That same officer leads the four of us over to a playground sandbox in the middle of Square Sarah Bernhardt. The entire playground is cordoned off, and there's a large mound of sand next to a hole.

"A child unearthed a boot while digging in the sand," the officer says in French, "and found that the boot wasn't empty. The mother called it in, and then we called you once we exhumed the body and discovered the victim's throat was slashed." He shakes his head. "The guy was buried completely upside-down if you can believe it."

"Do we have an ID on the victim?" Pierre asks.

The officer looks at his notes. "Yes, a Davit Muradyan according to the ID we found on him."

"Armenian," Seth says. Pierre agrees.

The officer continues, "Ran his name through the system and came up with a hit. Last year, he was charged with kidnapping and rape. An open-close case until the victim retracted her claims."

"Fits the victim pool," I say, satisfied.

"Thank you." Pierre surveys the area. "Have your boys clear out of here, but keep the perimeter guarded. We'll take it from here."

"Yessir." The officer walks off and starts barking orders to clear the area.

Minutes later, Pierre, Thérèse, Seth, and I stand alone in the sandbox.

From what I can tell, the hole is about six feet deep. Roughly matches the size of the outlined body lying beneath the tarp to the side of the hole.

Pierre pulls the tarp back, revealing a man who looks to be in his late thirties. Most of the sand has already been brushed away from his face, but it still clings to his dark hair and clothes. The man has his hair styled short but not buzzed. A well-manicured beard covers the lower half of his face, and his thick eyebrows have been recently shaved at the bridge of his nose. He wears stylish threads, but not too formal. Dark, narrow cowboy boots, likely made of snakeskin, rise over the tops of his dark jeans.

I look over at Seth who's standing with his arms crossed. "Well?"

His expression tells me he understands the question. He exhales loudly, nods, then comes to my side. "It's why we're here, right?"

Pierre eyes me. "I pray to God that you find answers." He steps back.

Thérèse stays silent. She hasn't said more than a few words since Pierre received the call back at the airport. Being wrong must've really hit her hard, and it serves her right.

As much as I'd love to gloat about it, Mr. Davit Muradyan awaits. I kneel next to him, touch his hand, and take a deep breath as I await the fire, sparks, and alien shift. They come quickly, and he pulls me in.

* * * * *

Davit Muradyan sits at the bar with his elbows on the counter and his head perched in his hands. An empty glass sits in front of him, right next to a basket with a half-eaten burger and a side of chile con queso fries. Once a month, he seeks out hole-in-the-wall taverns like La Tache Sombre to get his fix.

The low lighting gives him a sense of anonymity and the food gives him strength, but it's the beer—especially the beer—that he needs. Liquid courage he calls it. Too little, and he won't have the courage to acquire what's become a necessity in his life. Too much, and he becomes far too sloppy.

Sloppy isn't what he wants. He made that mistake once before and almost paid for it. Almost. But he's smarter than that now. Maintaining control of himself and the situation is a requirement. Plus, he always has a contingency plan if things go sideways. Sloppy gets people caught, and he'll never be caught again.

He glances down the bar. Drinks in the brunette at the far end with his eyes. She's homely but far from what he'd consider unattractive. No ring. No company. Just sorrow in her dark, downcast eyes.

The perfect prey.

Davit taps the bar with a finger, and the bartender replaces his empty glass with another pint of beer. It's the last round of encouragement he'll need tonight. One more bite of the burger and a handful of fries wash down easily, then he drains the glass.

Time for action.

Forty-five euros sit underneath the basket in front of him. More than enough to cover his tab with tip but not enough to make him memorable. Memorable works against men like him. It's just as bad as sloppy. Perhaps worse.

He slides off the stool, locates the sign for the bathrooms, and heads that way. Four beers require relieving himself before making his move. It always does.

A single toilet, urinal, and sink are the only things in the bathroom besides an overflowing wastebasket. For the record, it's the cleanest bathroom he's encountered in such a seedy place. Plus, he's alone.

Davit slides the lock into place on the door, preventing anyone else from entering and interrupting him. After all, there's nothing he hates more than being interrupted. He's always had issues urinating in public.

"You've got a shy little guy," his mother used to say. *He grins and unzips.*

Still do.

Nervous energy flows out of him and into the urinal, leaving him filled with a sense of calm. He zips back up and washes his hands. Twice, for good luck. A splash of cold water to the face refreshes him. He eyes himself in the mirror. Admires his reflection.

"Hello, Alice."

Davit spins around and faces a tall man wearing a black cloak drawn over his head. Only the man's green eyes remain visible within the deep shadows beneath his hood.

Davit scowls. "The hell, man?" He glances past the man. Verifies the lock on the bathroom door is still engaged. "How did you get in here? And the name's not Alice."

"The center is key," *the man says.*

"Ain't no key for that lock."

"No key is necessary. All are welcome to come inside and seek the truth."

Davit puffs out his chest. He's never been good at standing up to men. His father made sure of it. But it doesn't prevent him from acting tough.

"Truth is, you're gonna find yourself on the floor if you don't get out of my way," *he says.*

The man grins. "She's already gone, you know."

"Huh?"

"The brunette at the bar. The one you were about to kidnap and rape."

"You're crazy!" *Davit shoves the man, and the man grabs his wrists.*

"You should've stopped when you had the chance, but you just couldn't, could you? One more. Then another one more. It never ends, does it?"

Davit struggles to free his hands, but the man is surprisingly strong. "Let go of me!"

"When I do, you shall be set free."

An electrical charge surges through Davit. The man releases Davit's wrists, and Davit stumbles backward. Hits the sink with his back. The bathroom light dims, and he begins feeling strange. Can't feel his arms or legs. When he looks, they're gone. Then, the darkness swallows the rest of him.

* * * * *

Daylight rushes back in, flooding my vision and blinding me for a few seconds. Once my eyes adjust to the change, I realize something is off. The surrounding sand crawls around me, writhing like maggots, and a throbbing pain blossoms across the top of my head and behind my eyes. Alarms fire in my head as recollection hits me.

This same thing happened after I mind tethered with Sarah Johnson, my first victim.

Fear seeps into my pores, producing a cold sweat that covers me from head to toe. The world rocks around me as nausea churns within.

Please, God, I can't go blind again.

I lean back on my heels and take a deep breath. Seth's at my side.

"You look pale and a tinge green," he says, concern in his tone.

"Give me a minute, and I'll be fine."

The nausea passes, but the fear and headache remain. I can't help but wonder how much longer I have before my eyesight goes again.

Just don't think about it.

Seth helps me to my feet as Pierre and Thérèse approach. Pierre looks at me expectantly.

"The victim was at La Tache Sombre," I say. "It's a tavern."

"I know the place," Thérèse says. "In fact, I was there Wednesday night, too."

All three of us look at her, stunned.

Thérèse frowns. "Why are you all looking at me like that? I was supposed to meet a friend there for drinks and a possible sleepover, but he stood me up. I finally left around midnight." She scowls, then says, "Alone."

"You don't remember seeing the victim there?" I ask.

Thérèse glances down at the uncovered body. "No, but La Tache Sombre is known for its low lighting and intimacy. Hence its name."

"The dark spot," Pierre says.

"Yes," Thérèse confirms. "And trust me, it lives up to its name."

"I read something about that place a long time ago," Seth says. "It was rumored to have been a hangout for vampires back in the late 1800s and early 1900s. It served as the perfect place for them to lure their prey into."

Thérèse laughs. "The place still attracts bloodsuckers, but certainly not of the vampiric kind. At least none that I'm aware of." She waves her hand. "Anyway, I'll get one of the officers to take me over there. With any luck, not only will our victim be on some security footage but also our killer."

"I think you'll be wasting your time," I say. "The victim was taken or killed inside a locked men's bathroom."

Seth eyes me. "How do you know it was locked?"

"The victim checked to make sure he was alone and then locked himself inside."

"Why?" Pierre asks.

"Let's just say he had issues performing in a public setting."

Seth scrunches his face. "Ugh. Why would anyone want to do that in public to begin with?"

"Urinating, Seth. He couldn't go with others around."

Thérèse cocks her head and smiles wryly. "You see and feel everything the victim does, don't you?"

I shudder just thinking about it. "Yes, depending on the victim, but can we focus on the case?"

"Agreed," Seth says. He leans over and whispers in my ear, "But you and I will definitely have a longer discussion about this later."

I ignore Seth and continue filling them in on the details. "After finishing his business and washing his hands, the victim realized he wasn't alone."

"Same guy as the one you saw with Edelmann shows up, right?" Seth asks.

"Yes," I say. "I'm positive."

"I'll give La Tache Sombre a call," Pierre says. "See if anyone complained about the bathroom being locked from the inside." He pulls out his phone.

"Remember, it was Wednesday night," Thérèse says.

Pierre nods. "Got it." He turns and walks away.

"So that's it, then?" Thérèse asks. "Two men in a locked bathroom?"

"Yeah. Unfortunately, the encounter was quite short."

Thérèse sighs but seems less perturbed than she had been earlier. "Okay. I'll compile a list of relatives and known associates and pass your sketch around again. Maybe we'll finally get lucky."

"I hope so," Seth says. "I've never worked a case like this before."

"Neither have I," I admit.

"None of us have." Thérèse sweeps her hair behind her shoulders. "Go ahead and take the limousine back to the hotel. I'll catch a ride back to my car and pick Pierre up when he's finished here. We'll regroup tomorrow."

"Sounds like a plan," Seth says.

Thérèse flags down one of the officers on scene and then follows him over to a police cruiser. A few minutes later, Pierre returns.

"I just spoke with Natalia, the owner of La Tache Sombre," Pierre says. "It turns out that the bathroom door was locked from the inside Wednesday night. She said that they had to break the door down to gain access. When they did, they found the bathroom empty."

Seth looks at me. "I know you said that the victim locked himself inside, but I'm wondering if the door can be locked and then closed or locked from the outside, too."

"No. It was a keyless deadbolt," Pierre says. "Only lockable from the inside and impossible to lock and then leave."

Seth shakes his head. "This is just crazy."

"Stranger still, there was no sign of a struggle inside, either," Pierre says. "As it so happens, they have a camera positioned in the hallway just outside the bathrooms. Every man that went into the bathroom that day came back out except for the last man, who went in around midnight. Video footage confirmed that no other men were in the bathroom at the time. When I asked Natalia what the last man looked like, she described our victim perfectly, right down to the cowboy boots he's wearing now."

"And you're certain there's no other way out of the bathroom?" Seth asks. "No window or anything?"

"Nothing," Pierre confirms. "It's an interior room with solid floors, walls, and ceiling. It would be impossible."

"And yet it happened." Seth runs his hands through his hair. "Damn this case."

Pierre nods. "My sentiments, exactly."

Seth eyes me. "What the hell are we dealing with?"

"I'm not sure," I say, my mind churning for answers.

"A real-life magician," Pierre offers halfheartedly.

Seth shakes his head. "Is it even possible to catch this guy?"

"I don't know, but I'm certainly not going to stop trying," I say.

"Thank you," Pierre says. "It is hard to tread quicksand, but I assure you that we are making progress."

"And costing you a fortune in the meantime." Seth eyes Pierre. "How much longer can you afford to keep us here?"

Pierre waves his hand. "You needn't worry. Money isn't an issue. Solving this case and stopping the killer are our only two concerns."

"I can't imagine having your resources," Seth says.

Pierre chuckles. "I assure you, this case lies far from the ordinary. Not only does a case like this draw national and international attention, but it also affects the perception our people have of our president. The longer it drags on, the more scrutiny he draws. Plus, it's an election year."

Seth raises his hand. "Enough said. Politics supersede all rational thought and spending."

"Precisely." Pierre looks around. "I still have a lot to do here. How about you two return to the hotel and get unpacked?"

"Thérèse said the same thing," I say. "We'll be ready to go when you need us."

* * * * *

Back at the hotel, Seth and I check into our new suite and order room service. It arrives quickly, and I chow down on a ham and swiss sandwich. It's truly one of the best sandwiches I've ever eaten, and it helps drive away the headache I've been carrying with me since touching Davit's body.

As we relax on the sofa, Seth rubs my feet. It calms my nerves but doesn't extinguish my fears completely. Residual effects of the experience linger with my vision, the edges of everything a bit fuzzy.

Seth stares into the distance. He gets that way when he's contemplating something. We're so much alike in many ways.

"What are you thinking about?" I ask.

His brow furrows, but he doesn't look at me. "So, when you're inside someone's mind, you really feel and see everything?"

"Yes, I see everything, but feeling things depends on who the victim is. Or rather what the victim is. Centaurian, Shadow Priest, or whatever."

He glances over at me. "Like *everything* everything?"

"Yes, Seth. I've had the displeasure of watching two men who weren't you urinate, and I'd rather not think about it too much."

"Must be weird, you know, since you're not a guy."

I smile. "Yeah, but it's helped me understand the difficulty in aiming that thing."

Seth laughs. "Okay, now *you've* gone too far."

Guilt wells up within me. Not from what I said but from what happened earlier.

I stare at the stitching on the sofa cushion beside me. "Seth…"

He peers over at me. "I know that tone, and it's usually followed with something you've previously forgotten to mention."

The man knows me too well.

"You're not wrong." I close my eyes and return to the bathroom of La Tache Sombre. "I wasn't trying to keep anything from you, but I also didn't want to say anything in front of Pierre and Thérèse."

His hands stop rubbing my feet. "Anything about what?"

"When the killer appeared in the bathroom, he greeted the victim. But it wasn't like with René Edelmann. Instead of using the victim's name… he used mine."

Seth tenses. Squeezes the life out of my foot. "That's significant, Alice!" He smacks the bottom of my foot. "Why would you keep something like that from any of us?"

I pull my foot away from his grasp and begin massaging it, stalling for time. "Honestly, I wasn't sure what to make of it."

"Don't give me that, Alice. The killer *knows* who you are and *what* you can do. That's what you can make of it."

I nod. "You're right, but it doesn't help with the case. If I tell Pierre and Thérèse, they will worry and potentially send us home. I couldn't risk that."

Seth exhales forcefully. "Yeah, I hear what you're saying, but I still think they deserve to know. This kind of knowledge increases the risk for us all."

"I'm not sure I agree. So far, the killer has only gone after terrible people. I don't think he'll come after any of us. It's not what he stands for."

"What he stands for? Listen to yourself. It's almost like you sympathize with this guy and his brand of vigilante justice." He glares holes through me. "Do you?"

I yank my other foot away from his hand. "Are you being serious right now?"

"Wish I wasn't, but you do have quite the track record when it comes to vigilante tendencies."

"Don't you dare go there right now, Seth Allyn. I'm not in the mood. Nor am I like Thérèse."

"When did I say anything about Thérèse?"

"Ugh!" I push myself off the sofa and storm into the bedroom, slamming the door behind me before plopping down on the bed.

What hurts the most is the fact that Seth's not wrong. A small part of me wonders if catching this killer is the right thing to do. After all, he's likely prevented numerous future crimes and killings.

Killing is never the answer, Alice.

The down comforter pulls me into its fluffy, warm embrace as I lie back on the bed. My mind begins to drift as sleep knocks at my door. After a time, I give in and allow it to sweep me away.

CHAPTER FOURTEEN

ALL NIGHT, MIRRORS AND keys and circles fill my dreams. Cloaked men hiding in shadows. Wielding garrotes. Chanting damnation to those different from themselves. By the time I crawl out of bed I can think of little else. That is until the glorious aromas of maple syrup and bacon waft into the bedroom and fill my nostrils. An earthquake rumbles deep within my belly.

Seth's in the kitchen, slaving away at the stove. After what he's put me through the last few days, it's gonna take more than bacon and eggs to quell my wrath. But it's a good start.

A plate piled high with pancakes and scrambled eggs sits on the counter. Butter and syrup accompany the ensemble, each ready to be applied to the still steaming pancakes. Next to the plate stands a tall glass of chocolate milk. For his sake, it had better be made with Nesquik and not some nasty chocolate syrup.

I sit at the kitchen bar and prep the pancakes for consumption, bypassing the butter altogether. "Alright, you've made your way out of the doghouse, but that doesn't mean you've earned your way back into the bedroom just yet."

Seth glances over his shoulder and grins. "Maybe not, but I'm just getting started."

"Gear up. It's a tall mountain." The first bite of pancakes leaves me drooling as melted chocolate chips gush from it.

"I heard that moan," Seth says. "That's gotta get me a bit further up that steep mountain, right?"

"Farther, not further. And yes, you're heading in the right direction and at a pretty good clip. But don't wear yourself out before you summit."

"Never." He slides a plate with bacon and sausage links toward me and then carries another plate around the counter and joins me at the bar.

Minutes later, I'm scraping a dirty fork across an empty plate, vying for that last taste of maple syrup. The pancakes sit heavy in my gut, and it's a glorious feeling. Lunch will have to come much later today, if at all.

As I sit here and stare at the plate, circles begin filling my mind. Lots and lots of circles. It gives me an idea.

The last drops of chocolate milk cling to the edge of my glass and require me to tongue them out. After prevailing, I set the glass down and glance over at Seth. "We need to find a map of Paris."

He hops off his barstool and starts washing the dishes. "Why? You've got Google Maps on your phone."

I push my plate and glass across the counter and toward the sink. "I'm not looking for directions, genius. I need it to draw on."

"Oh." He looks up at me. "You've got an idea brewing, don't you?"

"I'm not used to working on a case without having all the resources to actually do it. You know, the boards and pictures and evidence sitting there, ready to be studied."

"Yeah, I get it." He smiles. "You want to plot out all the murder locations on the map. See if anything pops."

"I know Pierre and Thérèse have a map back at their office with the info already on it, but I want one of my own." I chew on my lower lip. "I've just got this feeling that there's more to it all."

Seth begins stacking the clean dishes on the drying rack. "And you think this because of the pattern you found in the killer's schedule?"

I nod. "Exactly."

"Yeah, I'm on board." He dries his hands off and tosses the dishtowel on top of the clean dishes. "Besides, it's not like we have much else to do at the moment, right?"

"I thought you'd be itching to interview associates of Davit Muradyan with Thérèse."

"Not in the least." Seth smiles at me in that special way of his, melting a good portion of the ice surrounding my heart. "My partner's right in front of me, and she's all I need."

My God, he's good.

I return the smile. "I'll admit, you're a fast mountain climber, Mr. Ryan."

"Doing my best to summit by lunch." He winks at me.

"Whoa, don't go getting ahead of yourself." I hop off the stool as Seth rounds the corner of the counter.

He grabs my hips and pulls me into a hug. "Never."

I'd pull away, but he smells so good, so I bury my face in his chest instead. The questionable move fully thaws my heart, and I find myself pushing him toward the bedroom. He doesn't even attempt to resist as we cling to each other and lock lips.

The map can wait.

* * * * *

Several hours and miles of walking later, we finally locate a shop that promises to sell more than a watered-down tourist attraction guide of Paris. Strong smells of old parchment and ink hit me as we step through the door and into the old shop. It's a reprieve from the musty, wet sidewalks we've traveled all morning.

Immediately, I feel as though I've traveled back in time a century or more. Maps of every size and color line the walls and hang from the ceiling. Many of them are yellowed with age and frayed on their edges. Some look so fragile I fear a heavy breath would destroy them.

Every type of map imaginable catches my eye, and the details of each are beyond comprehension. Maps of cities, countries, and the world. Terrain maps and sewer maps. I've never seen so many maps in my entire life.

An old man sits behind a counter at the back of the shop. His long white beard covers the better part of his chest and lays across the countertop. It takes several moments for me to realize he's missing his right arm, the beard a cloaking device.

He greets us as we approach. *"Les Américains?"*

Seth glances toward me. "Are we that obvious?"

"Welcome," the man says in English. "My name is Giovanni Romano. How may I be of service to you on this beautiful day?"

I lean on the counter. "We're looking to purchase an authentic, detailed street map of Paris. Preferably a recent one."

The man's gray eyes sparkle. "Well then, you've come to the right place, and I have just the map you need. Wait right there, and I'll be right back." He disappears through a pair of curtains and returns a minute later with a long cardboard tube. "Oh ho ho. You are in for a real treat, my friends."

I can't help but smile at the jolly man. "I'm sure we are."

He places the tube between his legs then reaches into its end and pulls out a rolled-up sheet of yellowish-white paper. He talks as he carefully places a weight on the end of the map and then unrolls it. "I drafted this map just a year ago for a client, but they never came to pick it up. As you can see, the details are second to none. If you were to compare it to some fancy online map, you'd find them to be nearly identical. However, you would never be able to match the beautiful, artistic style of this map with one generated by a computer. That, I guarantee."

The glorious map speaks for itself, every last detail perfection. It blows my mind to think that anyone has the skill to do such tedious work, let alone a man with only one arm.

I look up at Giovanni with awe. "You are indeed a master cartographer, sir."

His eyes beam. "Please, call me Giovanni." He proffers his hand.

My pulse quickens when I glimpse the strange mark on the inside of his wrist. It reminds me of a ship's wheel. "I… I'm Alice." I gesture toward Seth with my head, my eyes still anchored to the mark. "This is my husband, Seth."

Giovanni dips his head toward me, then Seth. "A pleasure."

"You're not from around here, are you?" I ask.

"The name gave me away, did it?" He smiles. "I came here from Italy almost three decades ago. Hard to believe it's been that long. Soon, it'll be time for me to move on again. I never stay in one place too long."

"I know what you mean." My gaze returns to the map. "This map will serve our purposes well."

Seth pulls out his wallet. "How much do we owe you?"

Giovanni shakes his head. "My friends, I could not charge you a single Euro and feel right about it. As I said, this map was commissioned and paid for in advance. Since it was never picked up, it is yours."

"You're too kind, Giovanni," Seth says, returning his wallet to his pocket.

Giovanni cocks his head and eyes Seth. "One can never be too kind, now can they?"

Seth shrugs. "I suppose not."

Giovanni points at a location in the middle of the map and smiles. "Did you know that *Cathédrale Notre-Dame de Paris* lies at the center of the city? It truly is one of the most beautiful if not *the* most beautiful site you'll see in all of Paris. Make plans to visit if you have not already. Trust me, you will not be disappointed doing so."

"Thank you for the suggestion," Seth says, "but I'm afraid we're here for business and not pleasure."

"Ah, I see. Well, that is unfortunate. You're missing out on all Paris has to offer." Giovanni rolls the map back up and returns it to the cardboard tube still wedged between his thighs before handing the tube to Seth. "All I ask is that you make good use of it."

"Trust me, we will," I say. "Thank you, again."

Giovanni dips his head. "It's been a pleasure."

Outside the shop, a strange feeling washes over me. Like someone's watching me. My skin prickles, and the hairs on my nape stand on end as I scan the sidewalks and streets for a source, but none seems to exist, and the feeling quickly fades.

I grab Seth's hand and squeeze it. "Is it just me, or did you feel someone watching us, too?"

His brow furrows. "It's not just you."

My pulse quickens. "You think it's our killer?"

"Either that or another Shadow Priest." Seth points toward one of the shops across the street. "It's a mirror shop."

"Yeah, I see that now." I swallow hard. "Could be Morgan."

"Maybe, but I'd rather not stick around and find out." He tugs my arm. "Come on."

As we head back toward the hotel with the map, both of us continually look over our shoulders and scrutinize every shadow, doorway, window, and dark alley we pass by. An attack in broad daylight would be unlikely, either from a Shadow Priest or our killer, but the knowledge does nothing to calm the brewing storm in my gut.

By the time we make it back to our hotel suite, my neck feels sore from twisting my head around so much. Plus, it's almost time for dinner. A remark Seth has made three times now. He orders room service as soon as we get into the suite. Honestly, I don't blame him since we skipped lunch.

While we wait, I take the map and lay it out on the dining room table. It takes ten minutes to locate and mark the eleven locations where our killer has dumped the bodies. Now, I've forever ruined Giovanni's beautiful map. But it's for a good cause. Or at least a good reason.

Unfortunately, the more I stare at the map, the more I begin to doubt my theory of a pattern to the locations. All I see are eleven random dots.

After a quick shower, Seth joins me in the dining room. He stares at the map. "Looks kinda like a poorly drawn circle to me. Or maybe one of those connect-the-dot pictures."

A circle…

My mind clicks. "The center is the key…"

"What's that mean?" Seth asks.

My eyes begin to cross as I continue to stare at the dots. "Something the killer said to Davit." I peer at the far wall and sigh heavily. "Now I'm thinking it might've been a clue meant for me."

Seth scoffs. "Why would the killer give you a clue about anything?"

I pull out one of the chairs and plop down on it. "Come on, Seth, think about it. It's a game to him, same as all the other serial killers we've hunted over the years. Given how little we know of him, I'm sure he's growing bored with us."

Seth nods. "Right. Time for him to up the ante."

I raise my hands. "Exactly. He wants that adrenaline rush. The thrill of being chased and staying one step ahead. Right now, he's a thousand steps ahead of us."

"And giving you clues helps narrow the gap." He leans over the table and stares at the map. "Okay, so how do we find the center of eleven random dots?"

"Well, we have two choices. Either we make a wild guess, or I send the data to Kenny."

"So, you're saying Kenny is really our only choice." Seth grins. "That boy can figure out just about anything, can't he."

"Guess it's settled then." I stand and grab my phone. "I'll take a picture and send it over to him."

Seth folds his arms across his chest. "And then we wait."

"Oh, I'm certain we can come up with some sort of way to pass the time, Mr. Ryan."

A grin spreads across his face. "Have I reached the summit already?"

"You summited right after breakfast, babe. Remember?"

He cocks his head and looks toward the ceiling. "Did I? Hmm. Maybe I could use a refresher."

A loud knock sounds from the suite door.

I smack his butt as he turns and walks away. "A raincheck, then."

"And I'll hold you to it," he says over his shoulder.

As much as I love his face, I thoroughly enjoy watching him walk away.

Count on it, babe.

* * * * *

A few hours later, Kenny calls while Seth and I are relaxing on the sofa and nursing bottles of beer. I answer and hit the speaker icon so Seth can hear the conversation too. "You're on speakerphone with Seth and me. Tell us you've got some good news, Kenny."

"Hey, Alice. Seth. So, I went ahead and took a look at the data you sent me about the killings. Had to use some crazy spacial statistics to get the mean center of those coordinates. Admittedly, it was quite fun. Anyway, I have an answer for you guys."

"Tell me it's not in the middle of a street or park or something like that," I say.

"Or a river," Seth adds.

"Nope. In fact, the data points right at the heart of Paris. I mean like *right* at the center. Notre-Dame Cathedral."

I glance at Seth. "You're joking, right?"

"Come on, Alice. You know I never joke about math," Kenny says.

Seth says, "Of course you don't."

Kenny chuckles. "Anyway, I just sent you an updated image with a circle drawn around all the coordinates. I also marked the center of it."

"Speaking of the center, did I tell you about the killer saying that the center was the key?" I ask.

"Nope, but it makes sense. The data proves it."

"You're amazing, Kenny," I say.

"I know, but you don't need to tell me every time we talk. You'll wind up exploding my head."

I smirk. "Funny, Kenny."

"Anyway, I gotta run. Kellie's asking for my help with something."

Seth says, "A superhero never rests, right?"

"Ain't that the truth! Anyway, take care, guys. Talk again soon!"

"You, too, Kenny," I say.

"Bye," Seth adds.

After hanging up, I pull up the image Kenny sent. Sure enough, Notre-Dame Cathedral and the center of Paris lie at the heart of our killer's trail of bodies. I hand the phone to Seth so he can see it.

"Damned if it isn't the exact center," Seth says after studying the image.

I take a swig of my beer and lean back on the sofa. "Not a coincidence."

Seth shakes his head. "Not even a little."

As I stare at the ceiling, my mind races with the implications of what it all means. Often, serial killers need validation and go out of their way to be noticed. To be discovered and awed. Worshiped, even.

But this… This is something else.

The longer I contemplate it, the more elegant the pattern becomes. In a sick, sadistic way, of course. But still, not only do the murders follow a time pattern, but the placement of the bodies form a crude circle.

A circle…

"Six ways to Sunday, it's an elaborate pattern," Seth says.

"Elegant." I take another swig of beer. "There's no way the killer wasn't giving me a clue. The center *is* key."

"Yeah." He scratches the back of his neck. "Plus Giovanni insisted that we visit the church."

"I'm certain it was a recommendation. And a coincidence."

"Maybe, and maybe not. I saw his wrist, too, you know." He chuckles. "You freaks seem to attract each other."

My brow furrows. "Freaks, huh?"

He shrugs. "As good a label as any, right?"

I turn and face him. "And I'm the freakiest freak of them all?"

"At least in the bedroom." He chuckles.

"I'll take that as a complement." I slap Seth on the thigh. "Now, let's get ourselves over to that church."

"I hate to curb your enthusiasm, babe, but it's kinda late to be visiting a church, don't you think?"

As usual, he's right. "Fine, but we're going there first thing tomorrow morning, got it?"

"Well, it's about time."

The word *'time'* sticks in my mind, but I'm not sure why. I take my phone back from Seth and study the image again. "What's that supposed to mean, anyway?"

"You going to church. We can attend the morning mass service."

"Tomorrow's Tuesday, Seth, not Sunday."

"Yeah, hence the morning part of it and not weekly."

"Oh, I see." I look up from my phone. "Hate to burst your bubble, but that's not what I had in mind."

He shrugs. "Maybe not, but it looks like God might have other plans for you anyway."

"No offense to God, but I'm pretty certain he has nothing to do with any of this."

"You're wrong, Alice. God has his hands in everything."

"The world is his cookie jar." I snort, picturing God as Cookie Monster from *Sesame Street*.

Seth rolls his eyes. "Stick to your day job, funny girl."

"Well, I guess we'll have to just wait and see about God's plan. Hopefully he'll deliver the killer right into *our* hands."

"He is the God of miracles. Anything's possible."

My eyes focus on Notre-Dame Cathedral. "I still don't understand what the church has to do with the killings, though."

"Yeah, I'm not sure, either," he says. "The killer doesn't strike me as a spiritual person."

Strike…

The beginnings of something profound form in the back of my mind, but I can't quite grasp what it is yet. "Right. He doesn't seem like a religious nut."

Seth frowns at me. "And you're familiar with religious nuts?"

"You've met my mother, haven't you?" I chuckle.

"She's no nut, Alice. She just loves you and wants the best for you."

"Keeping it serious, are we?" I sigh. "Well, you're not wrong about her. At least the part about her wanting the best for me."

"She really does."

My eyes roam the image again. Focus on the dots. The containing circle. *Why a circle?*

The thought keeps carouseling through my mind. Spinning round and round as I study the image further. At first, I glean nothing new, but then my mind begins piecing it all together.

Circle... Strike... Time... A clock!

Butterflies rise in my chest, their tiny wings fluttering with frenzy. "Hey, I think I might be onto something else."

"Oh yeah?"

I pull myself up off the sofa and walk over to the dining room table. The map taunts me with its secrets, but not for long. "I'm going to need a few things."

Seth joins me in front of the table. "As in we need to go back out?"

"Actually, no." I set my beer on the table then bend down and start untying Seth's shoe.

"Uh... you need my shoe?"

"No, just the lace." After finishing its extraction, I peer up at him. "Find me a pen and grab one of the thumbtacks out of my bag, too."

He frowns. "You have thumbtacks in your bag?"

"Yes, Seth. What do you think I use to tack the blankets over the window when we want to sleep in?"

Seth shrugs. "Never thought about it, I guess."

I stand up and shoo him away. "Hurry it up."

"Okay, okay. I'm on it." He heads for the bedroom.

A few minutes later, he finally returns. Six thumbtacks in hand but no pen. I push past him and grab a pen out of the desk drawer in the living room.

"And what are we doing with these things?" he asks, eying his shoestring and the thumbtacks.

"Watch and learn."

I take a thumbtack and stab it through one end of Seth's shoelace. Then I push the thumbtack through the center of Notre-Dame Cathedral on the map; the same place where Kenny had placed the center dot on his image. With a bit of effort, the thumbtack drives down into the surface of the table and anchors itself. Might be a ding to the room deposit, but it's too late to turn back now.

"Okay, now we need a good reference point." I hand him my phone. "Zoom in on the picture and find the best starting point along the circle."

Seth nods. "Okay, now I'm with you. We're going to draw the same circle on *our* map."

"Precisely."

After a few minutes, he points at Arc de Triomphe on the map. "Just east of that place. Where the first road circles around it."

"Got it."

I pull the shoelace tight and tie its loose end around the pen, securing the pen's tip right on top of the point Seth gave me. Slowly, I begin drawing the circle. Once I get back around to the starting point, I step back and take my work in. It looks just like Kenny's circle. And as expected, another pattern emerges.

I smile. "Yes, of course."

Seth stares at the map. "Yes, what?"

"Don't worry, you'll understand in a minute." I untie the pen and set it aside. "Take off your wristwatch and place it on the map over the church and the thumbtack."

Seth frowns but complies. "What are you seeing that I'm not?"

"Be patient, babe." I grab the pen. "Okay, make sure to keep the watch aligned with the map as best as possible. Twelve being north and six south. Got it?"

"Yeah."

"Good. I'm going to move the string around the circle and you're going to tell me when I've reached each hour marker. And try to be as precise as possible."

"Okay, but I still don't see where you're going with this."

"I know, but it'll be easier to show you rather than trying to explain it."

Once I get all twelve hours marked, I start adding in the minute marks between each of them. It doesn't take long, and the final product looks better than I'd hoped.

"Now, you'll begin to see what I'm seeing in my head. Go get that list of murders I gave you the other day."

Seth returns with the list. "Got it. Now what?"

"Read them back to me."

"March 25th, 2019. Sunday. Midnight to three in the morning."

I pull the string up to the midnight mark on our makeshift clock. The first body location aligns with it perfectly. "Write midnight next to it and give me the next one."

Seth jots it down on the paper. "Okay, April 30th, 2019. Tuesday. 1800 to 2100."

Again, I align the shoestring with the 6th hour mark on our makeshift clock. Then, I begin swinging it around until the shoestring aligns with the location of the second body. "Write down six thirty-three."

We continue through the list, noting the time on the clock with the placement of the bodies. My pulse begins racing with excitement as another thought strikes me. I grab Seth's wristwatch off the table and shove it into his hands.

"Pop out the small wheel that enables you to adjust the time and turn it until the hour and minute hands align at twelve."

"Done," Seth says.

"Okay, now you're going to tell me the time every time the hands align, and I'll verify it with the list. First one's obviously twelve o'clock."

"Obviously, yes." He turns the wheel until the hands align again. "One oh five."

"Got it."

He speeds through the rest of them. "Two eleven. Three sixteen. Four twenty-two. Five twenty-seven. Six thirty-three. Seven thirty-eight. Eight forty-four. Nine forty-nine. Ten fifty-four."

"Yes, to every last one of them," I say.

Seth looks at me, stunned. "That's crazy. What does it mean?"

It's a good question and one I have no answer for. "Dunno, but one thing's for sure. Our killer is obsessed with time."

"The Time Killer," Seth says. "Or in more modern terms, Facebook." He chuckles.

I laugh aloud. "Clever, babe. However, I'm sure Facebook would sue us if we started calling this guy the Facebook Killer. Plus, he's more than just your basic killer. He slashes the throats of his victims."

"Right." He scratches his chin. "So, we'll call him The Time Slasher then."

I frown. "I don't think so. It sounds too much like a book on productivity or something."

Seth shakes his head. "Never can win with you, can I?" He cocks his head. "So, what do you suggest, Mrs. Smarty-pants?"

"I think an alternative word for time would work better." I tap my chin with the pen. "Something like the Greek word for time, *chrónos*."

"The *Chrónos* Slasher?" He scrunches up his face.

"Yeah, but without the 's' at the end. The Chrono Slasher."

"Kinda sounds like that old RPG videogame from the nineties, *Chrono Trigger*."

"Exactly. Has a certain ring to it, don't you think?"

Seth shrugs. "Hey, it's your freak show, remember? You can call this guy whatever you want."

"At least you remember the rules. And for the record, that's what I want. The Chrono Slasher."

Seth slaps the table. "Well then, it's settled." He kisses my cheek. "We've got the important part nailed down, so now what? When will he kill again?"

I close my eyes for a moment as I think about it. "Based on the established pattern, we've got just over four weeks. That puts us at April twenty-fourth."

"Four weeks..." He sighs. "This case just sucks the life from me. I feel so hopeless."

"I know, but we can't give up now. We're getting closer every day."

"You really think so?"

I smile. "Yeah. Look at what we just solved."

"The center was the key to figuring out the pattern of the killings, but what does that get us?"

Thoughts swirl in my mind. "Maybe it has some sort of deeper meaning as well. I say we still visit the church tomorrow."

"And we attend the mass service."

I shake my head. "You're not gonna let it go, are you?"

"Nope. Besides, we might kill two birds with one stop. The killer might attend the mass service, too."

"One stone, Seth, and I'm pretty sure the killer isn't religious."

"No, it's stop. We make one stop and maybe kill two birds." He nudges me with his elbow. "Get it?"

I roll my eyes. "You're ridiculous."

"Yes, and also insistent. We attend the mass service, or we don't go at all."

"You're willing to risk failing to catch a killer just because I don't want to attend the mass service?"

"Trust me, it's far less risky than you toying with eternal damnation."

"Wow, you've been around my mother for far too long."

"Fine, don't do it for yourself, then. Do it for me."

"Ugh. You're impossible."

He leans close. "So, that's a 'yes' then?"

I push him back. "Fine, but don't expect me to do the whole sit, kneel, stand stuff. I'm not Catholic."

"Neither am I, and I wouldn't dream of it." He grabs my arm and pulls me into an embrace. "I swear, you won't regret it."

I stare into his big, beautiful eyes, and my stomach rumbles. "Maybe not, but you're gonna have a big regret if that food you ordered doesn't get here soon."

"Patience, my love." He kisses me, then lets me go. "How about you give

Pierre a call and fill him in on your breakthrough."

I glance back down at the map. "Not sure what good my breakthrough is just yet, so I think we should wait on saying anything."

"Fine, but I'm sure he'll be impressed with your killer's new name."

A knock at the suite door sends Seth hustling away. My gaze returns to the map. The circle. The clock. The patterns.

You're a clever one, Chrono Slasher. So, what else might I be missing?

CHAPTER FIFTEEN

TWO GOTHIC SQUARE TOWERS rise above the skyline in front of us. The famed West Façade of Notre-Dame Cathedral. Now that I stand before it, I realize that no picture could ever do the 800-year-old building justice. Its architecture is truly breathtaking. Between its arches and buttresses and its beautifully carved statues, chimeras, and gargoyles that line its outer walls, my eyes can't decide where to focus.

"She's magnificent, isn't she," Seth says.

"Worth the trip alone."

"Wait until you see the inside. The stained-glass windows are beyond incredible." He takes my hand. "Come on."

A dark-skinned man dressed in a black suit, black shirt, and wearing a clerical collar stands just outside the central portal. His warm smile greets us, as do his striking hazel eyes. A modest beard hangs from his lower jaw, dark but peppered gray and white. Matches the short-trimmed hair on his head.

The man sweeps his outstretched arm toward the building. "Welcome to Notre-Dame de Paris," he says in French. His accent further suggests that he isn't a native Parisian.

Most likely a Spaniard.

"My name is Father Toussaint." His gaze falls on me. "Based on the size of your bulging eyes, I assume that this is your first visit?"

"Yes." I can't help but stare at the magnificent, yet strange scene depicted above the central portal.

Father Toussaint cranes his head. "Ah, yes. What you're looking at is a rendering of the Last Judgment. The Archangel Michael uses the scales of justice to weigh souls against those gathered by Satan while Jesus and his heavenly hosts look on." His gaze returns to me. "Are you familiar with the Last Judgment?"

"Yes," Seth says, beating me to it. "But what's depicted in that scene isn't biblically accurate. The Last Judgment happens at the end of the millennial kingdom, not at the Second Coming. Jesus separates the sheep from the goats at the Second Coming." His French is impeccable.

Father Toussaint blinks several times, stunned by Seth's answer. It takes several moments for him to recover. "I take it that you are not Catholic."

"And you'd be correct." Seth points at himself. "Nondenominational."

"I see." Father Toussaint folds his hands behind his back. "Last Judgment aside, have you proclaimed your belief, hope, and trust in Jesus Christ as your savior?"

Seth nods. "Long ago, Father, but I have a tendency to stray from the path now and again."

"You are not alone, my son. We all fall short and must be vigilant in our daily walk." Father Toussaint's gaze falls upon me. "And how about you, my dear? Have you accepted Jesus Christ as your lord and savior?"

Suddenly, I'm all too aware of the crowd around us. Furthermore, we seem to be the only ones detained. It quickens my pulse.

Why has he singled us out?

The man smiles as though he's reading my thoughts. "You needn't be afraid to speak the truth, my dear. I am not here to judge but to simply point out the path to salvation."

Salvation.

That word drives icy shards of fear into my veins. Of its own accord, my traitorous hand reaches for the cross that hangs from my neck beneath my blouse. Trembling fingers latch onto it.

My gaze falls at the man's feet. "I do know God," I hear myself say with a scratchy tone.

His hand touches my shoulder. "It's a start." I finally meet his gaze and nod.

But is it enough?

Father Toussaint's brow winkles as his eyes continue to study mine. He wants to say more.

Despite my aversion toward the subject of religion, I find myself asking, "What is it?"

He strokes his beard several times before speaking. "Over the years, I have developed a keen ability to read people. When I look at you, it is obvious to me that you've struggled for a long time with your faith. Perhaps we could sit down for a spell and discuss the issues that hinder you from letting go and surrendering to the call we both know you hear."

I shake my head. "I'm sorry, Father, but you're wrong. It's impossible to struggle with issues that don't exist."

His eyebrows dip and meet over the bridge of his nose. "Are you saying that you do not feel him calling you to surrender, or is it something more than that?"

"Oh, I feel a calling, alright. But it doesn't come from God."

He crosses his arms and taps his chin. "Interesting."

"What is?" I ask, far too curious to leave it alone.

"As I am certain you know, a calling is an entirely different matter." The furrows of his brow deepen. "This calling of yours. Do you use it for good or for evil?"

The question strikes me as almost offensive. How many people actively seek to do evil and admit it?

None.

"Well, good of course," I say.

"And if you use this calling of yours for good, how can it not come from God? After all, the holy scriptures are not ambiguous when it comes to God's nature. It says that all things good come from him."

"Yes, but with the good comes evil," I counter. "It's a packaged deal."

"In life this is often true, but with God there can be no evil. He is perfect in his goodness, and his nature is unchanging."

"If that's true, then why does he allow evil to rule this world?"

"Ah, now that is a great question." He touches my arm again. "Please, come inside and we can discuss this further."

"No offense, Father, but we didn't come here to discuss religion," I say.

Father Toussaint bows his head. "Forgive me. I've taken enough of your time." He moves aside and ushers us toward the portal. "Please enjoy your day, and do not hesitate to seek me out if you'd like to discuss salvation and the nature of God further."

"Thank you," Seth and I both say.

We step inside the cathedral and fight our way through a sea of people. It's like trying to swim upstream as more of them are exiting the cathedral than entering with us. I'm just about to ask Seth why when I notice the sign. Apparently, we've just missed the morning mass. The knots in my stomach I've been carrying with me all morning unravel.

As we move into the nave, the cathedral darkens, much more so than I would've imagined. Modern sconces cling to the stone columns but remain stingy with their light. I'm not sure if the low lighting helps preserve the old cathedral or if it's simply done so that the plethora of stained-glass windows can be better seen and admired. Whatever the reason, the low lighting makes me feel right at home.

We continue to explore the cathedral and all its wonders for a solid hour, and we both enjoy every second of it, but it isn't the purpose of our visit. As remarkable as the cathedral is, I fail to find anything that connects it with our killer.

Back in the nave, I stare up at the "voice" of the cathedral, a symphonic organ built in 1733. The monstrosity of it astounds me, its 8000 pipes climbing high along the wall and blocking much of the western rose window.

Seth crosses his arms. "Man, what I wouldn't give to play a few notes on that thing."

"They actually let people play it on Sunday afternoons."

He glances at me. "Really?"

"Yeah. You can get your name added to the waiting list, but I think it's a few years long."

"Hmm." He frowns. "A return trip would take some careful planning."

"Like all of the murders. Speaking of which, I think I was wrong."

Seth continues to study the grand organ. "Wrong about what?"

I turn in a circle. "Nothing about this place screams serial killer."

He chuckles. "Well, I'd hope not. We're standing inside one of the most iconic cathedrals in the entire world."

I slide my hand around his bicep and pull myself against him, leaning my head on his shoulder. "You know what I mean."

He kisses the top of my head. "Sometimes, we try and over-complicate things because the truth seems far too simple."

Seth's right. I do it all the time, rarely adhering to the KISS principle. "So, you agree that the center was the key to figuring out the pattern and discovering the times but nothing more?"

"I have to at this point." He rubs the back of his neck. "For now, I think we need to figure out why time is significant to him. We do that, and we might just find this Chrono Slasher."

"Agreed," I say.

But where do we start?

My phone buzzes. After checking the screen, I touch Seth's arm. "It's Kenny. I'll be right back."

He nods and peers back up at the organ. "Don't worry, I'm not going anywhere. I could stare at this beauty all day."

As I seek out a quieter location, I answer the call. "Hello?"

"Hey, Alice, it's me again," Kenny says.

Just hearing his voice lifts my spirits. "I think I've talked to you more while I've been here in Paris than I had the last few months before coming here."

"Probably true, but not your fault. I've been way too busy with life and poorly managing it. Anyway, after you had me find the center of the body drops, I couldn't stop thinking about it. I began wondering if what the killer said held another meaning."

The kid reminds me of myself sometimes. "I'd been wondering the same thing. Turns out there was another pattern."

"Really?"

"Yeah, the location of each killing coincides with the victim's time of death if you assume that the circle is a clock. Not only that, but every point coincides with the hour and minute hands aligning."

"Now that's definitely not a coincidence," Kenny says.

"Right, but so far I've come up empty as to what it all means."

"Yeah, I had too, until I realized that it might be good to scour the video footage from around Notre-Dame Cathedral."

"Please tell me you found something."

"Well, I added a few more parameters to make my search a little more robust and actually got a hit."

"Are you saying that our killer goes to church?"

"At least once. Right after the last body appeared."

"The bastard's repenting for what he's done."

"Maybe, and maybe not. Honestly, it was kinda weird."

"Weird how?"

"Previously, I reviewed months and months of video footage from all across Paris without getting a single hit on the guy. Then, after he speaks to you through your vision or whatever, he's suddenly caught on video?"

"That doesn't seem like a coincidence, either."

"No, especially when you see the video. He stood directly in front of the camera and removed his hood."

"He sent me another message…"

"That'd be my guess. Anyway, I just thought you'd want to know as soon as possible. Oh, and I just sent you the clip."

"You're the GOAT Kenny, and I mean that sincerely."

Kenny sniffs. "Yeah, um, so, anyway. I need to run. Let me know if you catch the guy, alright?"

"I will, and I'll give you the credit if we do."

"Please don't, Alice. You're the one who saw his face. I just matched it to some video. Anyway, I'll talk to you later." He ends the call before I can say anything else.

A little bubble appears over my text message app icon, indicating I have a new message. It's the video Kenny just sent. Hands trembling, I click on the message and stare at the screen as the video plays. There's no sound, and it's dark outside, but it's impossible to mistake the ominous building looming in the background. My skin prickles.

Notre-Dame Cathedral.

Thirty seconds in, a cloaked figure moves into the frame and positions themselves directly in front of the camera. A breath catches in my throat as the figure lowers their hood. Blood pounds in my ears, and the hairs on my arms and nape stand on end as he peers into the camera.

A single green eye looks right at me. Captures my soul. Fifteen seconds tick by as he stands there. Still as the stone gargoyles peering down from the cathedral towers in the background. Afterward, he raises his hood back up and hobbles out of the frame.

I watch the video several more times, each time hoping to glean some sort of significance from it, but nothing beyond the Chrono Slasher stands out. Frustrated, I shove my phone back in my pocket and head back inside to find Seth.

He meets me at the back of the nave. "Kenny have good news?"

"Yes and no." I hand him my phone. "Take a look."

We sit down in the back row, and Seth views the video multiple times before saying anything. "This was definitely a message for us. And great job on the sketch. You really nailed his likeness."

"Yay, me." I sigh. "Now what?"

Seth hands my phone back and grins. "I think it's time we revisit Father Toussaint."

"Why? The Chrono Slasher didn't actually come into the church."

"Yeah, he stepped back out of the camera frame, but that doesn't mean he didn't come inside. He's proven how great he is at avoiding cameras." Seth stands and proffers his hand. "Either way, it can't hurt to ask Father Toussaint if he recognizes the guy."

Seth's right, but my hesitance isn't because I don't think the killer came into the church. It stems from not wanting to speak to Father Toussaint again. The man stirs feelings of faith in me that I'd rather stay dormant, and I fear what might come out of my mouth. Then again, it isn't like I have a choice in the matter. Cases always take precedence over any fears or misgivings I might have.

I exhale loudly, then take Seth's hand. He pulls me up.

"Lead the way," I say.

Father Toussaint still haunts the central portal when we return to the front of the cathedral. We stand to the side for a few minutes while he finishes his conversation with an older couple visiting from Austria. As the couple walks away, Father Toussaint turns his attention toward us.

Somehow, the man wears an even bigger smile than he did the first time we spoke. "Ah, you've returned. I had a feeling you would. Am I wrong to assume you want to talk about salvation further after touring my beautiful home?"

"Perhaps another time," Seth says. "At the moment, we have a more urgent matter to discuss."

"More urgent than the final resting place of your soul?" Father Toussaint shakes his head solemnly. "You must be mistaken, my friend. I assure you, no such urgency exists."

"Perhaps I should just start over," Seth says. "I'm Detective Ryan—" He motions toward me with his hand. "—and this is Detective Bergman. We're homicide detectives, and we've returned to you in a more official capacity, I'm afraid."

Father Toussaint's eyebrows rise. "Oh, I see." He pulls us to the side, away from the onslaught of visitors pouring in and out of the three portals.

"In that case, how may I be of assistance, Detectives?"

I pull out my sketch of the killer—the Chrono Slasher—and hand it to Father Toussaint. "Do you recognize this man?"

He studies the sketch for several seconds and strokes his beard. "I am afraid I do not. However, I am not always the only one here. May I ask what this is in regard to?"

Seth leans closer to Father Toussaint. "I'm sure you've heard news about the serial killer here in Paris, right?"

"I am sorry, but I have not." He looks at the sketch one last time before handing it back to me. "As you might imagine, I rarely spend time on matters that lie outside the purview of God's church."

Another dead end.

A long sigh ushers from my lips as I fold the sketch and shove it back into my pocket. "That's unfortunate. We have reason to believe that the man in the sketch might be our killer."

"I understand, and I am sorry I cannot assist you in this matter." Father Toussaint folds his hands together. "Again, if you do not mind my asking, are you visiting every cathedral and church in Paris with your sketch or just ours?"

"If you're asking if we're singling out Notre-Dame Cathedral, the answer is yes," I say. "We've obtained video evidence of the suspect on the cathedral grounds. Very early in the morning."

Father Toussaint nods slowly. "Oh, I understand." He holds up a finger and smiles. "In that case, you will want to speak with Father Rogelio. He handles the overnight affairs of the cathedral."

"And where might we find him?" I ask.

"I'm afraid Father Rogelio isn't here right now." He pulls up his right sleeve and eyes a gold wristwatch. "Given that it's Tuesday, he should arrive within the hour to prepare himself for confessions."

"Looks like we've got some more time on our hands," Seth says.

Father Toussaint sweeps his arm toward the central portal. "How about you go back inside and wait for him to arrive? I assure you that sitting in

God's presence will lift your spirits."

Knowing the way Seth thinks, I take his hand and squeeze it before he has a chance to respond. I quickly say, "Thank you, Father, but we'll wait out here. It's a terribly nice day for a change."

Father Toussaint considers the grayish-blue sky. "That it is, Detective. Praise God Almighty." He turns back with a smile. "Now that you've been granted a little more time, would you like to discuss salvation further?"

This man is relentless.

"Perhaps another time, Father. Right now, we need to stay focused on capturing this killer before he strikes again," I say.

Father Toussaint dips his head. "As you wish. Just know that I am here every day if you would like to explore your questions further." He looks past me and smiles wide. "It looks like today might be your lucky day, Detectives. Father Rogelio approaches as we speak."

Seth and I turn and watch a young man dressed just like Father Toussaint walk out of the central portal. Fiery hair sprouts from his head in luscious curls, framing his rotund face.

"Father Rogelio," Father Toussaint says, "you're just the man we've been waiting for."

Father Rogelio's sky-blue eyes sparkle with mischief. "Oh, I am, am I?" His baritone pipes shake the double chin hanging beneath his hidden jawline.

"Indeed." Father Toussaint gestures toward Seth and me with his hand. "Detectives Ryan and Bergman. *Homicide* detectives," he emphasizes.

Father Rogelio gasps. "My, my, my." He leans close. "I hope I'm not in some kind of trouble again."

Again?

I hand him the sketch of the Chrono Slasher. "We're hoping you might be able to identify this person for us."

Recognition sparks in the man's eyes almost immediately. He looks up from the sketch, the mischievousness previously in his eyes replaced with a tinge of sorrow. "A victim?"

Victim?

Seth and I share a glance.

"Afraid not," Seth says.

I roll my eyes. "What Detective Ryan means is that we're looking for that man—" I point at the sketch still clutched in Father Rogelio's hands. "—in connection with several homicides."

"Homicides?" His voice rises an octave.

"Are you familiar with the serial killer who's been leaving bodies all around Paris for the last year?" Seth asks.

"I am." Father Rogelio's gaze returns to the sketch. "And you're certain this is the man you're looking for?"

"Nothing is certain right now. We're looking to identify him and bring him in for questioning." I place my hand on one of Father Rogelio's and wait to speak again until he looks up at me. "You know him, don't you?"

Father Rogelio searches my eyes, then nods. "Yes, I do. He used to be a regular, along with his son, but that stopped about a year ago. Now, I see only him now and again. Perhaps once a month or so." He shakes his head and sighs. "My God in heaven. I just can't imagine Jacques involved in murder, let alone a string of them."

"Jacques?" I ask, my pulse ratcheting up.

He looks at the sketch one last time, then hands it back to me with a decisive nod. "Yes, Detective. Jacques Milan."

CHAPTER SIXTEEN

MY HEART FLUTTERS AS Seth, Pierre, Thérèse, and I stand just outside Jacques Milan's apartment door. After more than six weeks, I'm ready to close this case and get back home to Desert Springs and my life. But none of us know what we'll find on the other side of this door.

All records indicate that Jacques is an upstanding Parisian. No arrests. No parking tickets. No complaints lodged against him. Not even a late book return at the library he used to frequent.

There are only three things we know for certain about Jacques Milan: he's a self-published novelist, he has a teenage son named Raphaël, and his wife died in a car accident seven years ago. None of those facts add up to a father turned vigilante killer. However, an additional fact about his son piques my interest.

According to his high school secretary, Raphaël never finished his junior year last year and hasn't been in attendance since. She and the principal both attempted several calls to Jacques, but none were ever returned. The timing of the boy's apparent disappearance coincides with the start of the killings nearly a year ago, and none of us think that it's a coincidence.

But first we need to find one or both of them.

Pierre eyes Thérèse. "Ready?"

She nods, her expression grim and her grip tight on her weapon.

Pierre nods at Seth, and Seth swings a handheld battering ram at the door.

Crack!

A single blow, and the door explodes inward. Slams against the inside wall. Pierre rushes in, weapon drawn. Thérèse flanks him, and Seth follows behind them, discarding the battering ram at my feet.

Nice move, Seth.

Just as I'm about to step over the battering ram and head through the breached door, I glimpse movement at the far end of the corridor. My pulse quickens as a figure cloaked in black comes around the corner. The way they hobble along is a dead giveaway.

"Jacques Milan!" I yell, pointing the SIG Sauer Pro SP 2022 that Pierre gave me at him.

He halts. Stares at me for several moments as I cautiously approach.

"Hands in the air," I say in French. Seth joins me in the corridor.

Jacques turns and hobbles back around the corner.

"Dammit!" I holster the gun and sprint down the corridor.

Seth and I reach the corner at the same time. We draw our weapons and round the corner, him high and me low, but no one's there. A hundred yards away, the elevator stands closed. The indicator on the wall above its doors puts it down on the first floor. We're on the sixth, so there's no way Jacques could've taken it.

"Not the elevator," I say.

Seth points down the hallway. "Stairwell is on the right."

We head for the door, but it just doesn't feel right. Unless Jacques fakes his hobble—and I suppose he could—there's no way he could've reached the stairwell or the elevator before we rounded the corner. Nevertheless, he had to have gone somewhere. Inside the open stairwell, we wait, listen, and peer up and down the flights. No sounds usher from above or below, nor do either of us detect movement of any kind.

Seth looks at me. Points at me then toward the rising stairs. I nod and start the ascent as he heads down. Two flights lead up to the roof, but the door remains barred and locked.

Jacques didn't come this way.

Seth and I meet down on the fourth-floor landing. The scowl he wears says it all.

"He's gone," Seth says, shoving his gun into its holster.

"Ugh! We almost had him." I holster my gun and exhale loudly. "Now what?"

Seth scratches the back of his neck. "You think he could've ducked into one of the apartments after going around the corner?"

I shrug. "It makes more sense than him just disappearing, but we weren't that far behind him. I'm certain we would've heard a door open and then click shut if he had."

"Maybe." He cocks his head. "Unless someone already had their door open. Busting in his apartment door made quite the noise."

"True."

We head back up to the sixth floor. As we near the corner of the corridor, I notice that the last apartment has a camera mounted above the door. It faces the corridor at a slight angle, and a red light indicates it's on.

I point up at the camera. "Look at that."

"Maybe we can see where he went," Seth says.

Thérèse comes around the corner, weapon drawn. She lowers it when she sees that it's just us. "What happened to you two?"

"Jacques was in the corridor behind us," I say. "We chased him around the corner but lost him."

Thérèse sighs. "That explains why his apartment was empty."

"There's a camera here," Seth says, pointing up at it. "Think you can get us in for a look?"

"Not likely without a warrant, but it's worth a shot." She knocks on the door. "This is the police. Open up," she says in French. She takes out her badge and holds it up toward the camera.

A minute later, several locks disengage, then the door cracks open. A young woman with dark hair and glasses peers through the opening. *"Oui?"*

"Is your camera recording?" Thérèse asks in French.

The young woman nods. *"Oui."*

"Would you be willing to show us the last fifteen minutes of footage?" Thérèse pulls twenty euros out of her pocket and offers it to the woman.

The young woman frowns, then nods. The door closes for a moment as she slides the safety chain off, then she opens the door and lets us in. Thérèse hands her the money.

"I am Frederique," she says. "Follow me."

She leads us into a corner room filled with computer equipment and sits down in front of a massive computer monitor. It's almost as wide as her entire desk. A few keystrokes brings up a high-definition view of the corridor outside her apartment. Utilizing a dial control, she begins rewinding the feed. Twelve minutes in, Seth and I walk backward into the frame and disappear on the other side. Moments later, Jacques is heading backward.

"Stop it right there," I say.

Thérèse repeats me in French and Frederique halts the video with Jacques in the middle of the frame, right in front of her doorway.

"Move it forward," I say, this time in French. "Slowly."

The girl advances the video frame by frame. Jacques hobbles. Hobbles. Vanishes.

The four of us collectively gasp. Then, the room falls silent.

What did I just see?

Seth leans closer to the monitor. "What just happened there?"

"I don't know," I say.

"Run it back," Thérèse says to Frederique.

She does, and we get the exact same result. For some reason, I expected the second viewing to be different. Like she'd turned the dial too quickly the first time or something and skipped ahead in the video.

"Did you lose the feed?" Thérèse asks.

"No." Frederique moves the video forward and backward. Jacques is there in one frame and gone the next. Seconds later, Seth and I come into the picture. "Look at the time stamp in the top right corner. There are no missing frames." She rolls it back then forward again. Sure enough, the milliseconds on the time stamp tick upward without a jump before and after Jacques disappears.

"Damn…" Seth says. He shakes his head. "My eyes are seeing it, but my brain just can't wrap itself around what happened."

"Same," I say.

My heart thunders in my chest as thoughts churn in my mind. Pieces of the case begin falling into place. None of the victims were murdered where their bodies were found, and René and Davit were not killed where Jacques encountered them, either.

I gasp. "He teleported them somewhere…"

Seth looks at me. "What?"

"The victims. He teleported them somewhere to kill them. Then he dumped their bodies the same way."

"Teleportation is impossible," Frederique says. We all look at her, and she shrugs. "What? I speak English, too."

Thérèse draws her weapon and points it at Frederique. The young woman's eyes bulge, and she cowers against the desk. "You've got two choices, young lady. Either you can hand over the footage, or I will arrest you and confiscate everything in this apartment. Decide quickly."

Frederique turns and quickly pulls a cable out of the computer. The video disappears from the screen, and an error pops up about a missing hard drive. She offers up the detached external SSD to Thérèse. "Everything is on here."

Thérèse snatches the drive out of Frederique's hands. "And there are no copies anywhere else?"

Frederique shakes her head vigorously. "No, I swear."

Thérèse snarls. "If you tell anyone about this video or if I find a copy of it online, you'll be prosecuted and thrown into prison, understood?"

Frederique nods. "I promise. No one will ever know."

Thérèse holsters her gun then wraps the cord around the drive. "Good." She turns and walks out of the room and toward the front of the apartment. The rest of us follow her. At the front door she turns and eyes Frederique.

"Oh, and one more thing. Remove the camera from the corridor. It's illegal to have it there." With that, Thérèse exits the apartment.

"I'm sorry about her," Seth says to Frederique as we're leaving. "I swear she's not always so unpleasant."

Liar.

A minute later, I enter Jacques's apartment for the first time. Somewhat like Thérèse's apartment, it's sparsely furnished. However, there are photos of Paris hanging all over the walls.

Pierre walks out of one of the back rooms. "Where have you all been?"

"We almost had Jacques," Seth says.

"And then he teleported," I finish.

Pierre just stands there for several seconds. His brow furrows. "Did—did you just say he *teleported?*"

Thérèse holds up the drive she took from Frederique. "Evidence is right here. Trust me, I wouldn't have believed it if I hadn't seen it with my own eyes."

"Teleported…" Pierre strokes his chin, then shakes his head. "That's a new one."

"And it explains everything we've discovered," I say.

Seth crosses his arms. "Yeah, but there's one major issue I think you're all overlooking."

"What?" Thérèse asks.

"How the hell are we going to arrest someone who can teleport?"

Pierre sighs loudly. "That's a damn good question."

"Hate to say it, but we've got just one choice," Thérèse says. "We kill him."

Pierre raises his hand and glares at Thérèse. "Whoa, whoa, whoa. Hold on. No one is killing *anyone.* You say something like that again, and I'll have your badge. Understood?"

"No," Thérèse growls. "This man has killed eleven people and will keep on killing until he's stopped. Therefore, he must be stopped. And in order to do that, he must be captured or killed. Unless you know something that I don't, we can't capture someone who can teleport out of a locked room. So, what other choice do we have besides killing him?"

Somehow, I find myself on the same page with Thérèse again. Mostly. There's no doubt that the Chrono Slasher must be stopped, but there must be a way to capture him.

"I see two viable paths forward," I say. The others look at me. "First, we could make a call to our mutual friends and see if they have a solution to our teleportation problem. If they can't provide us with a solution, we turn to the other side."

"The other side?" Pierre frowns.

Seth's gaze hardens. "I know what you're thinking, Alice, and I don't like it."

"I don't like it either," I say, "but Reagan might be our only solution."

"And who is Reagan?" Pierre asks.

"An enemy of our enemy," Thérèse says. "We'll cross that bridge if we need to. Right now, we need to figure out how to track Jacques down."

"All three of you are getting ahead of yourselves," Pierre says. "Take a look around this place. Not only do we not have a single shred of evidence linking Jacques Milan to the murders, but we have no motive, either."

"That's not true," I say. "We have the picture of his hand in the video with Li Qiang, this new video proving he can teleport, plus what I saw while mind tethered to René Edelmann and Davit Muradyan."

"None of that will make a bit of difference in a court of law," Thérèse says. "Your testimony, no matter how compelling, is invalid. Plus, the video with the hand is blurry and could be anything. And who would believe that the man can teleport? Yeah, we have video evidence of him doing it, but I can find thousands of videos just like it online and in movies. We would look like fools."

"Okay, so what's our path forward?" Seth asks. "We have no evidence he's our guy and no way of capturing him long enough to interrogate him, either. Aside from killing him and having Alice dive into his mind, we're dead in the water, right?"

My eyes focus on the far wall. A single picture not of just Paris but of Jacques and his son Raphaël standing beneath the Eiffel Tower. It's another avenue.

"We need to focus on finding the son, Raphaël." The more I think about it, the more I believe he's the key that unravels this case. "His disappearance happened right around the time the murders began. It can't be coincidence."

"What are you thinking?" Seth asks. "He's dead or something?"

"Maybe, and if so, it could possibly tie him to our first victim," I say.

Pierre nods slowly. "I see where you're going with this. A revenge killing turns Jacques into a vigilante serial killer. Honestly, it's the first thing that's made half a milliliter of sense with this case."

Thérèse scowls. "I don't like it."

Seth looks at her. "Which part?"

"Any of it." She crosses her arms over her chest. "We're chasing a ghost that can't be captured and trying to find a kid who's apparently been missing for the last year. We might as well be blindfolded in the middle of a forest with a bow and a single arrow and a target a thousand miles away that we must hit or die." Thérèse raises her arms. "It's impossible."

After all I've seen and been through in my life, I no longer believe that anything is impossible. Our minds are capable of doing the impossible, like connecting with the dead.

Or teleporting.

Seth shakes his head. "So what? You think we should just give up? Let this guy go on killing forever because it's too hard?"

Thérèse shrugs. "At least his victims aren't innocent people, right?"

"According to the law they are," Pierre counters. "And the law is the only thing that separates us from people like our killer. If we fail to uphold it, we all lose."

"Well, we still have two paths to explore," I say. "Find the boy and find out if there's a way to contain someone who can teleport."

Pierre nods. "I'll contact our mutual friends. The rest of you figure out what happened to Raphaël Milan."

I walk over to the picture of Jacques and Raphaël and snap a photo of it.

* * * * *

Seth crashes on the bed as soon as we get back to the hotel, but there's no way I'll be able to sleep right now. My mind struggles to grasp the mechanics of teleporting. Oddly enough, my name for the killer fits even better than I knew. He slashes through time and steps into the rift.

The Chrono Slasher.

How strange the world has become in the last few years of my life, and it will become stranger still. Paris and all its glory stretches beyond the glass doors of the balcony, its lights breathing life into the dark skies. My mind conjures up *Interview With The Vampire* and Louis and Lestat. Once, I believed vampires to be fantasy. Monsters that lurked in the pages of horror stories but never outside of them. Now, I can't help but wonder if they exist, too. My gut says so.

How long will it be before I cross paths with one?

As much as I'd love to stare at Paris and fantasize about vampires, it won't bring me any closer to finding Raphaël. To my knowledge, there's only one thing I can do that might right now. I pull out my phone and speed dial my superhero.

Kenny answers. "You, again. Did you find your man?"

"We did, but he got away."

"Dang. Sorry to hear that."

"Yeah. Anyway, I was wondering if you might be able to do another search for me."

"Of course. Name it, and I'll jump right in."

"It could be a bit trickier than my previous requests. We're looking for a young man who disappeared a year ago."

"Oh, well that's gonna be a problem. No one keeps archive footage that long. Banks are at the long end, keeping records for about six months. Most other places only keep data for one to three months. It just takes up too much space these days with cameras having much higher resolution and recording nonstop."

"Right. Hadn't thought about that. Anyway, I'll send you the young man's photo. Maybe we'll get lucky and spot him somewhere recently."

"Sounds good." Silence hangs on the line for several seconds before Kenny talks again. "Oh, I also wanted you to know that everything Seth told you about his past checks out. At least as far as where he was born and serving time."

"You're certain?"

"Not one hundred percent, but I used some software I wrote a few years back to analyze Seth's facial features with those of Klaus Rein. They matched perfectly. Naturally, I have no way of checking Romanian records from the late eighties and early nineties as they're not online and may not even exist anymore."

I sigh with relief. "I understand, and thank you, Kenny. You don't know how much better that makes me feel."

"You're welcome. It's really weird thinking that Seth isn't Seth."

"I know." I sigh as I look at my reflection in the window. "How about we put the past back where it belongs and focus on the here and now?"

"Good idea. I'll let you know if I get any hits on the new search."

"Okay. Talk to you soon."

After hanging up with Kenny, I retreat to the sofa, both relieved and concerned as I sink into its soft leather cushions. If Raphaël can't be located via video footage, how will we ever get to the truth and capture the Chrono Slasher?

CHAPTER SEVENTEEN

SETH AND I LIE on the sofa in our hotel suite living room. He's fighting off sleep, but I can't keep my mind from thinking about Jacques's missing son.

I smack Seth's leg. "It's been weeks, and we're still no closer to locating Raphaël or figuring out what happened to him."

He groans. "Yeah, I know."

"None of his friends have seen him or heard from him since the week before the first murder back in March of 2019. It concerns me, especially given his age. He could've been trafficked."

"You're right, and I'm concerned about his wellbeing just as much as you are, but what can we do about it when we've got nothing to go on?"

"I don't know, and it frustrates me to no end."

Seth strokes the back of my hand. "I know it helps for you to hash things out, so keep talking. What else do we know?"

I close my eyes. "Well, let's see. Raphaël posted on Instagram and Twitter multiple times a day right up until his disappearance, but he's posted nothing else since."

"Right, and we both know what it likely means."

I shoot Seth a glare. "Don't you dare say he's dead."

His brow furrows. "Never would without a body or evidence, but it isn't looking good for him. He hasn't made or received a single phone call or text message, nor has his cell phone pinged any cell towers in almost a year. For all intents and purposes, Raphaël has vanished from the face of the earth."

"Ugh." I shake my head. "What sucks even more about all this is that Jake and Dakota offered no solution as to how we might detain someone who can teleport."

"Like it matters," Seth says. "We have no way of locating Jacques, and he hasn't been seen since that day outside his apartment."

"I know." I close my eyes again.

What else could possibly go wrong?

My phone starts buzzing back on the kitchen counter. Seth gets up and retrieves it. "Looks like Jake's on the line." He hands me the phone then heads for the bedroom.

I lie flat on the sofa and stare at the ceiling. "Hello?"

"Sorry to bother you darlin' but I've got bad news."

Seriously, God? Now what?

Every muscle in my body tenses up. "Let me have it."

"As you're aware, we've been monitorin' and searchin' every last unit at Dunharrow Storage, top to bottom. Unfortunately, we came up with nothin'."

My gut wrenches. "You're not pulling my leg, are you?"

"Lord, I wish I was. We practically tore the place apart lookin' for that Shadow Mirror."

"Ugh." Anger stirs in the pit of my stomach, and I sock the sofa. "Reagan must've lied to me."

"Afraid so. We've had eyes on the place for two months and searched every vehicle leavin'. Not a peep."

"Sounds like I need to pay the little bastard a visit."

"Might be worth another go at him, but if he lied to you while under the influence of sodium thiopental, I'm guessin' your odds are low."

"I know, but I have to try."

"I hear ya. Well, be safe, darlin'."

"Thanks, Jake. Talk to you again soon." I shove the phone into my front pocket and brood.

Seth returns and settles down next to me, lifting my legs onto his lap. "Bad news I take it?"

"Reagan lied about the stupid mirror."

"Mmm." He nods. "I had a feeling the truth serum wasn't working."

"Me, too. But I lied to myself about it anyway."

He leans over and kisses my cheek. "Sounds like we need to pay him a visit."

"No doubt about that." I sigh. "Guess I'll call Pierre and see if he can get us in to see Reagan."

Seth raises an eyebrow. "Really? Didn't think you wanted Pierre involved in any of the Reagan business."

"He certainly doesn't need to know anything about what happened in our prior hotel suite, and he won't need to. I'll just tell him that Reagan is an informant of mine and that I heard he was locked up here in Paris."

"Alright. We'll play it your way." He lifts my legs up and slides himself off the sofa.

"Where are you going now?" I ask, not wanting him to leave.

Seth pats his stomach. "Thought I'd whip up some breakfast for dinner." He cocks his head. "You not hungry?"

The bombardment of bad news today should've killed my appetite, but my stomach is tough. Just the thought of food makes it rumble loudly. "Oh, I'm definitely hungry."

Seth smiles. "Good. You just relax, and I'll have breakfast ready in no time." He walks back toward the kitchen.

I retrieve my phone and dial Pierre's number. It rings once and goes straight to voicemail. After leaving him a brief message about Reagan, I lie back and close my eyes. The constant clinking and banging Seth makes in the kitchen fades as I return to each of the crime scenes in my mind. The futile task keeps me from brooding over all our failures.

Pierre calls me back right after Seth summons me to the kitchen for bacon and eggs.

"Hi, Pierre." I turn in the chair and face the living room. "Please tell me you can get us in to see Reagan."

"I'm afraid that won't be possible."

"It's because we're Americans, right?"

"No, it has nothing to do with either of you. It turns out that we are not detaining a Reagan Clark."

My pulse spikes. "They let him go?"

"No, no. I checked back several months. No Reagan Clark has ever been detained."

He wasn't detained?

All thoughts of food die as my stomach knots. "Okay, Pierre. I guess I must've been misinformed. Sorry I bothered you."

"If you don't mind me asking, who told you we had detained him?"

"I'd rather not say, but thank you."

"I understand, and you're welcome." He pauses, then, "Look, I need to run. If anything comes up, give me a call."

"I will." I hang up and throw my phone at the back of the sofa. "Ugh!"

Seth rounds the counter and stands in front of me with his arms crossed. "What's happened now?"

"The bitch lied to us," I say with vitriol. "She never took Reagan into custody that night."

Seth scowls. "That doesn't make any sense. Why would Thérèse lie about it?"

I ball my hands. "Because she's a liar."

He glances back at the sofa. My phone lay in pieces on the floor next to it. "Guess I'll give her a call."

"Make her come over here. I want to see her face when she finds out we know."

"I'm not sure that's the best idea right now."

"I don't care what you think, Seth. Call her and get her over here right now, or I will."

"Fine." He dials her number and walks over to the balcony doors.

She'd better have a damn good explanation, or I'm gonna kill her.

* * * * *

An hour later, Thérèse stands outside our hotel suite door. Water drips from her rain jacket and folded-up umbrella, leaving small puddles on the floor. Unfortunately, she looks no worse for wear, her perfect hair and makeup undisturbed.

I hate her.

"Well, are you going to invite me in or what?" she asks.

I step back and open the door farther. "Come on in."

She doesn't even make it over to the sofa before I extend my claws and lay into her.

"You've been lying to us for two months, and I want to know why."

Thérèse turns and faces me, her eyes narrowed and shoulders tense. She obviously knows what I'm referring to. "Lied to you? About what?"

I stalk toward her, fists balled and ready for action. "I'm in no mood to play games, Thérèse. You never turned Reagan in."

Tension eases from her shoulders. "Yes, I did, but we had no evidence to detain him."

"Even if that were true, which it isn't, why would you keep it from me? You saw what he did before."

"All the mirrors were removed from this suite, so I figured you'd be safe from him."

I stare her down. Pummel her with daggers. "Stop lying, Thérèse. I spoke with Pierre. He confirmed that no one with the name Reagan Clark was ever brought in by you or anyone else."

Seth joins my side, his arms crossed and muscles flexed. "What did you do, Thérèse? Take him somewhere and kill him?"

God, I love this man.

Thérèse forces air through her nostrils. "That's absurd."

"Hardly." I scoff. "You wanted to kill the spray paint guy the first day we met you, so it's far from absurd."

She scowls at me. "I never would've shot him."

"I'm not sure I believe you, but it doesn't matter. What does matter is Reagan. Where is he? What happened?" I demand.

Thérèse closes her eyes for a second and sighs heavily. "Fine. I'll tell you the truth."

"So spill it," I say.

She retreats to the sofa and sits down. After a long pause, she begins. "When you two left the old suite and came up to this one, I began escorting Reagan out of the building. We walked down the corridor and were waiting for the elevator when I thought I heard a door open back down the corridor.

"I turned to see if anyone was in the corridor, but it was empty. When I turned back, Reagan was gone. Vanished into thin air. I searched everywhere for him even though I knew it was pointless, and I've been keeping an eye out for him ever since."

"There's a mirror by the elevators," I say, remembering it when I'd paced the corridor earlier that same evening.

Thérèse nods. "I know, and I haven't been able to stop thinking about it since that night."

I continue my thought, "But Reagan said he couldn't use another mirror."

Seth takes a seat on the opposite end of the sofa from Thérèse. "Unless that was a lie, too."

Reagan the liar.

"Nothing surprises me when it comes to that man. He's a pathological liar. And damned good at it, too."

I begin pacing in front of the sofa. It seems this case contains just three things: bodies, questions, and lies. As much as I hate that Thérèse lied to us about taking Reagan in and that I wouldn't trust her as far as I could throw her, I still believe her story. What would she have to gain at this point by lying further?

Nothing.

After Thérèse leaves, Seth warms up our dinner in the microwave. The eggs are beyond rubbery, and the bacon has gone from crispy to floppy, but both satisfy my renewed hunger all the same. Nevertheless, unrest stirs deep within me. I need some fresh air to clear my head, and a trip to the balcony won't cut it.

Jacket in hand, I head for the suite door.

Seth arm bars me at the door. "Where do you think you're going?" His brow creases. "It's late."

I push his arm down. "I need some air."

"Then I'll go with you."

"No. It's been a rough day, and I need to be alone for a while."

He raises his arm back up. "If you think I'm gonna let you wander the streets of Paris alone at night, then you're crazier than I thought."

"Don't play the tough husband right now, Seth. I'm not in the mood for it. Just let me go."

Seth draws a deep breath and exhales slowly. "Okay, but only on one condition. You take Reagan's gun with you."

"Fine."

He looks back toward the living room. "And my cellphone since yours is in pieces on the floor." I nod and wait for him to return with the gun and phone.

A few minutes later, I step outside the hotel and into the frigid Paris night. My breath plumes in the moist air, but at least the rain has stopped for now. Heading east, I aim for Arc de Triomphe. The monument isn't necessarily my destination, but it's a good starting point.

In the distance, the bells of Notre-Dame Cathedral catch my attention as they sound out the nine o'clock hour. Thirteen strikes in all counting the four that signal the top of the hour. The beautiful sound leads my mind back to the map. Back to the clock. Back to what Jacques said to Davit. Or rather to me.

The center of everything.

Several moments pass before I realize that my feet have started carrying me toward Île de la Cité and Notre-Dame Cathedral. By the time I reach the desolate cathedral, its bells are chiming the new hour once again. They sound even more beautiful and haunting up close.

Shadows veil parts of the gothic structure, giving it a menacing air with the chimeras and gargoyles guarding its balconies and towers. Curiously, a faint light emits from the Portal of St. Anne to the right. As I approach, I notice that one of the doors sits ajar.

Why would the door be open at this hour?

My skin prickles as I ease the door open and slip inside. Ahead, the nave sits empty, save one spot toward the front on the left. No doubt remains in my mind as to who the cloaked figure is that kneels in front of the chair.

After silencing Seth's phone, I draw Reagan's golden gun. A deep, ragged breath expels from my lungs. My hands tremble, and my heart quakes as I watch the Chrono Slasher from afar.

Seconds tick by as I stand here and listen, but the cathedral refuses to stir. No priests. No caretaker. Just him, me, and the deafening silence between us.

It's now or never, Alice.

CHAPTER EIGHTEEN

THE LAST NINE WEEKS led me to the doors of Notre-Dame Cathedral. Through them and into its nave. To this very moment. Yet I never expected it to turn out this way. How could anyone have?

The cathedral's 800-year-old limestone walls rise around me. Encase me like a stone sarcophagus. Ribbed vaults soar far above my head, dark with night. Wings of bats or perhaps dragons. Beneath my feet sits a checkerboard of black and white marble tiles. Mesmerizing, they anchor me to the floor.

Ahead loom the golden altar and cross. Both luminous, soaking in the faint light and shining bright. But neither object holds my gaze. It remains locked onto Jacques Milan—the Chrono Slasher.

Gooseflesh prickles my skin as it ripples down my arms and legs, his last word still hanging in my mind, ready to be plucked.

"Him."

My mind teeters on the edge of understanding yet fails to take the plunge. How would killing him put someone else's life in danger? The moments of our conversation replay in my head.

"One more step, and I'll send you straight to hell," I'd said.

His reply came slowly. *"One more step will end my suffering, and I so long for it, but doing so will not save…"*

Tears fell from his eyes. Splattered on the tile floor. Eroded portions of the wall of hatred I'd built up around him.

Empathy filled my voice. *"Finish what you were going to say, Jacques. Killing you will not save what?"*

Silence. Deafening silence filled the cathedral. Then, a haunting, hollow whisper emitted from his lips. *"Him."*

Him.

The word reverberates in my chest. Shakes my heart to its core. Leaves me breathless.

Him.

My mind focuses on Seth. Losing him would not just devastate me. It would kill me. Rip my heart to pieces. If Seth is the "him" Jacques speaks of, I must know more. Must know everything.

Emotions overwhelm me as Jacques and I stare each other down, neither of us willing to make the first move toward an inevitable death.

Time marches forward all around us, yet we boldly stand outside of its constructs. Alone in a bubble of silence. At odds with ourselves and with each other.

As the seconds tick away, Reagan's FNX-45 Tactical FDE clutched in my hands becomes a lead weight, slowly pulling my arms ever downward. I fight against fatigue and take a step back, distancing myself from Jacques the only recourse I have. Even so, it's futile.

No matter how hard I concentrate, understanding of his words fails me. Finally, I shatter the shroud of silence hanging between us. "Killing you won't save *him*? What's that supposed to mean?" My voice echoes through the dark nave, notes of anger sending its pitch an octave higher. "A bullet through the back of your skull will make the world a better place."

"Hatred distorts your vision, Detective. Because of it, you've become far more blind than you were when you were a child."

"Congratulations, Jacques. You've looked me up on the internet. Studied my past like any good psycho would. So what? You think that gives you some sort of advantage over me?"

He shakes his head slowly. "You misunderstand."

"Do I? Then help me fill in the blanks. What great secret do you keep that I've failed to unbury?"

"I am little more than an obstacle altering and blocking your view of the truth, Alice. Open your eyes, and you will discover that I am not the monster you claim me to be."

"Monster. An interesting word choice. Have you not looked in the mirror recently? You're a perfect example of God's wrath. His judgment manifested in flesh."

"Am I?" Jacques smiles faintly. "Not minutes ago, you led me to believe you didn't really know God. And now you think my sins are the cause of my deformities. That's quite interesting."

"You know I was in your apartment the other day. I saw all the pictures from your past. A few years ago, you had no physical deformities from what I could tell. One might've considered you handsome, even. But now… Now, it's hard to look at you without fighting off repulsion. If what's happened to you isn't a manifestation of your wickedness, then what is it?"

Jacques gestures toward one of the chairs. "May I sit?"

I nod, then take the chair on the opposite side of the nave isle, keeping the gun aimed at him as he settles in the chair.

"Thank you," he says. "As you can imagine, I haven't the strength to stand for long periods anymore."

"So, what am I missing?"

Jacques raises his left sleeve, exposing his wrist and the reddish mark on the inside of it. Unfortunately, his deformed arm makes it impossible to know what the mark once looked like.

"Like you, I am different than others in this world," he says.

My gaze lingers on his wrist. "Yes, I know. You can teleport."

"I suppose that's one word for it." He tilts his head to one side and studies me. "I cannot be certain, but I assume using your gift comes at a cost. Am I correct?"

"Yes." That's all he's gonna get from me.

"Then you do understand." Jacques sweeps his arms down the length of his body. "All these deformities are the costs I've paid for using mine."

"You mean…"

He nods. "When I teleport someone or something other than myself, a piece of me gets lost."

God, I thought the price of my gift was high.

Another thought strikes me.

"Killing doesn't restore you?" I immediately regret asking the question. It reveals a truth about me that he has no right knowing. But I can't take it back now.

Jacques leans forward. Regards me with his single, green eye. Finally, he shrugs. "Perhaps it would, but the cost would be too high."

Rage pulls me off the chair and halfway across the aisle. "Don't you dare pretend you're innocent! There are eleven bodies with your name to them, Jacques. Eleven!"

He nods solemnly. "Yes, I know, and their deaths are tragic. However, we have not reached the end. Yet another must die."

"Why? Haven't you fulfilled your sick ritual? All the hands on the clock have aligned."

"Yes, Alice, but it must end where it began. Night must become day."

His words have twisted my mind to the point where I don't even know what he's saying anymore.

"If another must die, then it should be you," I growl. "I can end it right now with a single bullet."

He sighs, clearly frustrated. "Have you not heard a word I've said? You cannot stop time, Alice. Events are already in motion and cannot be altered."

"You're not making any sense." I step closer. "What are you not telling me? Do you have an accomplice?"

"An accomplice?" He scoffs. "Look at me, Alice. Do you think I give up my flesh willingly? Certainly not. Each time I use my gift on someone other than myself, I draw nearer to taking my own life."

The man is clearly delusional. "How can I believe a word you're saying?

You're obviously aware of my gift, so you know all that I've seen. René and Davit died from your touch."

"Did they?" He shakes his head slowly before lifting it and his gaze to the vaulted ceiling. "God, you have blinded her."

I'm really getting tired of people telling me that. My hands squeeze the gun in a death grip. "I'm not blind, Jacques. I know what I saw," I growl.

Jacques sighs. "Then your mind is made up about me."

"You haven't given me a single reason to believe otherwise."

"Have I not?" He regards me with a sense of compassion. "Then listen. I am but a tool. I gather the grapes but do not press them for wine."

I shift my feet and regrip the gun. "If you're being used, then tell me why and by who. Give me a name, and I might be able to help you."

By putting you down.

His one-eyed gaze hardens. "Even if I knew, I would never tell you. The risk would be far too great."

I groan. "What's that supposed to mean? Who is in danger? Who is *him*? Is it Seth? Your son?"

His gaze remains defiant. "The answers lie within the blood. Within the symbols it powers."

"Enough with the riddles, Jacques. This is your last warning. You either explain yourself or you die."

"Listen to me. When the time comes, you must enter the darkness that hides beneath the light of the cross. Remember, only a sacrifice will make the path known. Heed the cross, and never forget that another life hangs in the balance." He sighs heavily and closes his eye. A sorrowful groan rises from within him. "Forgive me, but I can tell you no more."

"That's not good—"

Jacques launches off his chair. Knocks it over.

Thwack!

My finger slides over the gun's trigger.

Pulls it just as he collides with me.

Muzzle flashes red.

Jacques's face contorts with pain.

Then, a flash of liquid lightning consumes me from the inside out.

Light fissures splinter across the cathedral ceiling, creating a shattered mirror effect across my vision. From those fissures pour forth deep shadows. Then the shadows come for me. Rip me apart and devour me until nothing remains but perfect darkness.

* * * * *

Jacques's hands wrap around my throat. Two vises.

Hatred burns in his single eye, his green iris flickering like flames as he glares down at me.

"You shouldn't have come, Alice."

Clang!

The cathedral bells ring in my ears as I fight to break free from his grasp. But then he plunges my head into the water. Deep down until his face and the world distort above its surface.

Flailing does nothing but tire me out, his strength far surpassing mine.

Clang!

The water ripples as the bells sound again.

Then, my body betrays me.

Does the unthinkable.

Draws a breath.

Water fills my mouth. My throat. My lungs.

Sends me into a coughing fit.

Lungs afire, I fight harder.

Struggle to free myself from his grasp.

Bubbles float to the surface when I scream his name. "Jacques!"

* * * * *

My eyes snap open and the nightmare fades. Rain pelts my face and fills my gaping mouth as I stare up at a dark, brooding sky. I turn my head and empty the water from my mouth. Cough up more from saturated lungs and spit it out.

Blades of grass scratch against my cheek, disorienting me further as I lie there and catch my breath. Pain pulses through my head as I pull myself up into a sitting position and work to gain my bearings.

At first, nothing about my surroundings looks familiar. Grass lies beneath me, and an outcropping of bushes and flowers rise in front of me. A short, chain-link fence made of green pipe stands just beyond the bushes. Farther still, I finally see something familiar. The Fountain of the Virgin rises toward the eastern horizon.

Clang!

The Notre-Dame Cathedral bells startle me. A hundred yards behind me looms the gothic cathedral, its flying buttresses lit up against the night sky. I wait for the next strike, but no more follow.

One o'clock in the morning.

I can't remember what time it was when I entered the cathedral, but one thing's for certain. "Seth's gonna kill me."

It takes a great deal of effort to pull myself up, my head still pulsing with anger. Reagan's golden gun lies a few feet away from me, nestled in the rain-slicked grass. A quick check of the chamber and magazine confirms what I'm beginning to recall: there's a bullet missing.

I… I shot Jacques.

Shoving the gun into my waistband, I head back toward the right portal on the West Façade. Unlike earlier, the doors stand closed and secured. Two questions immediately come to mind: did Jacques dodge the bullet I fired, and did he close the doors? Either both are true, or both are false. If the latter, he must have an accomplice. These thoughts trigger another epiphany and freeze me where I stand.

Jacques must've opened the door. He was waiting for me.

* * * * *

As I begin the trek back to the hotel, I call the hotel suite.

"Hello?" I can tell right away that Seth's upset.

"Hey, babe. It's me."

Seth screams into the phone, "Good God, Alice! Where are you? I've been trying to reach you for hours. I thought you were dead or worse."

That phrase has always annoyed me, but now's certainly not the time to bring it up. "Don't worry, I'm on my way back now."

"On your way back from where?"

"Notre-Dame Cathedral."

"Seriously? You said you just needed some air. I wouldn't have let you go alone if I'd known you were going there. Ugh! What were you thinking?"

"I don't know, Seth, okay? I didn't intend to go there. It just happened."

"You realize that's almost four miles from here, right?"

"No, but it does explain why my calves and feet are a bit tired."

He sighs loudly. "I'm so relieved and pissed at you right now."

"I know, and I'll make it up to you. I promise."

"What are you not telling me, Alice? What happened?"

Two years ago, I promised Seth I'd never lie to him again, and I've kept that promise to this day. It's the only way I can live with myself. "Jacques was there."

"At the cathedral?"

"Yes. I… confronted him."

"Dammit, Alice! What's wrong with you? You should've called me as soon as you saw him."

"I thought about it, but I also didn't want to lose the opportunity."

Seth groans. "You're reckless."

"I know I am, but I don't mean to be."

"So what happened?"

"We talked. He made me mad. I got in his face, and he attacked me. The gun went off, and then I woke up in a small park on the south side of the cathedral."

"Wait, what? He attacked you?"

"Yes, but not in a violent way."

"You're not making any sense. How can someone attack you in a non-violent way? Especially when it causes you to shoot them?"

"I don't know. He lunged at me. I panicked. Shot him. Or thought I did. Then I woke up in the grass with a mouthful of rain."

"You shot him and then he carried you outside?"

My mind plays back through the entire confrontation. "No… he teleported me there I think."

"Why?"

It's a fair question, especially given what Jacques told me about what it does to him. The more I contemplate it, the less it makes sense.

"Honestly, I don't know. He could've just teleported himself away."

"Yeah, that's what I meant."

"Right."

So why did you teleport me, Jacques? Why would you risk your life doing so?

It takes a minute for the answer to become clear. "I think he wanted me to understand and feel the experience for myself."

"Okay, but why?"

"Because… it explains why the victims had no memories beyond him teleporting them." The more I ponder it the more certain I become. "Yes, that's it. It was before midnight that we fought and before he teleported me. I didn't become conscious again until right at one o'clock. I know because I heard the bells chime once."

"One? Seriously? What the hell happened after that?"

"Nothing. I tried to get back inside the cathedral, but the doors were locked. That's when I called you."

"It's three-twenty, Alice."

"Three… oh, I see. That single chime must've been the third and not the first."

"So you were knocked out for several hours."

"Yeah, I guess so."

"No wonder his victims have no chance."

"Yeah."

"You're lucky he didn't kill you."

"No, he's lucky I didn't kill him."

"Where are you at now?" he asks.

"Um… I just passed the Luxor Obelisk."

"That's still two miles from here."

"I know, and talking to you on the phone is slowing me down."

"Don't hang up, Alice."

"Relax, Seth. I'll be there as soon as I can."

I end the call and run like my life depends on it.

CHAPTER NINETEEN

IT'S SATURDAY NIGHT, AND we're back at Thérèse's apartment for dinner and discussion of the case. Pierre's been quiet most of the evening, brooding over something. He says it's nothing when I ask, but I'm no fool. I'm confident his mood has everything to do with me and my encounter with the Chrono Slasher, and I don't blame him. Going into the cathedral and facing Jacques alone was a foolish move. Not only that, but I'm certain I gained nothing from doing it, either.

Seth takes a long draw from his beer bottle, then peers at each of us. "It feels like we've come to another roadblock in this case. Any ideas on how we should proceed?"

No answer comes to mind as I stare at the plate of unfinished fish and shrimp tacos sitting in the middle of the table. The thought of eating another bite makes my stomach cramp, and the once pleasant smell now tortures me.

"That's a good question," Thérèse says. "Thanks to Detective Bergman, we know a lot more about our killer than we did a few months ago. Having said that, it feels like we're destined to play cleanup forever."

I push an abandoned piece of shrimp around my paper plate with my fork. "You know you can call me Alice, Thérèse."

She cocks her head as she stares at me from across the table. "We've moved past all the formalities then?"

It's amazing how she still finds ways to annoy me. A rare art form. But I'm good at the game, too. "Tonight, I'm a guest in your home."

Her eyes narrow. "Oh, I see. It's the setting that determines the formality. I'll remember that."

"I'm sure you will." I turn my attention toward Pierre. "Jacques told me that the killings aren't done."

Pierre removes his glasses, closes his eyes, and pinches the bridge of his nose. He looks far older than the man I remember meeting a few months back. This case not only drives him toward an early retirement but perhaps an early grave.

Don't think like that, Alice.

"And why should they be? We have no solution to stop him." Pierre pulls out a cloth and begins cleaning his glasses. "Even if we maintain surveillance of his apartment and Notre-Dame Cathedral indefinitely, I fear it will make little difference. By the time we react to his presence at either location, he'll have vanished into nothing."

Seth nods. "Hate to say it, but you're right. He's a ghost."

"And bulletproof." I close my eyes for a minute and relive my encounter with Jacques in the cathedral. "I shot him pointblank, but you said there was no evidence of it in the cathedral."

"None," Pierre confirms. "Nothing damaged. No bullet casing. No blood. Absolutely nothing."

Thérèse eyes Pierre. "Do you think Jacques cleaned it up himself?"

"No." Pierre returns his glasses to his face. "We used fluorescent lights to examine the central aisle from one end of the nave to the other and didn't find a single drop of blood anywhere."

"Maybe someone had already cleaned the cathedral by the time you arrived," Seth says.

Pierre shakes his head. "I personally interrogated Father Toussaint. He unlocked the cathedral himself and was the only one there when I arrived. If someone had used a cleaner, I would've smelled it."

I turn to Seth. "I think I know why."

"Well, we'd all like to hear your explanation," Thérèse says.

Pierre nods when I look at him.

I stare at the empty beer bottle next to my plate. "What if the bullet didn't leave the gun until after Jacques teleported me outside?"

Seth leans back in his chair and cocks his head. "You think it happened that fast?"

"Yeah. The last thing I remember after he touched me and before the shadows consumed me was the muzzle flash."

Thérèse leans over the table. "Did you hear a bang?"

A bang?

The moment plays over and over in my mind, but I don't recall hearing anything after Jacques's chair hit the floor. "I'm not sure, but I don't think so. When he touched me, it seemed to suck the air out of the room like a vacuum, and each moment expanded into seconds."

"Then we'll likely find the spent casing near where you woke up in the grass," Pierre says.

"Maybe, but even if we do, what good will it do us?" I ask.

Seth scowls. "Well, we'll at least know if you shot Jacques or not."

I skewer the lone shrimp with my fork, imagining it to be Jacques's heart. "Unless he turns up dead somewhere, does it matter?"

"No," Pierre admits, "and it scares me."

"You know what scares me?" Thérèse asks. "Empty glasses and bottles. I'll grab us some more beers from the refrigerator and fetch some cookies, too." No one argues with her as she gets up and heads around the wall and into the kitchen.

While Thérèse occupies herself in the kitchen, Seth and Pierre continue the conversation about the case, or the lack thereof. For me, it's time for a breather. I rise from my chair and head into the dark living room. It takes a few seconds to locate the knob on the floor lamp. A single turn brings the lamp to life and casts shadows across the barren room.

The same stack of books sit on the TV tray next to the leather recliner, seemingly untouched from the last time we were here. It's not surprising at all. Thérèse works as much as Seth and I do.

As I settle into the recliner, I notice a book wedged between the left arm and the side of the cushion. Its brown leather binding blends well with the chair, giving it the perfect camouflage. I'm uncertain if it was there the last time I was in this room, and I wonder if its placement isn't a coincidence.

I unwedge the book and hold it beneath the yellowish lamplight. No title graces its cover or spine, but there are many strange symbols stamped into the leather. As my finger glides over them, a realization strikes me. I've seen them all before.

The Shadow Mirror's frame.

Hairs on my nape rise, and my pulse doubles. Triples as I crack the book open. The first page is stamped with black ink. It says "PROPERTY OF" in German with a line below it. Scrawled across the line is the name Klaus Von Astner.

The next page contains a title handwritten in German: "Bridging Worlds: A Theoretical Guide."

Bridging worlds…

Someone's drawn a crude picture below the title in black ink. Two stone arches angled away from each other with a brick path or bridge spanning the distance between them. A person stands beneath each arch, the two of them facing each other.

Every following page is handwritten and contains more crude drawings of arches, platforms with troughs, clocks, and other things I can't identify. Many things are scribbled out or written over, and notes line the margins on both sides of the pages. Most are in German, but there are several in French, too. The handwriting of the ones in French does not match the German. I close the book and study its cover again.

Why would Thérèse have this?

Thérèse walks into the living room and halts when she sees me sitting in the chair. Her gaze immediately focuses on the leather-bound journal in my hands.

"What are you doing?" she asks. Her tone sounds pleasant enough, but I can tell she's perturbed. The question is why.

"Needed a break, so I'm just sitting here." I raise the journal. "Found this book stuffed in the chair. Its title sounds quite interesting."

"Does it?" She approaches slowly, her hands folded behind her back and her eyes locked on the journal. "I don't read German, so I wouldn't know."

You're lying, Thérèse, but why?

"Really? Then why did you have it stuffed between the cushion and the arm rest?"

She shrugs. "I guess it must've fallen off the TV tray."

And wedged itself into the crack? Nice try.

"Where did you get it?" I ask, expecting yet another lie.

"Oh, I found it at an old bookstore in Munich several years back. The symbols stamped into the cover fascinated me, so I had to buy it."

My attention returns to the journal. "Do you know what they mean?"

She reaches forward and snatches the journal out of my hands. "Wish I did. I tried searching for many of them online but failed to come up with anything of meaning." She smiles. "I don't know if it's the feel of the leather or the symbols themselves, but sitting in that chair and running my fingers across them after a long day calms me."

She's still lying about something, but I'm not sure about which parts. Maybe all of it.

"It does have a nice feel to it," I say. "As it turns out, I'm familiar with many of its symbols. Would you mind if I borrowed it for a few days?"

Thérèse pulls the journal to her chest and scowls down at me. "Borrow it?" She scoffs. "For what purpose?"

"Well, for starters, I'm pretty good with German."

"Really?" Thérèse flips the journal open. "Then you can tell me what wel-wel-ten uber bruck-in means." She stammers over the two words on purpose.

Still, I humor her. "It's pronounced *Welten Überbrücken*, and it means 'bridging worlds.'"

"Bridging worlds..." Her gaze moves from me to the ceiling as though she's considering it for the first time. We both know she's not. A quick Google search would've given her the answer long ago. She pulls the journal to her chest once again and peers down at me. "Do you believe we're not alone?"

The unexpected question throws me off. "I assume you're talking about aliens?"

She bobble-nods her head. "Yeah, I suppose so, but not in the way most movies and books portray them. I'm thinking more like humans that came from a different planet."

"Like me, right?" I roll my eyes.

Thérèse frowns. "Well, you *are* different."

"Maybe so, but I still don't buy into the idea that my family came from another world."

"If not, then why are you different? Did you somehow evolve? Transcend the limitations of humanity?"

"Isn't it just as likely as me being from another planet?" I counter.

She chews on her lower lip for a few moments. "I suppose so, but it makes more sense to me that those like you are from somewhere else. For instance, you have that mark on the inside of your wrist. If you've done nothing but transcend humanity, then why the mark?"

I rise from the recliner. "You know I don't have an answer for that."

"And neither does this journal." She turns and walks away with it still held against her chest.

I follow her into the dining room. She escapes into her bedroom and shuts the door behind her. I'm about to throw the door open and barge right in but Seth grabs my hand. We exchange scowls.

He says, "What's wrong with you? You don't invade someone's privacy, especially in their own home."

"She's hiding something," I say.

"It's her home," Seth counters. "She can hide anything she wants."

"He's right," Pierre says. "Going in there without permission would cross a line you don't want to be crossing, especially with Thérèse."

I ignore Pierre but join him and Seth back at the card table. "That journal is Centaurian, Seth. She has no right to keep it from me."

He frowns. "First of all, it doesn't matter what it is. If it's hers, she can do whatever she wants with it. Second, I didn't think you believed in Centauria."

"Did you miss what I said?" I exhale through my nose. "Look, it doesn't matter if I believe in the existence of life on another planet or not. Centaurian artifacts exist no matter where they originated from. Either way, she's not Centaurian and I am. I have a greater right to it than she does."

Seth shakes his head. "I know you don't believe that, on either count." He leans over and places his hand on top of mine. "No matter what, Thérèse obviously has her reasons for keeping it from you."

Thérèse exits from her bedroom and closes the door behind her. "I do."

"Well, I'd love to hear it," I snark.

She settles into the last chair at the table, directly across from me. Our eyes meet. "Look, I'll be honest with you. When I saw the journal in your hands it upset me. I immediately switched into defensive mode and made up the story about where I got it."

Vindication always tastes sweet. "I knew you were lying about it."

Thérèse leans on the table and weaves her fingers together. "The truth is, that journal means a lot to me. I knew the man who wrote it. More than knew, actually. Klaus Von Astner was my great uncle. He obsessed over this idea of creating what he called a 'bridge between worlds' for decades.

"My grandmother tried talking sense into him for many years, but her words fell on deaf ears. Eventually, his obsession with the idea consumed him to the point where he became a recluse. He never married and locked himself inside his Münster home.

"When he died, his body laid there for almost a year before anyone discovered it. The journal he left behind is the only possession I have to remember him. So, yes, I have good reason to be possessive of it."

Well, now I feel like a horse's ass.

I lean back in my chair. "Why didn't you just tell me that from the start?"

She shrugs. "Sometimes, I find it far easier to lie rather than open myself up to people."

I certainly know how that is. I've been doing it my entire life. But she doesn't need to know that.

"And you do know German, don't you," I say. It's not really a question at this point.

"*Ja ich spreche deutsch,*" she says.

Seth chuckles. "What we have here is a room full of linguals."

I reach over and squeeze his hand. "Um, I believe you mean linguists, babe."

He frowns. "Isn't that what I said?"

"No," Pierre says.

We all laugh, but our collective joviality quickly transitions into an awkward silence. It persists and morphs into an uneasiness I can't shake.

Pierre smacks his hands on the table, jolting the rest of us out of our stupors. "According to the pattern Alice discovered, we've got thirteen days to catch this Chrono Slasher before he kills again."

No matter the dire circumstances, I can't help but smile a little. It's the first time Pierre has referred to Jacques Milan as the Chrono Slasher.

"We don't need a reminder," Thérèse says, "we need a solution."

"You're right, but my mind is spent." Pierre polishes off his beer and sets the bottle back on the table. "For now, we've reached the end of meaningful conversation and of the night." He pushes his chair back from the table and stands.

I'm inclined to agree, standing myself and stretching my legs and arms.

Seth takes the hint and rises from his chair, too. "Yeah, I think we should head out as well."

Pierre grabs his coat off the back of his chair and slides himself into it. "I'll be happy to give you a ride back to your hotel."

Seth beats me to the punch. "Appreciate the offer, Pierre, but Alice and I will manage. It's a nice night, and I could certainly use the fresh air."

An uneasiness settles in my gut.

Seth's up to something.

Even though I'm apprehensive about what might be happening, I find myself saying "Ditto."

The three of us thank Thérèse for her hospitality again, then we exit her apartment. Outside, Pierre offers us a ride one last time. We decline, bid him farewell for the evening, and then begin our three-mile trek back to the hotel.

*　*　*　*　*

"You were holding back in there," Seth says as we walk along the poorly lit sidewalk.

"Was I?" I keep my eyes trained on the sidewalk, both to avoid Seth's gaze and to keep from tripping over any cracks or buckles.

"Yes, and I'm not talking about Thérèse's journal, either. Jacques said something important to you, didn't he?"

"...doing so will not save him."

That final word thunders through my mind. Crashes into my heart and prickles my skin. It's the only thing I've held back from Seth, and it's my cross to bear.

"I told you about the cryptic riddle."

"The darkness hiding beneath the light." He takes my hand and pulls me to a stop beneath a streetlamp. "Yeah, I remember, but that isn't it, is it?"

"It's the only thing he said of significance."

Seth lifts my chin. Forces me to make eye contact. "We both know that's not true."

Nothing good will come of me telling him, but he's left me no choice. I love and hate him for it.

"Jacques said something else when I first threatened to kill him. He said it would end his suffering and that he longed for it, but..."

"But what?"

"...but doing so would not save him," I finish.

Seth frowns. "I don't get it. Killing him won't save him? I mean from a salvation viewpoint, I'd agree. Otherwise, it doesn't make sense."

"No, Seth. He wasn't talking about himself. He said *him* as in someone else."

"Oh, I get it now." He sighs, then hugs me. "You think *him* means me."

"Yes. Well, maybe." I pull away and stare into his beautiful grayish-blue eyes. "I don't know."

"What are our options?" He stares at his hand and counts with his fingers as he lists off a few names. "Me. Pierre. Another victim. Who else?"

"Maybe his son?"

"Think so?" He rubs his chin. "I've already got him pegged as killing his son."

I scoff. "Based on what evidence?"

"Oh, you know, like the lack of any significant possessions in their apartment. I mean seriously, what teenage kid doesn't own a computer or gaming system or have posters hanging in their room? There was nothing personal of either of them, Alice."

"Not true," I say. "You forgot about the photo of them standing beneath the Eiffel Tower."

"It's the single meaningful event Jacques had with his son."

I rub my arms, the night a bit airish just standing here. "I spoke with the man, and I just don't see it."

"Okay, here's another thought. What if we've got it all wrong? What if Jacques isn't the only one in the family who can teleport?"

"You're saying—"

"The son might be the real killer," he finishes.

The revelation stuns me. Every moment with Jacques plays back in my mind. The sorrow and tears. The cryptic words. His faith.

"Killing Jacques wouldn't save his son's soul."

"Yes." Seth claps his hands together. "Exactly!"

"My God, Seth. You're..."

"Brilliant." He kisses me on the lips. "I know."

"That's not exactly what I was going to say, but if you're right, we have an even bigger problem on our hands."

He nods solemnly. "Two killers who can't be caught."

"We need to tell Pierre," I say.

"He's not going to be—"

Lightning flashes across the sky and thunder quickly follows, rumbling deep inside my chest. A pitter-patter of large raindrops pelt the sidewalk and street just ahead of us. Moments later, the slow pitter-patter gains momentum and morphs into a symphony as it heads straight for us. Seth grabs my hand, and we start running.

CHAPTER TWENTY

ONE HOUR REMAINS BEFORE the bells of Notre-Dame Cathedral ring sixteen times, signaling the noon hour. In one hour, a twelfth victim will die. One hour, and we'll be out of time again.

Right now, it's a fact, and it's eating me alive because we're no closer to figuring out Jacques's cryptic riddle than we were two weeks ago. I'm almost certain we're in the right location, and Pierre has staked his reputation and put his neck on the line for me, shutting down the cathedral at my request.

Why didn't you just give me the answer, Jacques?

Seth stands at the front of the nave. His head teeters back and forth as he examines the ceiling and the floor. "What was the clue again?"

"When the time comes, you must enter the darkness that hides beneath the light of the cross. Only a sacrifice will make the path known."

Seth peers down at the black and white checkered floor. "Well, we're standing at the center of the crossing of the transept. It's the center of the cross." His brow furrows as he continues to stare at the floor. "Maybe we should smear some blood on the tiles here."

"That's a terrible idea," Pierre says, "and I will not allow it. We will not defile the greatest church in all of Paris by smearing blood on its floors."

"Admittedly, I agree," I say, turning in a circle. "Maybe we're looking in the wrong place. He said something about symbols, too."

"Okay, then what do you suggest?" Thérèse ask.

My gaze shifts toward the choir. "It's not as noticeable in the daylight, but the night I encountered Jacques, the cross behind the altar reflected every bit of light that it could."

Thérèse turns around and considers the cross. "I think you might be onto something."

The four of us head through the choir section and beyond the shining, golden altar. Unfortunately, nothing looks amiss or out of alignment. As I run my hand along the back edge of the altar, I notice the surface isn't smooth in one spot, and it's right about where the center of the altar should be.

I kneel to get a better look, but it's too dark. "I think I might've found something, but I need more light." I proffer my hand toward Thérèse. "Hand me your flashlight."

She does, and I shine the flashlight at the backside of the altar. Sure enough, the light reveals a small engraved cross. Lines extend outward from the top of the cross like sunbeams.

The light of the cross.

A circular depression lies just beneath the engraved cross. Pressing on it and the cross don't trigger an event. I'm not sure what I was expecting to happen anyway.

An Indiana Jones moment?

I glance at Seth who's kneeling next to me. "Now what?"

"We do as Jacques said and make a sacrifice." We all turn toward Thérèse. A fresh drop of blood rests on the pad of her thumb. "Move aside."

Seth and I move out of her way, but I keep the flashlight beam trained on the cross and the circular depression below it.

"Thérèse, you can't defile the—"

She presses her bloody thumb into the depression, silencing Pierre.

At first nothing happens, but then the engraved cross glows with golden light. The four of us step back as the altar's back panel vibrates. Quakes. Then, it slides down into the floor, revealing a large opening. Several of the tiles behind the altar begin sinking into the floor. We all step back farther and watch as a stairway forms.

Pierre gasps. "My God…"

Seth rubs his hands together. "It's just like in the movies."

Now this is the Indiana Jones moment I was anticipating.

Pierre and I shine our flashlights into the dark void, revealing the beginnings of a circular stairwell. The four of us share glances as the cathedral bells clang once, signifying that it's fifteen minutes past the hour already.

Forty-five minutes remain.

"We're running out of time," Thérèse says, echoing my thoughts, "and we have no idea where this leads or if it's even the right place."

Eying the gaping hole, no doubt remains within me. "We've located the darkness beneath the light of the cross."

I offer the flashlight back to Thérèse, but she waves her hand. "Keep it, I've got another one."

"Thanks." I turn back and stare into the darkness. "The only thing I'm uncertain of is what we'll find below."

Pierre draws his weapon and his flashlight. "We have no choice at this point but to get in there and find out." He takes the first two steps down beneath the altar, then says, "Follow me."

* * * * *

The temperature plummets a good fifteen degrees as we descend into the darkness beneath the altar on a stairway carved straight from the limestone foundations. Damp walls, worn with age and water, reek of brine and mildew and leave a sticky, gelatinous film on my fingers as they slide along its rough surface. The four of us move slow, each step slick and treacherous, as we circle ever deeper.

Into the bowels of hell.

My head spins atop my shoulders as we reach the lower landing, the circular stairwell leaving me dizzy. Then, the bells sound, causing the walls and floor to quake. Putrid, stale water rains down on us. I grab hold of Seth's arm to steady myself just as the second chime shakes us again. After a time, all becomes still. The four of us share glances, each of us knowing the significance.

Thérèse echoes my thoughts again. "It's the half-hour bells. We need to move quicker." Urgency fills her voice.

It's strange given the callous way she always speaks of the prior eleven victims. Perhaps she's more human than I give her credit for after all. Either way, she's not wrong. We're running out of time.

Less than thirty minutes before someone else dies.

The thought sobers me. Drives away the dizziness in my head. Releasing Seth's arm, I focus on what lies ahead.

A crooked, narrow passage leads into the darkness ahead, extending beyond the reach of our flashlight beams. Pierre continues to lead the way, plunging into the passage with renewed urgency. I stick close behind him and Seth behind me. Thérèse brings up the rear.

Deep within the passage we round a sharp bend. Farther ahead, a flickering light becomes visible as it reflects off the walls. As we draw closer, the walls and floor become drier, and the mildew scent begins morphing. Its pungency fades as notes of pine and tar enter the passage and become stronger.

Torches.

Now that I've identified the light source, I can hear the torches crackling and popping. Furthermore, two low voices carry through the passage. Both are too faint to identify or understand, but my mind immediately conjures the picture of Jacques and Raphaël standing beneath the Eiffel Tower.

Father and son. Serial killer duo.

Ahead and to the right, the passage opens up. Pierre halts and raises his hand, signaling us to stop. Just then, I recognize one of the voices. I reach forward and tap Pierre's shoulder. He glances back at me.

"Jacques," I mouth.

He nods, then switches off his flashlight and clips it to his belt. The rest of us do the same with ours. With his hand still raised, Pierre begins counting down with his fingers.

Four.

Fear and anticipation catch my breath. Drive chills down my nape and spine.

Three.

Sweaty palms press against the grips of my gun. Safety off. Pointed low.

Two.

Thunderous bells quake the passage. Kick up a cloud of limestone dust. They sound and quake again. Then again before falling silent.

Only fifteen minutes remain.

Pierre lowers his arm and storms around the corner, leading with his weapon. "Make a move, and I'll drop you right where you stand," he shouts in French.

Seth, Thérèse, and I turn the last corner and step into a massive chamber. Pulse racing, my focus zeros in on a steel bar cage to the right. For several moments I can do nothing but stare, the shock of what I see petrifying.

Inside the cage stands a bald man with his hands cuffed behind him and the cuffs chained to shackles clamped around his ankles. His shirt and pants are ripped in several places and soiled brownish black. Yellow limestone dust clings to his clothes and skin. A thick beard peppered with yellow dust clings to his gaunt, dirty face, and green eyes peer out of dark, sunken sockets.

Even from where I stand, the man's stench overwhelms. Stale sweat. Urine. Feces. I try not to think about it, but there's more. A nidorous, foul odor. Infection, rotting flesh, or both.

Recognition sparks as our eyes meet. I know the man. Loathe the man. Wish him dead most nights.

Reagan.

It's then that I notice Jacques standing next to the cage. His arm extends through the bars, and his hand rests on Reagan's shoulder. At first, none of it makes sense.

Why is Reagan here?

Then, I realize Reagan's wearing the same clothes he wore when he came through the mirror in my hotel suite bedroom.

"My God, he's been down here for months," I whisper.

Immediately, I'm torn. Reagan's a vile, evil piece of garbage who doesn't deserve to live, but he also doesn't deserve to be treated like a caged animal. No one does. I'm on the verge of feeling sorry for him, yet I know his death would hurt no one.

Except maybe Morgan.

"Detectives and special agents," Jacques says, the words slithering from his deformed tongue. "I am pleased you all made it in time."

Reagan presses himself against the cage bars. "Kill this psycho and get me out of here!"

"Patience, my friend," Jacques says to him. "Your time has not yet come, but it will soon enough."

My gaze drifts toward the center of the chamber and a round, raised platform made of limestone. At the center of the platform stands a stone arch at least ten feet tall and seven feet wide. Curiosity pulls me toward the platform so I can get a better look at it.

Carved roman numerals circle the top edge of the platform. One through twelve, laid out like a clock. Twelve fissures extend inward from the edge of the platform, eleven of them dark red and filled to the brim. The last one, parallel to an identical one extending down from the number twelve mark, remains empty. Based on their positions, I'm certain each fissure coincides with the eleven times the minute and hour hands align.

A plastic tube runs from the empty fissure over to a crude trough hewn from limestone and connects to its underside. Thick chains with several hooks hang from the ceiling above the trough.

My gut churns as I face Jacques once again. "What the hell is all this?"

"It's the end of the road." Thérèse steps forward, gun aimed at Jacques. "Step away from the cage."

Jacques peers over at Thérèse. "You know I cannot do that."

"Cannot or won't?" Pierre asks, joining Thérèse.

"Sometimes, both are the same," Jacques says.

Thérèse steps closer. "You're the one who snatched Reagan from the hotel, aren't you?"

"I am."

"How did you know he was there?" Seth asks.

"You're asking all the wrong questions," Jacques says.

Seth and I join Pierre. "Why are you doing this, Jacques?" I ask.

He peers down at a pocket watch, then sighs. "I have no choice."

The bells sound and the chamber quakes.

Reagan's no longer standing in the cage.

Bells. Another quake. Chains rattle.

Jacques collapses into a heap and clutches the left side of his chest.

No bang, but more bells and another quake.

I rush over to Jacques as the bells sound and another quake shakes the chamber. There's no blood. No wound.

Torchlight flickers as limestone rains down from the ceiling as the chamber shakes again with the sound of bells.

More bells and quakes come in succession. Seth and Pierre appear at my side. But no Thérèse.

I glance over my shoulder. Reagan hangs from the chains over the trough.

Thérèse stands next to him, her gun no longer in her hands but secured in its holster. She holds her hands out in front of her, balled into fists.

Another quake shifts the light as the bells ring out.

Metal glints between Thérèse's hands.

Reagan screams and writhes as Thérèse loops the wire around the front of his neck.

As the bells sound and the chamber quakes again, she grunts and pulls back, her face contorted with rage.

Blood gushes from Reagan's severed neck and pours into the trough as he hangs from the chains like a butchered pig. It flows through the tubing, heading toward the platform and the final fissure.

I scramble to my feet and take aim at Thérèse with my gun. "What the hell have you done?"

Thérèse drops the garrote and smiles. "What was necessary."

In this moment, understanding hits me.

She's the one. She's the Chrono Slasher.

CHAPTER TWENTY-ONE

BLOOD CONTINUES TO DRIP from Reagan's lifeless body as the bells ring and the chamber quakes for the sixteenth and final time. We've reached the pinnacle. Witnessed the twelfth death. But to what end?

Thérèse retreats onto the platform as Seth, Pierre, and I close in on her.

Pierre holsters his gun. He's never looked more haggard than now. "It was you all this time, Thérèse?" He shakes his head. "Why?"

Thérèse glances back at the arch, clearly distraught. "No matter what I say, you wouldn't understand."

"Try me," Pierre says.

"It's the journal," I say.

"Yes, and it should've worked." She looks back at the arch again. "I followed every step meticulously. Met every requirement and deadline even as you breathed down my neck."

Seth crosses his arms. "I don't understand. What are you talking about?"

"That Centaurian journal lays out a blueprint on how to create a bridge between worlds, isn't that right, Thérèse?"

"Yes, and I believed every word of it," she says.

"You actually thought it would create a bridge by killing people?" Seth shakes his head. "And you fell for that, Thérèse?"

She looks back at the arch and sighs. "According to my great uncle, blood is magic."

"That's absurd." My eyes scan the platform. "Another world doesn't—"

The chamber quakes as the last fissure fills with the last drops of Reagan's blood. No bells accompany the quake this time, but then a groan rises out of the platform and blasts a ring of air outward. It sweeps across the chamber and extinguishes all the torches, casting the chamber in darkness.

Seth clicks his flashlight on.

"Turn it off," I whisper.

He does, then we wait.

One by one, the twelve fissures begin glowing red. Undulate as the blood contained within them starts flowing up the sides of the arch. As the blood covers the arch, previously undetectable symbols along the arch's outer edge take form.

Once the blood reaches the top of the arch and fills in the last symbol it stops flowing. Then, from the bottom of each side of the arch, the symbols grow brighter, their reddish hue shifting to white. As each one finishes its transition, its glowing light flashes bright and sounds a unique tone akin to that of a bell. After the last one sounds, the symbols fade, leaving us standing in the dark again.

A few seconds pass, then the area in the middle of the arch begins to fill itself in with a brilliant, blue light, moving from its outer edges to its center. As the last of the area fills in, its brightness lessens, revealing what looks like a solid blue surface across the inside of the arch. Then, a violent ring-shaped shockwave made of pure light blasts outward from the arch, nearly knocking me off my feet.

The torches around the outer edge of the chamber burst to life once again as the ring of white light expands outward and passes through them, filling the chamber with light as the ring fades. An ethereal glow emanates from the area within the arch, and its beautiful, blue, sparkling surface flows and ebbs like water.

Pierre gasps. "My God… What is that thing?"

"It's a bridge," Thérèse says breathily, "to another world."

Even as the bells sound again, quaking the chamber, we all stare at the arch, captivated by its beauty. The longer I stare, the more aware I become of its draw. It's as though it's alive. Straining my ears, I swear I can hear it calling my name. Beckoning me to finally go home.

Centauria…

* * * * *

Thérèse turns and faces me, a grin etched upon her face. "You know what lies beyond that watery surface, don't you, Alice?"

For several years, I've fought so hard to disbelieve. To prove to myself that our existence in the universe is unique. But now, I stand at the cusp of what must be another world.

My world.

Still, I hesitate. Resisting its pull will keep me from experiencing true belief. Protects me from the truth that I've always known deep within.

"How could I?" I ask.

"I see it in your eyes. In your face." She cocks her head. "It calls to you, doesn't it?"

"No." Not an ounce of conviction lies in that hollow word.

She proffers her hand toward me. "Come with me, Alice."

Seth puts his arm in front of me. "She's not going anywhere."

"Why would you do this, Thérèse?" Pierre shakes his head. "Even if that thing can take you to another world, why would you do it? Why kill those twelve people?"

Thérèse lowers her hand and glares daggers at Pierre. "I rid the world of twelve vile lowlifes, Pierre, not people." She peers at me again. "And how could I not attempt it after discovering my great uncle's journal? It's another world, Alice. One filled with magic greater than anything we could ever imagine."

The truth finally hits me. "You're jealous of what Jacques and I can do, aren't you?"

"How could anyone not be?" She glances back at the arch. "Once I step through that portal, I'll be like you."

Such a notion borders on the absurd. "I may know little about Centauria or mezhik for that matter, but I'm fairly certain it doesn't work that way. Even in this world, I was born with my gift, Thérèse. A gift passed down to me by my father. You have no such gift."

"You don't know that." Thérèse glances down at the inside of her left wrist. "I'm certain that my great uncle was a Centaurian. That means there must be Centaurian blood in my veins."

"I think you would know if it did." I peer up at the arch. "Do you feel it pulling you?"

She huffs. "No, but maybe my gift lies dormant."

"Or you have no gift at all," Seth says.

Thérèse turns and faces the arch. "There's only one way to find out."

Pierre draws his gun. Pulls the slide back. "Take another step, and I'll put a bullet in your back."

Thérèse scoffs. "You don't have the balls, Pierre."

"Maybe he doesn't, but I do," Seth says.

"Wait," Jacques cries out.

I'd all but forgotten about him. Somehow, he's managed to drag himself all the way over to the platform.

"Stay out of this, Jacques," Pierre says.

"My… my son," he rasps.

Thérèse turns back. A wicked smile parts her lips. "Yes, of course. How could I have forgotten about Raphaël? My glorious bargaining chip."

The truth of Jacques's words hits me. The *him* Jacques mentioned to me in the cathedral always referred to his son.

Jacques wheezes. "I did everything you asked of me."

"Oh, and much more, too." Thérèse snarls. "I told you to keep quiet, but you just couldn't help yourself, could you? You nearly ruined everything."

"I told Alice nothing. How could I when I didn't even know who'd taken my son?"

Thérèse takes a step backward, toward the arch.

Bang!

Seth fires a round into the far wall. "The next one won't be a warning."

Pierre takes a step toward Thérèse. "What have you done with Raphaël?"

"If I tell you now, you'd kill me," she says.

"How about this scenario." I join Thérèse on the platform. "Tell us where he is, or Seth will kill you and then I'll extract the location from your dead head. Does that work for you?"

"Do you find me so naive, Alice?" She laughs. "Trust me, I've thought of everything. You cannot extract information that I don't possess."

"If you don't know, then you're as good as dead," Seth says.

"If I die, the boy dies." She looks at me. "Let me go, and I'll tell you how to find the boy. Deal?"

"Please," Jacques moans. "Raphaël has done nothing wrong."

Seth moves around the platform to the left. Thérèse turns with him. The only reason I can think of as to why he would do so would be to stop her from diving into the portal.

Good plan.

Seth lowers his gun. "You know what I don't get, Thérèse? How did you hook up with someone like Jacques?"

Thérèse smiles. "Some kids like to brag about their fathers, especially the ones who have a father that can teleport." She glances back at Jacques and laughs. "Just think, it was your own son who betrayed you."

"Raphaël knew about it?" Jacques collapses on the edge of the platform and weeps.

Pierre steps up onto the platform. "Where will we find the boy, Thérèse?"

Thérèse reaches into her back pocket and pulls out her cell phone. As she does, the cathedral bells ring in succession, quaking the ground. She waits for it to cease, then says, "Listen carefully to everything I say."

Seth steps up onto the platform, his gun raised once more. Thérèse steps back. One more step, and her back will touch the arch's undulating surface.

"We're listening," Pierre says. His hands are visibly shaking.

Thérèse punches some numbers into her phone, then sets it down on the platform in front of her. "Once I step back, you'll take the phone and press send. You'll receive coordinates on where to find the boy. Do it before the clock strikes one, or you'll find him dead. Understood?"

"Yes," I say.

Jacques groans, then exhales loudly. In that moment, Thérèse kicks her phone toward me and dives through the arch.

It takes several moments for the *bang* to register in my mind even as my ears ring. It's then that I realize Seth and Pierre are staring at me. The barrel of my gun feels a bit warm to the touch, and a spent brass casing lies on the platform next to me.

As my ears continue to buzz, I pick up Thérèse's phone and hit send. The message fails to go through. "Damn. There's no signal down here, and we've only got seventeen minutes left."

Pierre sighs loudly. "That doesn't leave us enough time to get back up to the cathedral."

Seth holsters his gun and sticks out his hand. "Give me the phone. I think I can make it."

"No," Jacques groans. He looks at me. "Touch my hand, and I will send you up."

Pierre kneels next to Jacques. "I thought you were dead."

Jacques pushes himself up on an elbow. "It will not be long now." He draws a ragged breath. "Let me do this one last thing for my son."

"You'll knock me out," I say, remembering what'd happened to me a few weeks ago.

"I can control it to a degree." He reaches out. "Please, Alice. Trust me."

The screen on Thérèse's cell phone dims and sets my pulse racing. If it locks, I'll have no way to get back in and send the message. That would be the worst scenario I can think of. I access the phone settings and remove all the locks on the phone.

"Okay," I say.

"No!" Seth yells, but I've already touched Jacques's hand.

As before, the world fissures with light as my skin ignites. Shadows race toward me, disintegrating the chamber and everything in it.

CHAPTER TWENTY-TWO

SECONDS LATER, I'M WAKING up with another blistering headache. The golden altar sits in front of me, shining with splendor. Sitting up intensifies the pounding in my head, but I don't have time to think about it. I must send the message.

Clang!

The sound of the bells startles me and rattles my head.

Clang!

For some reason, the phone is no longer in my hand.

Clang!

It lies several feet to my left, beyond my reach.

Clang!

The fourth clang.

Four clangs!!!

What felt like a few seconds between when Jacques touched me and when I regained consciousness must've been seventeen minutes. Now, I'm out of time.

Panic envelops me as I thrust myself toward the phone and grab it.

A single bar of signal.

Clang!

I press send again.

It takes several seconds, but the message finally goes through. I exhale with relief and await a response.

Thunderous drums pound in my ears as the moments pass like hours. The phone refuses to buzz or chime, and the screen doesn't update.

Breathing becomes more difficult with each passing moment. A minute passes. Then two. Three.

God, was I too late?

I lie back on the floor, close my eyes, and pray.

Exhale.

Repeat.

Six minutes later, the phone buzzes in my hand and a response appears on the screen. The new message contains two numbers. GPS coordinates. I pull up Google maps and punch in the latitude and longitude coordinates. The map zooms in on a section of the map just to the north of Île Saint-Louis.

Four times I verify and re-input the coordinates, but each attempt yields the same result. My heart sinks as I stare at the marker on the map.

The Seine River…

Tears well in my eyes. "God, this can't be right."

Minutes later, Seth emerges from behind the altar. He's completely winded and dripping with sweat as he bends over next to me with his elbows on his knees. It takes him a full minute to catch his breath long enough to speak.

"Well," he gasps, "did it work?"

I shake my head, still in shock with the response. "Not in the way we'd hoped." I hand Thérèse's cell phone to him as I fend off a torrent of emotions.

Seth straightens and stares at the phone. His brow furrows. "Why am I looking at a map of the Seine River? I need more context."

"Those are the coordinates." My stomach roils. "That's where we'll find Raphaël Milan."

* * * * *

After several hours and phone calls, Pierre emerges from the cathedral. He strides across the concrete, his face stoic, but his eyes bleed with pain and betrayal. It could take years for him to get past what Thérèse did to him—to us all—if ever. The only thing I have to offer him right now is a solemn nod and a hope of closure.

Pierre scowls at nothing in particular. "I don't like the thought of that portal or whatever it is sitting beneath my city."

"Neither do I," I say, "but maybe Thérèse's journal details a way to shut it down."

"God, I hope so, but it'll have to wait." He removes his glasses and wipes his eyes, then puts the glasses back on. "I've got several officers stationed around it for now and an assurance from Father Toussaint that the cathedral will remain closed for a few more days while we get everything worked out."

I peer over at the cathedral. "That's good, but I'll feel better once Dakota and the others from Mirador arrive."

"As will I." He clears his throat. "Now, we need to go fish a body out of the river."

The walk over to Vedettes du Pont Neuf, the nearest boat dock to our location, takes about fifteen minutes, yet each minute feels more like a lifetime with Pierre as he suffers in silence. It saddens me that he has no one left to talk with or confide in now that Thérèse is gone. Not that her still being here would be any better.

A police boat awaits us when we arrive at the dock. Only three officers are on board: one female and two males. Seth, Pierre, and I board the vessel, and then Pierre makes quick introductions. Blanchet is the female officer, and the other two are Auclair and Rousseau. Blanchet and Auclair are already suited up for their impending dive, and Rousseau stands behind the wheel.

Rousseau fires up the engine, and then we head upstream toward the coordinates on the north side of Île Saint-Louis. The brackish water flows at a good clip, making visibility and diving a lot trickier. Rousseau positions the boat just east of the coordinates and drops anchor.

Blanchet and Auclair clip safety lines onto the anchor line then enter the water. Every moment following ratchets the tension up another notch and brings me closer to the edge of a nervous breakdown.

God, if you truly are the God of miracles, please let them find Raphaël alive.

The prayer borderlines absurd given where we're searching for him, but what else can I do but wait for them to pull something out of the water?

Seth wraps his arm around my shoulders, and I lean into him. This simple act both comforts me and gives me hope. At least for a few minutes.

Just when I begin to think all is lost, Blanchet breaks the ten-minute radio silence. "We've located some sort of metal box wrapped in heavy chain. Give us a minute or two, and we'll attach it to the wench. Over."

"Roger that. Over," Rousseau says.

"Unless the boy was fitted with an oxygen tank…" Pierre doesn't finish his thought. There's no need to.

A minute later, Blanchet's voice blares through the radio. "We've got the box attached. Let her rip. Over."

"Roger. Over." Rousseau nods to Pierre, and Pierre starts up the wench.

Forty-five seconds later, the corner of a box emerges from the water and the wench halts. The waves and brackishness of the water make it impossible to see just how big the box is. Seth and Pierre reach over the edge of the boat and haul the box aboard.

Every last ounce of hope withers as I stare down at the two-foot-cubed metal box wrapped in heavy chain. If Raphaël is in there, it's only part of him. Blanchet and Auclair surface, and we help them back onto the boat before examining the box.

Given the cleanliness of the outside of the box, it hasn't been in the water long. A large padlock secures the chain to the box, and whoever wrapped it also wire-tied its key to it. Rousseau hands Seth a knife and Seth cuts the key free. The lock opens without hesitation, and the chain falls to the sides.

One of the lines from the movie *Se7en* repeats in my head: *"What's in the box?"*

It's a terrible, haunting question. One I wish I never needed an answer to. But now, I do. If not for me, then for Jacques.

Seth stands and moves to the side, then gestures toward the box with his hand. "It's all yours, Pierre."

Pierre nods, then kneels in front of the box. Two latches secure its lid. He unlatches them, takes a deep breath, then lifts the lid. The entire boat gasps collectively.

"Wow, not what I expected," Seth says. "Or rather not *who* I expected."

"Yeah, it's certainly not Raphaël," Pierre says.

The severed head of a black man lies in the box, his eyelids stapled open and his lips stapled shut. A small piece of something yellow protrudes from his lips, nestled between two staples.

Pierre snaps on a pair of latex gloves and sets to work extracting two of the staples from the man's purple lips. His touch is far more delicate than mine would be. The dead man could care less if someone rips holes in his lips at this point.

The sun must've risen and set at least five times before Pierre finally gets the two staples removed. He tosses them aside before pulling a yellow piece of paper out of the dead man's mouth. He offers it up to me as though I'd want to touch it with my bare hands. It looks like it's still wet with blood and saliva.

"Let me get some gloves on first," I say.

Seth eyes the severed head. "He hasn't been dead long."

"Definitely not." Auclair leans closer to the open box and sniffs. "Three or four hours, tops."

After donning a pair of latex gloves, I pull my phone out of my pocket and check the time. It's almost 1700 hours. "The text I sent from Thérèse's phone must've been what killed him."

"You don't know that," Seth says. "And now that I think about it, this head has been in a sealed, submerged box. He could've died several more hours ago."

My gut says he's wrong, but it doesn't make a bit of difference now. What matters is what might be written on the paper. I proffer my hand to Pierre. "Give it to me."

The paper has a single fold, and the blood and saliva act as a bonding agent. It takes a few seconds to pull it apart without ripping the damp paper. Inside are seven sentences written in black marker.

I read them aloud: "Couldn't keep his mouth shut, so I shut it for him. Imagine the surprise on his face. Looked something like it does now. And don't worry. He's got everything you need in that bald head of his. Happy hunting, Detective. Clock's ticking."

Auclair, Rousseau, and Blanchet exchange looks of confusion. "What's that supposed to mean?" Auclair asks.

Seth and I share a look, then he sighs heavily and nods. "Raphaël's life depends on it."

Pierre holds up his hand, understanding what Seth's agreeing to. "Wait." He stands and peels off his latex gloves before eying Rousseau and the other two. "What you're about to witness cannot leave this boat, understood?"

The three of them look between each other, still confused. Rousseau says, "I think we've missed something."

Pierre frowns. "Detective Bergman—Alice—has a gift."

Blanchet nods knowingly. "She's a psychic. I've worked with one before."

"Something like that," I say. "But more… hands on."

After a bit more convincing, the three of them agree to keep anything they witness out of their reports. I'm not one for an audience, but we're short on time. Pierre stands to the side, and I take a knee in front of the open box. I push away every thought but one as I stare at the severed head.

Help me find Raphaël Milan.

I take a deep breath, then place my fingers on the man's clammy, cold cheek. Time slows, and the biting wind fades. Fire spreads throughout my body, and that familiar, alien shift occurs within me. The bodiless man grabs my hand and pulls me down into the depths.

* * * * *

He stares at his phone. Broods over the message he received from the anonymous number an hour ago. Torn despite how clear it is. He reads it again: "Tomorrow. 1300. Silence the kid for good."

He groans and shoves the phone in his pocket. It's not like he has anything against killing. In fact, he's gotten pretty good at it over the years.

But the kid?

He's kinda grown fond of the little bastard after taking care of him for more than a year now. Formed a connection he's never had with anyone before. Felt kinda nice having a friend. But a job's a job, and he never fails to finish anything.

He walks along the overgrown railroad tracks and into a dark tunnel. It's musty and pungent, but he's grown accustomed to it. Hardly even smells it anymore.

A ways in, he checks to make sure no one's following him before slipping behind a mass of tree roots that cover the secret entrance into the network of abandoned sewers. He knows the way by heart and never uses a light.

Right. Right. Left. Left. Left. Right. Right.

The pattern reminds him of playing video games when he was a boy. "A. B. B. A. Select," *he muses. Those are the days he clings to. A far simpler life than killing and kidnapping. But he knows one can never truly go back. At least not outside of the mind.*

Back inside the place he calls the compound—it's more like a network of adjoined maintenance rooms, but he doesn't care—, he sits down on a folding chair and watches the kid through the steel cage bars. As usual, the kid lies on his cot and stares up at the dark ceiling.

After a time, he says, "Looks like today's your last day with me, kid."

The kid sits up. Stares at him through the bars. "What's that mean, George?" *His voice rises several octaves and his eyes bulge.* "Can I finally go home?"

George.

He feels bad about lying to the kid about his name, but he can never be too careful. It probably wouldn't hurt for the kid to know that his real name was Manny since the kid would be dead soon, but it still isn't worth the risk. "Yeah, something like that."

Guilt stabs at him again even though what he said is kinda true. He's heard many people refer to death as going home.

The kid slides off the cot and approaches the bars. "I can tell something's wrong,

George. What is it?"

Manny sighs and rubs the top of his head. "I'll be straight with ya, kid. Your old man must've failed to deliver on his end, and now ya gotta pay the price."

The kid grabs hold of the bars, fear in his eyes. "I don't want to die, George." His lower lip trembles, but no tears come.

He's given all he had.

Manny chews on his lip. "And I don't want to kill ya neither, kid, but I ain't got no choice. We all have our roles to play. Ya know that, right?"

The kid shakes the bars. "Please, George! Just let me go. I swear I'll never tell anyone about you."

"I do that, and I'll be dead before morning." He rakes his hair with his fingers. "Look, kid. If there were any other way, I'd take it, but I ain't sacrificing myself no matter how much I like ya. Got it?"

The kid slides to the floor, still clutching the bars. He wails. "I thought you were my friend."

Damn, that hurts.

Manny stands when his phone buzzes. Sighs heavily. "Ya know we was never really friends. Not possible, given our situation." He starts walking away as he pulls the phone from his pocket. "Another lifetime, kid."

"Don't leave me here, George!" the kid yells.

"Be back before ya know it."

He exits the compound and closes the door behind him. After locking up, he slides the key into a small space between the bricks where the mortar is missing. It's the perfect hiding place for it, and he never has to carry the key with him or risk losing it.

Another set of instructions awaits him when he finally looks at his phone. He reads it aloud. "Change of plans. Meet at the warehouse in thirty minutes. Don't be late."

Why is it always thirty minutes?

Manny shoves his phone back into his pocket. "Your luck might've just turned for the better, kid." He smiles. "For your sake, I hope so."

It takes just nineteen minutes to exit the sewers and climb his way out of the small ravine where the abandoned train tracks lay. He looks over at the blue street sign just before crossing Rue Manin.

It's his usual route to the warehouse, and one he's grown fond of as it takes him right past McDonald's. His stomach rumbles at the thought of a triple cheeseburger and fries. He'll have to stop in once he's finished at the warehouse.

Maybe I'll get the kid something, too.

Seven more minutes and he reaches the warehouse. Just outside the warehouse door, Manny takes his gun out and checks the magazine. Six rounds. Seven including the one already chambered.

The money's been good for this job, but he's no fool. An unexpected meeting in the middle of the night tends to be bad juju. He hates bad juju.

Manny unzips his jacket, then slides the gun into his pocket, keeping it ready in his hand. After one last deep breath, he enters the warehouse. Naturally, it's dark, and there are no windows to provide outside light. But he's never feared the darkness.

What's curious is the crinkly sound his shoes make on the concrete floor. They've never made noise before. Concern rises in his gut.

Bang!

The door slams behind him. Startles him. Causes unexpected pain deep in the left side of his chest. Right through his shoulder blade.

He reaches up. Feels a hole in his jacket. His shirt. His fingers come away wet and sticky.

He staggers forward a few steps. Drops to one knee. "What just happened?"

A light turns on overhead. Chases away most of the darkness, but not the parts encroaching at the edges of his vision. Ten feet in front of him stands a blonde woman. She holds a gun in one hand and a... a sword in the other.

No, that can't be right.

He blinks away tears. Fumbles in his coat pocket. But the gun won't come out.

Bang!

He falls back. Hits his head on the concrete slab. Stares up at the ceiling. Chokes on what tastes like blood. Coppery, like a penny.

Manny grasps at anything to keep him grounded in this world. His fingers meet thick plastic. Then, the light dims.

He exhales a final breath as the light extinguishes.

* * * * *

I grab my stomach and breathe deep, fighting off nausea as the world rocks back into focus. Manny Lambert's lifeless eyes stare up at me from the metal box. His severed head and the motion of the boat fighting against the current prove more than my stomach can handle, so I purge what remains of breakfast over the side of the boat.

Everyone stares at me as I wipe remnants of bile from my lips. Rousseau hands me a bottle of water. It's not cold, but it helps flush the acidic taste from my mouth and soothes my burning throat.

I hand the half empty bottle back to Rousseau. "Thank you."

"Did you get what we needed?" Pierre asks.

I look up at him and nod. "She was all in. Thérèse killed Manny herself."

Pierre peers down at the metal box. "And I'm guessing that's Manny."

"Or at least what's left of him," Seth says.

"Yes, Manny Lambert." Nausea strikes again, but I manage to keep it under control this time.

I need to get out of this boat.

Sharp pain burrows deep into my temples, forcing my eyes closed. The implications of what it might mean aren't lost on me, but it isn't something I want to deal with or even think about right now, either. An assessment of my health, both mentally and physically, can wait until after we rescue Raphaël.

I lean back against the wall of the boat. "We need to get over to the intersection of Rue Manin and Rue de Crimée. From there, I should be able to retrace Manny's steps back to where he's holding Raphaël Milan."

* * * * *

Two hours later, Seth, Pierre, and I stand just inside the sewer entrance behind the mass of tree roots. Beady eyes reflect our flashlight beams, and scurrying feet echo from every direction. It's musty and wet and smells of feces and decay.

I really hate rats.

Despite consuming another one of Pierre's "famous" granola bars and several Excedrin, my headache has intensified. Now, I'm finding it difficult to recall details of my mind tethering session with Manny.

"Maybe we should wait this out," Seth says, his voice laced with concern.

"I agree," Pierre says. "These old sewers join with the catacombs all over the place. One wrong turn, and we could find ourselves lost or worse."

"No," I bark, holding my head. "Just give me a minute."

God, please help me. Otherwise, Raphaël will die down here.

Tears moisten my eyes.

No more blood on my hands. Please, God, I'm begging you.

An old, square Nintendo controller pops into my head. "Video games," I blurt out.

"What about them?" Seth asks.

Ignoring the pulsing spikes of pain shooting through my head, I imagine Manny holding the controller and focus specifically on the direction pad.

What was it you were thinking as you walked through these dark sewers?

"*Right,*" Manny says in my mind. I repeat the word aloud, and we move forward into the sewers, taking the first right we come to. Turn by turn, Manny guides me. "*Right. Left. Left. Left. Right. Right.*"

At last, we come to a steel door. "The compound," I whisper.

Seth eyes me, then the door. "The compound?"

"That's what Manny called it. It's more like a network of maintenance rooms."

Pierre pushes on the door, but it doesn't budge. "Seems to be locked."

"It is," I say.

Seth scowls. "Would've been good to know ahead of time, seeing as we didn't bring any tools with us."

"Everything we need is right in front of us." I stare at the cement bricks around the door. "Manny shoved the key into one of the cracks in the mortar. It should be easy enough to find." No amount of concentration helps me remember, though.

The three of us spend several minutes searching for the key before Pierre finally locates it. Inside the door lies a maze of rooms and equipment, but thankfully we don't have to rely on my mind to locate the one where Raphaël is because there's a worn path in the layers of filth on the concrete floor.

"Raphaël?" Pierre calls out as we move deeper into the dusty maze. "Can you hear me?"

One last room lies ahead. I remember the blue door, and its clean handle proves it's been used recently. Pierre shoves the door open, and the stench of feces and urine overwhelms me. Thankfully, I have nothing left to purge.

In the corner of the room sits a six-by-six-by-five steel cage. Its bars gleam in Pierre's flashlight beam. Inside the cage stands a young man, his hands gripping the bars.

"Raphaël, are you okay?" I ask in French.

His voice rasps, barely above a whisper. "Yeah, I think so. I'm so thirsty."

Pierre hands me a bottle of water. I open it and offer it to Raphaël. He takes it and guzzles its entire contents.

Seth locates a ring of keys hanging on the wall outside the room and hands them to me. "One of those must open the cage."

I fumble through the keys and find one that looks like it might open a cage. Thank God it does.

Seth and I stand back, and Pierre opens the cage door. Raphaël stumbles out.

"Who are you?" Raphaël asks, looking at the three of us.

"I am Special Agent Pierre Lamont with the French Police. Everything's going to be okay."

Pierre lowers his flashlight and offers the boy a hand. Raphaël takes it. The boy's much scrawnier than in the picture Jacques had hanging on the apartment wall, but he looks otherwise healthy.

"Where's George? Is he okay?" Raphaël asks.

"I'm sorry, Raphaël, but George is dead," I say.

"Who's George?" Seth asks.

"George is Manny," I say.

"And my father?" Raphaël asks. "Where is he?"

"He's at the hospital," Pierre says. "Somehow, he's found a way to keep hanging on, and I'm certain it has everything to do with you." He smiles at Raphaël. "Once we get you out of here and cleaned up, I'll take you to see him."

I smile to myself.

Raphaël and God have kept you alive, Jacques.

CHAPTER TWENTY-THREE

THE FOLLOWING MORNING, WE rise with the sun. My head still hurts, but nothing like it did yesterday after mind tethering with Manny Lambert. Unfortunately, the bedroom door looks a bit fuzzy from here, and rubbing my eyes does nothing to clear it up. Nausea grips me.

Please God, don't let me go blind again.

I leave it at that, knowing there's nothing else I can do.

After a quick shower, Seth and I meet Pierre outside and head over to Thérèse's apartment to find the journal. It doesn't take Seth long to locate her hiding spot underneath the floor in her bedroom. I study it in detail on the drive over to Notre-Dame Cathedral.

Once we reach the chamber beneath the cathedral, I'm surprised to see nothing has changed. Reagan's dead, limp body still hangs from the chains. The portal surface still ripples and undulates.

Pierre dismisses the seven officers who have been guarding the portal all night after verifying nothing had changed.

"Any word on when Dakota and the others will arrive?" I ask.

Pierre steps up onto the platform and stares at the portal. "They landed earlier this morning, so it shouldn't be long."

Despite the slight blur in my vision and what it implies about my future,

I head toward Reagan's hanging corpse. "I want to take a peek inside his mind while we wait."

Seth grabs my arm before I have a chance to move. "Not a chance in hell, Alice. It's not just a bad idea but a terrible one. He's a Shadow Priest."

"Yeah, and he knows where we can find the mirror."

"I don't give a damn what he does or doesn't know. It's not worth risking your life."

"So then, what is? How about all the people who will die because Morgan still controls the mirror? Are their lives meaningless?"

"You know that's not fair. No lives are meaningless."

"Then let go of my arm."

Seth huffs. "Dammit, Alice. You're too stubborn for your own good." He releases my arm. "If anything happens to you, I'm gonna be pissed."

"Yeah, well, me too." I rub my arm and walk over to Reagan.

A voice in my head urges me to reconsider what I'm about to do, and I'm all too aware about the implications of my headache and blurry vision. But this could be my last and best chance at finally putting an end to Morgan and the Shadow Priests.

But he is a Shadow Priest.

I survived mind tethering to a Shadow Priest once before and lived to tell about it, so why wouldn't I again? And if I do go blind again, there's a good chance I'll have to kill someone again anyway. Morgan would be the perfect target.

God, what's wrong with me? I'm as bad as Thérèse.

Consequences aside, I must know. Not knowing will eat me alive. It must be done.

I reach out with trembling fingers and touch Reagan's arm. Not his skin but his shirt. A few inches over, and we will mind tether. I close my eyes and take a deep breath.

Now or never, Alice.

My fingers crawl down his sleeve, millimeter by millimeter.

"Alice, stop!" someone yells.

My eyes snap open. Fingers lie on the cusp of touching Reagan's skin.

I know the voice.

Dakota.

Why would she want me to stop? The information contained within Reagan's head is as vital to her as it is to me. Reluctantly, I retract my hand and turn around.

Dakota grabs me and embraces me. "I thought I might be too late."

"Too late for what?"

"I had a glimpse of the future on the way over here and tried calling each of you but couldn't get through. I knew what you were going to do. Saw you touch Reagan and then you dropped dead." She hugs me tighter. "God, I thought I was too late."

My heart pounds in my chest. "You're certain of what you saw?"

Dakota releases me and looks into my eyes. "Without a doubt, and I'm never wrong."

I glance over at Reagan. "Then I guess I owe you my life."

"You owe me nothing," she says.

Out of the narrow passage walks Rico, then Jake. My stomach flutters with excitement.

"Rico!" I run over to him.

"*Hijita!*" He picks me up off my feet and twirls me around. "My God, it is so good to see you. It's been far too long."

Once grounded, I kiss his cheek. "I've missed you so much."

Jake walks over to me. "And what about me, darlin'? Do I get the same kind of reception?"

I hug him, too. "Thanks for coming, Jake."

"Wouldn't miss a portal to another world for nothin'."

The five of us join Pierre on the platform and stare at the portal contained within the arch.

"Now what?" Seth asks.

"That's a good question." Pierre looks over at Dakota. "How do we shut this thing down?"

She shrugs. "I don't have a clue."

I wrap my arms around myself, still chilled by what I'd almost done with Reagan. "I read through Klaus Von Astner's journal, but there was nothing in it about reversing the process and closing the portal."

"Can I see the journal?" Rico asks.

Pierre hands it to him. "You read German?"

"Enough to get by." He flips through the journal, obviously looking for something specific.

"What is it?" I ask.

Rico scowls at the journal. "I'm searching for any details as to when and where this portal leads."

"I don't follow," Seth says.

"Simple, really." Jake adjusts his cowboy hat. "Basically, there are two points that anchor or bridge two worlds. First, you have the when. When, as in what point in time does our current timeline intersect with the timeline of the connected world. Second, you have the where."

"Where in that world was the other side of our portal created," Seth finishes.

Rico closes the journal and pats Seth on the back. "Good job, *hijo*. I'm sure you'll be an expert on portals in no time." He turns to me. "Unfortunately, this indeed seems to be a bridge."

I stare at him, confused. "As opposed to what?"

"Well, there are two types of portals," he says. "The ones that go both ways, like a bridge, and the ones that go a single direction."

"There are really three types if you think about it," Jake says. "A single-direction portal could either lead *to* somewhere or *from* somewhere."

"Good point." Rico hands the journal back to Pierre. "Needless to say, this one is of the multi-directional variety and far more dangerous if you ask me."

Pierre places the journal under his arm and adjusts his glasses. "What makes it more dangerous?"

A grim look spreads across Rico's face. "Anything on the other side of it can come through to our world, and trust me when I say that there are far more dangerous and deadly creatures in Centauria than there are on your planet. Walking nightmares and cunning foes you'd never want to face."

"So, the question remains. What do we do now?" Seth asks.

Rico broods. "There's only one thing that can be done." He lifts his left sleeve and removes the shiny, solid black wristband. With a sigh he turns and places it in my hand.

The wristband that controls the nanotech in his basement…

I just stare at it, dumbfounded. "What's happening?"

He takes a set of keys out of his pants pocket and places them in my hand, too. "You must take care of my shop."

My pulse begins to race, causing my headache to flare up again. "I don't understand. Why can't you take care of your own shop?"

Rico places his hands on my shoulders and smiles. "*Hijita.* You are like the daughter I never had. I trust you with *everything.*"

The pieces begin clicking together in my mind. I shove the wristband and keys at him. "No, Rico. You take these back."

"Until a way to close the portal can be found, going through it is the only way I know of to safeguard this world. You must understand that."

"Why can't we guard it from this side?" Seth asks.

Rico regards him, then smiles. "We wouldn't be able to see what was coming until it was too late. As I said, Centauria has far deadlier threats than you could ever imagine."

"Dragons," Jake says.

Everyone looks at him.

Seth gasps. "Seriously?"

Rico nods. "Yes, and many of them loathe humans." He touches my shoulder. "It is time."

Tears fill my eyes. "How can I let you go? I still need you."

"You never needed me, *hijita.*" He smiles and wipes a tear from my cheek. "It was I that always needed you."

"That's not true!"

"Trust me, it is. And you must also understand that I've been running from my past for far too long. It's time I return home and face the demons I left behind."

"I don't understand. *This* is your home, Rico."

"A second home for certain, but you must trust me, *hijita*. I must go."

"Will you ever return?" I ask, wiping tears from my face.

He smiles, then kisses my forehead. "One cannot know the plans of God, but if his will deems it, then I will return."

I grab hold of him and draw him into a final hug. "And all the artifacts?" I whisper in his ear. "I don't know what most of them are let alone what they can do. Do you keep some sort of record?"

"I'm sorry, *hijita*, but I've kept it all in my head." He pulls away. "Don't worry, you'll figure it all out. I have faith in you."

After wishing everyone goodbye, Rico steps up to the portal. My heart breaks as he takes a deep breath and then steps into its watery surface and disappears.

Goodbye, my friend.

* * * * *

A knock on the hotel suite door pulls me from the depths of my mind. Jake and Dakota Barnes stand in the corridor when I open the door. I invite them in.

"Thought you guys would be gone by now," I say.

"We're on a tight schedule, but we've got one more item of business left here in Paris." Dakota withdraws an envelope from an inside coat pocket and hands it to me.

I stare at the black envelope for a moment. "What's this?"

Jake winks at me. "Just open it, darlin'."

I turn it over. It's not sealed, and when I open the flap, I see that it's empty. The only thing of significance is the white rook on the underside of the flap.

My brow furrows. "I don't understand."

"It's obviously an invitation," Seth says, joining us in the entryway.

Jake points at Seth and pretends to fire a bullet at him. "Right you are, bucko."

Dakota smiles. "Welcome to Mirador. That is, if you're ready."

Mirador…

I stare at the envelope, not quite understanding what joining them would entail. "I am, but ready for what?"

"To do what you've already been doing on your own, darlin'." Jake raises his arms and spreads them wide. "Savin' the world and others like yourself."

I peer over at Seth. "And what about him?"

Dakota cocks her head. "I'm not sure I follow. What about Seth?"

"We're inseparable. He goes where I go."

Jake laughs.

Normally, I enjoy his laughter, but right now it's just annoying. "And what's so funny about that?"

Jake grins, then smacks Seth in the stomach. "Bucko here's been a part of Mirador for years. How did you think you got on our radar in the first place?"

The weight of his words hits me. Stirs anger within me as I turn and face Seth. All those years he knew about me and kept it to himself. Feigned hurt when I finally told him the truth. Scoffed at the thought of me being different. Laughed about another world existing.

And I thought Reagan was a good liar.

But the anger fades as I stare into his eyes. The love he showers upon me exceeds anything I deserve. What other man would put up with me and all the baggage I carry? All the lies?

No one.

Even so, his deceit cannot go unpunished. I smack him in the gut. Much harder than Jake did, but he can take it. "Seriously, Seth?"

He clutches his stomach. "Okay, I probably deserved that, but you have to understand that I made an oath of secrecy."

I feel like such a fool. "Who else knows about this? Frost?"

"Lieut. Frost?" Seth laughs. "Definitely not, but he will soon enough. That is if you've decided to join us."

"I guess I have, but there's one thing you might want to know."

"And what's that?" he asks.

"It's going to be one helluva long flight back home for you."

"Overhead compartment?"

"Worse. You're getting checked like the dog you are."

"Man, that's harsh," Jake says.

We all laugh, Seth included.

CHAPTER TWENTY-FOUR

A week later…

IT FEELS STRANGE BEING back in Desert Springs again after spending the last three months in Paris. It's not so much the city itself that feels off to me—although the climate change is freaking my hair and skin out—but being back at the precinct again. I'd kind of gotten used to not going into an office and basically answering to no one.

Several new faces fill the locker room, but it's the old ones that leave my stomach fluttering. Feels like I'm fresh out of the academy again.

"Bergman." I turn and watch Detective Terry Roland stroll toward me. "Where's that worthless partner of yours?"

I shrug. "Late, as usual."

He chuckles. "Are the two of you still married, or did you finally dump his sorry ass while you were on extended vacation?"

"Extended vacation." I shake my head and close my locker door. "That's certainly one way to describe the last few months."

Seth walks up behind Detective Roland. "Terry, Terry, Terry. I heard that, buddy, and you'd better back off. Alice isn't on the market and never will be again unless my cold dead body lies six feet under."

Detective Roland raises his left hand and grins. "As it turns out, neither am I." He wiggles his ring finger, drawing attention to the black ring around it.

"You dirty dog!" Seth wraps his arms around Detective Roland from behind and pats him on the chest. "Who's the delusional fiancée?" He lets Terry go.

"Men don't wear engagement rings, Seth." As I stare at Detective Roland, my gut wrenches with guilt. "It's Veronica, isn't it?" I don't even need a response, his face answer enough.

How long has it been since we last talked, Vee?

"We eloped a month ago. Spent a few weeks down in Mexico." His grin returns. "She's a firecracker, that one."

After getting to know each other at my wedding, the two of them had started dating. I knew their relationship had become more serious, but I never thought they'd elope. Furthermore, I'm hurt that Vee didn't even bother to call me and tell me herself.

I swallow the lump in my throat. "Congrats, Terry. I'm really happy for the two of you."

"Thanks." He turns toward Seth. "Both of you."

"We'll have to get together and celebrate," Seth says.

"Definitely." He claps his hands together. "Anyway, I hear you've got an appointment with the boss man upstairs."

"Don't remind me," I say, already dreading it.

Seth looks at his watch. "Speaking of which, we're gonna be late."

The second-floor corridor sits empty and dark, save the light pouring out of Lieut. Frost's office through the drawn blinds and open door. As usual, his cologne greets us before we enter the office. But something's different. It doesn't threaten to peel the skin from my face, nor does it trigger my gag reflex. In fact, it smells quite pleasant.

We must've come back to an alternate universe where skunks don't exist or have been replaced with spices.

I stifle a snicker as Seth and I settle into the two wooden chairs facing the front of Lieut. Frost's desk. A single glance into the man's brown eyes sobers me right up. The man's gaze falls upon his desk, and my eyes follow. The black business card with the white rook is unmistakable. If I were to flip the card over, I'd see the same image, only the colors reversed. No writing of any kind.

Mirador.

Lieut. Frost pushes air through his nose as he reaches out and picks up the business card. He taps its edge on the desk as he regards Seth, then me. The man wears an excellent poker face, leaving me wondering if he's pissed, upset, indifferent, happy, or a combination of them all.

Finally, he speaks. "This is how things are going to work around here going forward. First and foremost, all cases go through me. That includes ones you work with your little friends. Second, you will continue to work cold cases while dealing with matters outside the purview and jurisdiction of this office. Third and final, welcome back. Your presence and expertise have been missed by many around here."

He stares at the business card as he taps it on the desk. "As much as I hate to admit it, this place hasn't been the same while you've been gone." He looks up at us, and his stare hardens. "Tell anyone that, and I'll bury you. Got it?"

"It's good to be back, sir," I say.

"Ditto, sir," Seth says.

"Good." He gestures toward the door with his head. "Shut the door, Ryan." Seth reaches over and pulls the door closed.

Now what?

Lieut. Frost leans down and opens one of his desk drawers. He pulls out a blue case file, sets it on the desk, and pushes it toward us. My eyes widen when I see the name on the file: Frost, Derek.

"As you might imagine, this case requires your full discretion." Lieut. Frost leans back and folds his massive arms across his chest. "I've held onto it for far too long."

Seth scans through the case file, then hands it to me. A murder-suicide thirteen years back. The first a gunshot execution style. The second a self-inflicted gunshot underneath the chin. Gunshot residue found on the suicide victim's hand. No witnesses. No suicide note. It looks pretty straightforward, especially given one important fact.

I glance up at Lieut. Frost. "It says this case is closed, sir."

Lieut. Frost leans forward and slams his fist on the desk. Veins bulge in his neck. "To hell with them!" He exhales loudly and scowls. "Look, I'm not saying that Detective Miles screwed things up on purpose, but there's no way in hell my brother did what it says in that file. I knew him as well as I know myself. Better, probably. Derek was a family man. Loved his wife more than life itself."

He pulls off his glasses and tosses them on the desk. "Work the case as you have time, and dammit, don't you dare feed me any BS about it being true. Understood?"

I nod. "I'll treat this case as though Derek's my own brother."

"We'll uncover the truth, sir," Seth says. "No matter how long it takes."

"I know you will." He returns his glasses to his face, then scowls. "Well, don't just sit there like you've got nothing better to do."

"Yessir," Seth and I echo. We rise from our chairs, the case file clutched in my hand.

"Leave the file," Lieut. Frost growls. "It stays with me."

"No problem." I toss the file back on the desk. "I've got all I need from it anyway."

Lieut. Frost takes the file and shoves it back into his desk drawer. "I'm sure you do, but it'll be right here if you need it again."

Seth and I exit the office and head back downstairs. First day back, and my head's already swimming in turmoil. I just can't wait to see what tomorrow might bring, but it'll have to wait. Right now, I need go see my father.

* * * * *

A few hours later, my father and I pull up in the alley behind Rico's Cane

Shoppe. Graffiti covers the walls, and broken glass litters the ground, pieces of it sparkling in the afternoon sun. One of the doors farther down the strip hangs open on its last hinge, mangled and twisted. I wouldn't be surprised if I found a druggie or homeless person in there right now, but it's not why we came.

"I still don't understand why we're here," Isaiah says. "I have no desire to run a white cane shop."

"I know, and neither do I, but it's far more than that."

"You keep saying that, but offer no further details."

"And that's why we're here." I throw my door open and step out of the car. "Come on."

It takes a minute to get through the obnoxious number of locks on the door and disarm the security system. The lights are automatic but slow, buzzing and flickering before fully coming on. Once inside, I lock us in.

Isaiah trolls around the workshop. "I thought you said this was a white cane shop, not a manufacturing plant."

"The shop's in front." I follow him around as he explores. "Rico makes every white cane he sells."

He shakes his head. "And you expect me to learn how to make them?"

"No, and that's not why we're here. Besides, Rico's already got plenty made. Now, let me show you why we're here."

I lead him over to the back corner section of the right-side cabinets and open the last cabinet door. Reaching up inside of it, I locate the switch and press it. A soft click emits from within the cabinet, then the magic begins.

Sounds of grinding gears, squeaking pulleys, and whooshing gas shocks fill the room. The entire twelve feet or so of the middle section of cabinets slides out from the wall—about five feet in total—and reveals a narrow stairway that leads down into the dark basement.

Isaiah looks at me, his eyes wide. "Well, that is certainly unexpected."

"I know, but wait until you see what's down there. It'll blow your mind."

As we begin our descent, the basement lights below come alive. When we step off the final step, the cabinets above slide into place, sealing us inside.

Isaiah steps into the single-room basement, and his lower jaw unhinges. I laugh, remembering the way I felt the first time I came down here, too. As we tour the glass enclosures spread throughout the massive room, I begin to realize that I don't understand what most of the items are or what they do. The thought frightens me a little.

He stops in front of one enclosure containing a golden shield featuring a dragon's head. "My God…"

"This place is magnificent, isn't it?" I say, nearly breathless myself.

My father looks at me. "Where did this all come from?"

"Most of the artifacts came from—" I cringe. No matter how many times I say the word, it's still a hard truth to swallow. "—Centauria. The others are inventions of Rico's. He always said that the artifacts had a way of finding him."

He sighs. "This is a lot to take in, even for me."

"And now you understand why Rico left the cane shop in my care." I tilt my head back and forth. "And why I need your help with it."

He frowns and looks around the room again, then sighs. "I guess I'm in. What do you need from me?"

"I know it's a big ask, but I need you to test and catalog every item in here."

"That could take months."

"I know, and you're the best and *only* person for the job."

"Am I?" He frowns. "And what about Kenny? His mind is far sharper than mine."

"One day, perhaps, but right now he has enough on his plate to deal with."

Isaiah runs his hand through his hair. "I'll do it, but on one condition."

"Name it."

"We bring your mother in on this, too."

Mother?

As much as I want to argue with him, I realize he's right. The two of them have become inseparable. Plus, she'd be a great person to run the actual shop.

I proffer my hand, and he takes it. "Deal, but you're the one who gets to explain Centauria and everything else to her."

He smiles. "She's going to lose her mind."

If I don't lose mine first.

CHAPTER TWENTY-FIVE

Two years later…

MY ARMS GLISTEN WITH perspiration, and rivulets of sweat run between my shoulder blades and down my spine, saturating my underwear. The air hasn't been hooked back up yet, and my desk fan provides little more than a wisp of air. Much more of this heat, and I might just move my desk outside to cool down.

I peer over at Seth who's sitting at his own desk. "Is it just me, or has summer come early?"

"Not sure, but Lieut. Frost might have a mutiny on his hands if he doesn't get the air flowing in here soon."

Sam Barrow, our internal mail handler, rolls his cart up to the door and sticks his head in. As much as I enjoy his exuberant smile, it's not enough to make me forget about the sweltering heat even for a moment.

"Afternoon, Detectives Ryan and Ryan," Sam says.

He's the only person in the precinct that refers to me as Detective Ryan, and it makes me feel a tad special every time he does. It's like it's our little secret even though it's no secret at all.

I wipe sweat from my brow and smile at him. "You're looking good, Sam.

Lose some more weight?"

He peers down at his belly and pokes it. "Think I did, but I ain't gonna report the theft."

I chuckle. "Well, you're in the right place if you change your mind."

"That I am." Sam grabs a manila envelope off his cart and walks in. "Looks like I have just one piece of mail between the two of you." He sets the envelope on my desk, then tips his hat. "Hope the two of you have a mighty fine afternoon. Catch them criminals."

"Thanks, Sam. You have a good afternoon, too," I say.

Seth looks up and nods. "Sam."

Sam whistles as he exits the office and continues down the hall with his cart.

It's rare that either of us get mail unless it's internal. The envelope contains no return address and just says Bergman across the front in large, brown, handwritten letters. The "e" and the "m" are the only two letters not capitalized. It strikes me as a bit odd.

A quick examination confirms that whatever the envelope contains isn't much thicker than a piece of paper, nor does it weigh much. It also has room to slide around inside. I flip the envelope over and run my letter opener underneath the flap, ripping the end open. Rather than dumping the contents out on my desk, I squish the end open and peer inside. It looks like pictures, but it's too dark to tell.

I dump the contents out. Three pieces of black plastic framed in white slide across the top of my desk.

Seth looks over. "Are those polaroids?"

"That's what it looks like," I say.

As I start to flip one of them over, I stop. There's something brownish red on one of the corners of each of them. It's more than likely nothing, yet instinct tells me I should put on a glove first.

The latex feels slimy and gross on my skin and makes my hands sweat even more than they already had been. But it's a good reminder that I should be using gloves right now anyway.

Seth gets up and walks over to the front of my desk just as I flip the first polaroid over. The image isn't what I expected to see. It's of an old wooden shed. Stained dark but weather-beaten. The shed's door hangs from its top hinge, tilted forward yet still latched. There's not much else remarkable about the photo other than the brownish-red fingerprint on the bottom edge. From what I can tell, it looks like paint.

After the first photo, I'm not sure what to expect when I flip over the second one.

"Oh my God," Seth says.

The image churns the contents of my stomach, but I can't stop looking at it.

A limbless, female torso.

Naked.

Meat cleaver embedded in her stomach.

Seth looks at me. "And the third?"

It's days like this when I hate my job. Yeah, I live to solve murders and put psychopaths behind bars, but seeing a dismembered body never gets easier. In some way, I think it might actually get worse.

I take a deep breath and hold it, then turn over the last polaroid.

A severed head sits atop a pike or garden tool. Something with a long, wooden handle.

Blonde hair. Mid-twenties. Most likely the owner of the limbless torso.

Someone's written "Say Cheese!" underneath the picture.

Here we go again…

TO BE CONTINUED...

Visit **danielkuhnley.com** for more information.

PLEASE TELL OTHERS WHAT YOU THOUGHT

Thank you for taking this journey with me. If you'd like to show your support for my work, please leave a review wherever you purchased this book. It's free to do so, and it'll only take you a minute to write a quick sentence expressing your thoughts about the book.

Your review is especially important to independent, self-published authors like me. Internet and online bookstore algorithms favor books with reviews. They display in search results and at the top of search results more often than books without reviews.

Did you know that there's a minimum number of reviews needed to purchase certain advertising? It's true. Help me reach that threshold by leaving a review. Doing so will help more people find this book and will in turn help me sell more books, which means I can keep authoring more books for you.

Go to danielkuhnley.com/reviews if you need a link to where you can leave a review.

Thank you!!

READ *BIRTH OF A KILLER* FOR FREE

Curious how Alice gained her sight as a teen?
Want to read about the attack that started it all?

danielkuhnley.com/become-a-conqueror

Sign up and read *Birth Of A Killer*, An Alice Bergman Novella. Be the **FIRST** to get sneak peaks at my upcoming novels and the chance to win **FREE** stuff, like signed books.

A paranormal serial killer thriller that'll keep you turning the pages.

Be careful what you dream when murder is on your mind.

My name is Alice, and I'm a sixteen-year-old ghost. No, I'm not actually dead, but I was born blind. The sad thing is the world's more blind to me than I am to it.

That is, until the day he noticed me. A bully. He ruined my life and turned my dreams into nightmares, so what could I do? The same thing any girl my age would do—I wished he'd die.

Then… he turns up dead. Naturally, I freaked out. Am I to blame? Did my nightmare kill him? Would anyone believe me if I confessed?

It's absurd. I know it. Nightmares don't come true… do they?

Birth of a Killer is the suspenseful prequel novella to *The Braille Killer*. If you like unique sleuths, origin stories, and a hint of the supernatural, you'll love Daniel Kuhnley's nail-biting tale.

Buy *Birth of a Killer* today to see how Alice's story began!

EXPLORE CENTAURIA

Curious about the portal Thérèse and Rico went through? Explore Centauria in Daniel Kuhnley's Epic Dragon Fantasy series, *The Dark Heart Chronicles*.

Read *The Dragon's Stone*, book one in the series.

Available on Amazon and other retailers. Visit danielkuhnley.com for more details.

ABOUT THE AUTHOR

Daniel Kuhnley is an American author of Epic Dragon Fantasy, Supernatural Serial Killer, and Christian YA Sci-Fi/Fantasy stories. Some of his novels include *Reborn*, *The Braille Killer*, and *Kiara Kole And The Key Of Truth*. He enjoys watching movies, reading novels, and programming. He lives in Albuquerque, NM with his wife who also writes.

CONNECT WITH DANIEL

danielkuhnley.com/connect

ACKNOWLEDGMENTS

As always, I thank my Lord and Savior Jesus Christ. Life has no meaning without you.

I'd also like to thank Teri and Nikki for doing some beta reading to make sure this story was on the right track.

And to my wife, Marsha. She is the driving force behind everything I do and accomplish. Without her, these books would never see the light of day. I love and appreciate her more than words could ever express.

Thank you all,

Daniel